Drowning Barbie

Books by Frederick Ramsay

The Ike Schwartz Mysteries
Artscape
Secrets
Buffalo Mountain
Stranger Room
Choker
The Eye of the Virgin
Rogue
Scone Island
Drowning Barbie

The Jerusalem Mysteries
Judas
The Eighth Veil
Holy Smoke

The Botswana Mysteries
Predators
Reapers

Other Novels
Impulse

Drowning Barbie

An Ike Schwartz Mystery

Frederick Ramsay

Poisoned Pen Press

Poisoned Pen Press
6962 E. First Ave., Ste. 103
Scottsdale, AZ 85251
www.poisonedpenpress.com
info@poisonedpenpress.com

Printed in the United States of America

Preface

A response made by a mother about her daughter playing in the family swimming pool with her doll: "What is she doing?" she was asked.

"It looks like she's drowning Barbie."

That was not the first time I had a title in search of a story. *Stranger Room* had a similar birth—great title, no immediate story.

The core story here, the *A* story, if you will, has little or nothing to do with swimming pools or dolls. It is about childhood, but not the idyllic sort that involves either. In fact, the two narratives that weave in and out of the book had their origins from disparate sources. One was told to me by a former Santa Barbara cop about a body found in a lumberyard in New York City. I'm not sure why a California law enforcement officer had an interest in the New York City crime scene, but he did. The second, the *A* story, had its origins in an encounter with a young woman I met at a writers' conference—a story about herself, as it happens. They are both true. I have fictionalized them. The first, because there is a widow involved whom I had the opportunity to meet and who is looking for a new start, and in any case doesn't need the *tsuris*. As for the second, I felt I needed to protect the young woman. She has a burden to bear most of us can scarcely imagine and she doesn't need either the notoriety or our sympathy—only a chance to make a new life for herself.

The title, then, should be understood as a metaphor for the *A* story and a pun for the *B*.

When she told me about her childhood, if you can call it that, my young friend announced, rather proudly, that she had that very week made it to her twenty-third birthday and since she did not believe she would be alive at age twenty-three, she was celebrating. She will be twenty-five or twenty-six by now.

I hope.

This book is dedicated to her.

Frederick Ramsay
2014

"It shouldn't hurt to be a child." *

Picketsville, Virginia

Early June

From a distance you couldn't be sure how old the girl might be—sixteen, twenty-six—no way to tell. She could have been any of a hundred, a thousand displaced and forgotten young women who wander around the shabbier streets in America's cities. Only this wasn't the city, unless you believe Picketsville, Virginia, population sixty thousand, more or less—lately, less—qualifies as urban. And she was not wandering. She stood perfectly still, staring at the earth at her feet. The usual accumulation of leaves and plants seemed askew, unnatural in their arrangement, and recently turned dirt lay in places where it didn't belong. A stand of hardwoods, untouched for a century or more, filtered the early summer sunlight and softened the lines on her face, but not the anger in her eyes. She stood a little straighter, but her eyes never left the ground. Her lips moved as if reciting a private litany.

"We used to come here back before all that. Like, we had picnics over by that old spring. A long time ago and what was I? Six or seven—maybe a year away from the hell you put me in. I don't know, maybe I don't remember things so good anymore. Too many of my days are out of focus because of all that shit you shoved in your body and mine. There're things that I can't pull out of my head anymore."

A vehicle sounded its horn from the road fifty yards behind her. The girl stopped mumbling and dropped a scraggly bouquet of wildflowers at her feet. She took a breath, wiped her nose on her sleeve, and walked away.

Sometime Later That Month

A breeze disturbed the otherwise sleepy afternoon. Andy Lieux decided to walk his dog in the woods by the old spring. This was a special spot, known to only a few, or so he thought. In fact, the small rivulet- and fern-laced area was a spot most of the long-term residents of Picketsville also thought of as their special place.

In the springtime, after the area's scant snow melted and the rains came, the little mountain spring would gush and the low area beside it would become a marsh. Skunk cabbage and bluets and quaker-ladies would poke through the soft loam. By late May, the ground would dry a bit and the rank earthy aroma of the naturally composting detritus would abate. Ferns would poke through and unfurl their fronds, eventually to cover the entire quarter acre or so of the site. By late June the skunk cabbage gave way to a by-now impenetrable carpet of ferns that helped hide the smaller fauna from the ever-present predators—the circle of life. The spring water flowed at a more sedate pace, slowed by wild watercress lining its short course, into a larger creek ten yards away. There its crystal water mixed with the more turgid creek.

The dog drank noisily from the spring and, its thirst slaked, began its ritual zigzag exploration of the area, pausing here and there to mark its territory and occasionally pawing at the soil beneath the ferns in search of…who knows what? He snuffed here and there and paused at some newly turned earth. His nose twitched, he let out a small yip, and scratched at the one place not covered with leaves, moss, or verdure of one sort or another. When a gray-green hand surfaced, Andy pulled his dog off, and at that moment Picketsville, Virginia, would have another murder for the sheriff's office to solve. Two murders, actually, but that would be discovered later. Identifying the remains of Ethyl Smut and finding her killer would be problem enough.

Too many people believed she deserved it.

Chapter One

Ike Schwartz jerked back the blinds. White hot Nevada sun streamed across the room and, laser-like, assaulted Ruth Harris' eyelids. She grunted, sat up, and forced them open a millimeter or two. Big mistake. She groaned, closed them, and eased her throbbing head back against the pillows, vaguely aware that Ike stood grinning at her at the end of the bed.

He waggled his fingers. "Good morning, Sunshine. And how are we feeling this fine morning?"

"How are we…what's with the *we*? You are the cop, Schwartz. I assume you got the license number of the truck that ran me over."

"Sorry, not this time. The pain you feel this morning is all self-inflicted. I've ordered breakfast, by the way, toast, eggs, orange juice—" Ruth groaned again. "But first I think you need to drink a lot of water and spend about fifteen minutes in a very hot shower. You probably should open your eyes. I don't want you bumping into things and falling down."

"If I open my eyes they will fall out of their sockets and probably get lost under the bed. That could be very inconvenient. Just coffee, Ike. I need a gallon of coffee and a straw to drink it with so I don't have to move. My God, even my hair hurts."

"Wages of sin."

"Shut up and get me coffee or I will kill you. It will be self-defense and no judge in the world will convict me."

"Yes, of course, but first listen to the sweet voice of reason. Most of the pain in your head is due to the fact that alcohol, a substance you should be familiar with after last night, dehydrates. You are dehydrated and your brain is protesting. Coffee also dehydrates, but more slowly. You do not want coffee yet. You may think you want coffee, but you'd be wrong. You need water and a few aspirin. I have put several bottles of water, thoughtfully supplied by this hotel at an outrageous price of five bucks a pop, in the shower with a bottle of aspirin which I discovered in your makeup bag. Drink and sluice off. Then, you may have coffee and breakfast."

"No coffee?"

"Water first, inside and out."

Ruth eased out from under the sheets and stared at her bare knees. "Where's my nightgown?"

"You never got that far. It was all I could do to get you out of your other things."

"What did I…? Wait a minute." Ruth frowned and forced herself to remember. "Okay, after our latest fiasco…I will kill Charlie Garland the next time I see him…we flew to Las Vegas and booked in this hotel what…three days ago, right? Right. Three. We toured the city. We admired the fountains at the Bellagio and played blackjack, took in a racy show, and had dinners at all the expensive restaurants we could manage. We witnessed the dumbing down of American culture in the streets, as people who should know better did their best to look like thugs, or hookers, and then awkwardly attired tourists when they weren't taking pictures of the ones who were trying to look like hookers or whatever, gawking. We gambled. Then, last night after we had dinner and a few drinks, we played the slots and…Hey, I won two thousand dollars last night. Is that right? It is. Where's my money?"

"As to that, a substantial portion of it went to pay for the party."

"The party? We had a party?"

"You really don't remember?"

"Maybe. Crap, Ike, I never do things like this. Even when I was a pain in my parents' collective rear end and acting out big-time—"

"I remember."

"Shut up. Even then, I never behaved like this. I've never been more than moderately tight, and that was a special occasion. What happened?"

"Well, as you just now retrieved from your addled cerebral cortex, you won a substantial sum at the dollar slots and proceeded to buy hooch for a group of folks who came to congratulate you and soon became your new best friends. It grew into a party."

"Did you try to stop me?"

"Yes and no. To be honest, I was feeling pretty relaxed myself after all that we'd endured lately—guns and explosions, to name but a few of the most significant. I figured we deserved to blow our tops and, after all, it was found money. It didn't take much in the way of hooch, by the way. Either you have a low tolerance for tequila or your body just needed a little shove. You popped some of your painkillers before we went out, so maybe you had some help flying your plane."

"Oh, Lord. I'm going to shower. When I come out you can tell me where the rest of my money went, and you'd better offer coffee. Maybe I will find a better excuse for what my head is going through while trying to keep the soap out of my eyes. Is there anything else I should know?"

"Oh, yeah. Say, do you like my robe? The hotel gave it to me. It even has my initial on it, see? A big red *S* on the pocket. The *S* is for Schwartz."

"Ike, the *S* stands for Sheraton."

"No, I'm pretty sure it stands for Schwartz. You have one, too. It's hanging on the bathroom door."

"Right. I have a hotel robe with an *H* for Harris and not for Hilton on it, or is this joint a Holiday Inn?"

"No, it's an *S*, too. So, go shower and see how much comes back to you as the gremlins in your head shut down the jack hammers they're using in their attempt to escape."

Ike led her to the shower. Sooner or later she would remember. When she did she'd need something stronger than coffee.

Room service arrived and he had breakfast laid out in the sitting area of their suite when he heard her scream. The previous night's gaiety had finally been located in her memory's lost luggage department. The scream was followed by a series of groans and a very loud, "yaaahh!"

The bathroom door flew open and cloud of steam billowed out followed by a very wet and naked Ruth.

"We're married!"

"Yep."

"And you didn't try to stop me?"

"Nope."

"Why didn't you?"

"Several of the nice people whom you declared earlier were your new BFFs tried. Two policemen had a few words on the matter as well. Do you remember Officer Hornick?"

"Who?"

"Officer Hornick. You insisted on calling him Ossifer Horney."

"My God, I did? What did he do?"

"Remanded you into my custody—professional courtesy, you could say."

"And then…when did we get married?"

"That would be shortly after you had finished discussing your First Amendment rights with Ossifer Horney. By the way, the Constitution does not guarantee your right to stand on the middle of the Las Vegas Strip and sing, 'I'm too sexy in my shirt.' Anyway, before he finished Mirandizing you, you invited him, his partner, and the aforementioned BFFs to be in your wedding and we all traipsed down to the Budding Rose Wedding Chapel where, for a small fee, we got hitched."

"Oh my God, no!"

"In the case of the Budding Rose Wedding Chapel, God had very little to do with it. You should be very thankful for the Budding Rose. We almost ended up at the local McWedding."

"Ack!"

"Precisely. Now wrap a towel around yourself and have some breakfast. It's our honeymoon."

"But why didn't you stop me?"

"The party business—I did try. You were spending your winnings like a drunken sailor or college president with a government grant, the latter of which, of course, you are. But stop the wedding? Sorry, no, you made a solemn promise—well a promise, I'm not sure about the solemnity of it—that if we survived being shot at and generally abused by friend and foe alike last week, a wedding date was a certainty. We did survive and I, assuming the sincerity of that declaration, acted on it. I figured I might never get you that close to an altar ever again."

"So we're a couple."

"We have been a couple for years. Now we are now a *married* couple. I'm as sorry, as I suspect you are, that it happened this way, but you were insistent and the cops were losing their sense of humor, not to mention patience. The term *drunk tank* came into play several times. Besides, as I said, who knew when?"

Ruth wrapped the towel into a sarong and sat. "Let's face it, we are the 'odd couple,' aren't we? About the only thing we agree on is that we are better people together than apart. Given that, this escapade isn't even unusual, is it?"

"Well…"

"Don't answer that. Ike, you have been amazingly patient with me about turning an engagement into a wedding. I don't know why, but for me the finality of it always seemed so…I don't know…help me out here."

"Final?"

"Exactly. I expect there is some Freudian worm wiggling around in my subconscious somewhere that suggests that I deliberately got falling-down drunk in order to do what I really wanted to do, but was afraid to do sober. Does that make any sense?"

"Probably, but who the hell cares?"

"Not me. But first I have to say it, I am not regretting this at all, Ike. I am happy to wear the customized robe with the big *S* on it and be Mrs. Sheraton, okay? I've wanted this, I think, since the night you smooched me up in the mountains. I just never had the nerve to…you know. So now what?"

"We eat this ridiculously expensive breakfast and pack."

"No, that's not what I meant. We need to have a real wedding when we get back, Ike. You know, cake and reception and rice and all that. I need to brace up my mother. You have your father and Dolly to think about, and all those folks who love us and also give us heartburn will be upset. We owe them something formal—official."

"Right, we need to formalize the irrational. Got it. We have a plane to catch in three hours."

"Okay, eat and pack without passing GO and collecting… rice in your cuffs. You have to make good on your end of the deal too."

"My end? What's that?"

"No more Charlie Garland and your old CIA buddies. No more international shoot-outs, bombs, conspiracies, or missed meals."

"Right, no more Charlie et al. Just local murders, mayhem, parking tickets, and breaking up underage keggers in the woods. Done. Now, eat your breakfast and pull that towel up or your eggs will be cold before you get back to them."

"You are such a romantic, Ike."

Chapter Two

Ike Schwartz, Picketsville's sheriff, missed the old days when his town was only a dot on the map set back from the interstate and not on anyone's list of "must see" destinations in the Shenandoah Valley. Sadly, those days were gone and he blamed the university for it. When Callend University had been merely Callend College, a women's institution more nearly resembling a late nineteenth-century ladies' finishing school, the town slept peacefully in a cultural backwash. But then, Dr. Ruth Harris had been appointed its president and yanked it into the twenty-first century. Through skillful mergers, fund-raising, and recruiting of top level faculty and students, Callend was transformed from a stereotypical way station to the altar for Southern belles to a full-scale university, training young men and women in the skills needed to manage the future. Picketsville became a place to visit after an obligatory stop at Luray Caverns and Lexington, to experience back-to-back the campuses of Washington and Lee and VMI, and before traveling further south to Hollins University or east to Sweet Briar and Randolph colleges.

That Ruth Harris was, in the words of Essie Sutherlin, Ike's "main squeeze," did not alter Ike's conviction that the university was the source of his *tsuris*.

"Your what?" Essie asked.

"It means pain in the ass but with frustration, if you follow."

"It's one of them Jew words, ain't it?"

"Yiddish."

"Thought so. So when are you and the lady going to get married and end the 'sore ass' we all is being put through from waiting on you two to do something?"

"Essie, you should concentrate on dispatching and leave my private life alone."

"Ike, you're the sheriff of a small town where everybody knows everybody else's business. You ain't got a private life. So, when are you going to do the deed?"

"Working on it, and why is that a problem for you? Answer the phone."

"It ain't rung." At that moment the phone bank lit up and several rang at once. "How do you do that? I swear you know when the thing is going to ring and who's on the other end almost every time. Okay, which line do I answer first?"

"Six is trouble. I'm guessing four is your husband, Billy, and three is not important. Pick up six."

Essie answered the line he suggested, shook her head, and said, "You're right. It's Andy Lieux and he says his old dog found a body in the woods. Hey, didn't we already have one of them this year?"

"That was two years ago, and as we don't have a public trash dump or a surfeit of dumpsters, the woods is where the bodies always go. Where in the woods is this body?"

Essie returned to the phone. "Where you at, Andy?" She scribbled on a tear sheet and handed it to Ike.

"Now, pick up line four and find out where Billy is and send him to the scene and then call the medical examiner, the evidence techs, and get them all headed out there too."

"Don't you want to know who's on two?"

"No…yes, I think I probably do." Ike picked up the phone, punched the blinking red button numbered two. "Yes?"

"That you, Ike?"

"It's me. What can I do for you, Pop?"

"Well, me and Miss Dolly want you and your lady to come out to the farm for dinner this Sunday if you can."

"I don't know. I'll have to ask. It's still summer, but believe it or not, with vacations and academic planning, it's a busy time for Ruth."

"Yeah, well you ask her and let me know. Oh, and there's this other thing."

"Other thing? What other thing would that be?"

"Well, maybe it's nothin' but I could'a swore someone spent the night in the old hay barn down by the road earlier in the week."

"And you're telling me now? Why?"

"Well, it's like this. I don't usually pay that no mind. I worry it might burn down, you know, if they was to light a fire in there. I been meaning to tear the thing down so burning wouldn't bother me much either, but I'd hate to see somebody get hurt. Anyway, I was down to the barn this morning and they left some stuff behind."

"They probably got spooked and ran without picking up."

"Yeah, maybe, but this stuff looks like it ain't been used for a dozen years. Old stuff."

"Okay, listen, I have to go. I'll talk to Ruth and see if we can make it Sunday. I have a crime scene to check out. I'll look at your barn on my way. Probably some people dumping their trash the way they do."

◇◇◇

Deputy Billy Sutherlin had the yellow crime-scene tape strung between five or six trees and had isolated roughly a third of an acre when Ike arrived.

"Over there, Ike." He pointed to the pile of freshly turned earth in the center of his scene.

"What do we know, Billy?"

"So far, nothing. The dog dug up part of an arm before Andy pulled him off. We ain't touched nothing since. The ETs ought to be here pretty quick. They called maybe fifteen minutes ago."

"Did you get Andy's statement?"

"Yeah. Got that wrote down in my book and sent him packing because his dog was like to go crazy trying to get at the body."

"Okay. Get some help out here. I want to sweep this area for anything that looks like it doesn't belong. And I mean anything."

Chapter Three

While deputies shuffled through the accumulation of leaves and fallen branches in their search for anything that might prove useful, Ike set the evidence technicians and the medical examiner, who'd arrived with them, to work exhuming the body. As he watched, a face, then a torso, and finally an entire body of a middle-aged woman came to light. She had on faded and torn jeans, a blood-stained t-shirt with a slogan silk-screened on it that he couldn't read, and a bandanna that had probably bound her going-to-gray and cheaply dyed hair. Crusted blood filled a too-deep depression on the side of her head. Her feet were bare and very dirty. Lying close—but buried in the dirt and evidently tossed in as an afterthought—was a pair of lime green flip-flops.

"Probable death by blunt force trauma. I won't know the TOD until I get her on a table and start poking around, but she's been here awhile, Sheriff. So, how was your vacation?"

"Do all medical examiners have your level of sangfroid or are you a special case, Tom? You have a positive knack for blending the awful with the mundane. I need an ID on this lady ASAP and the vacation was...exceptional, I would say."

"Exceptional? That begs a question."

"Judging from her face, I think we have a meth head here. Sunken cheeks...that's a meth face for sure."

The ME glanced at the dead woman's face and nodded, then signaled for the ETs to lift the corpse over to a black body bag. As they did so, one slipped and her foot slid into the shallow grave.

"Careful there, Anderson," the ME snapped. Ike glanced into the now-empty grave site and saw what appeared to be clothing of some sort.

"Pull that coat or whatever it is out. There may be some useful information in it, on it, or about it. What question is being begged, Tom?"

The ETs zipped the bag shut over the dead woman and returned to the shallow pit. The tech who'd slipped reached in and lifted the cloth away. It tore.

"Cripes, this coat is rotten and…Jesus, there's another one."

As she lifted the cloth scraps away, the skeletal remains of a second body came into view.

"I hope you don't have an early tee time, Tom. It appears you just got yourself another job."

The ME bent and brushed aside some of the cloth and dirt. He called for the ETs to bring brushes and they set to work uncovering the second body.

"I'll tell you here and now, these are two separate cases, Sheriff. This one was planted here at least ten years ago. If they're connected at all it would be because the killer had a thing about this particular burying spot for his victims, but what are the odds? Or, I suppose, our latest murderer could have been plain lazy. If he'd dug a proper grave, he'd have found this guy and moved over a few feet."

"Or maybe he was absentminded and, after a decade, forgot where he planted his first victim."

"This would be a case of the snail serial killer—slow but deadly."

"Or," Ike said, ignoring the ME's bad joke, "he wanted this dead guy found because the two people are related somehow."

"A much more sensible possibility, to be sure, but would you like to calculate the odds on that?"

"Nope. I need your report as soon as, etcetera. I'm thinking this second stiff won't be so easy to ID. Can you think of anybody who's been missing for ten years or so?"

The ME lit what appeared to be a very rotten corncob pipe. "I've been on this job in this state less than six months. You're kidding, right?"

"I wish." Ike turned and called out to his deputy. "Billy, anything?"

"I don't know, Ike. We have this bunch of flowers left on the grave. I don't reckon they'll tell us much, though."

"I got something," Charley Picket called out. "There's a piece of oak branch over here and I'm pretty sure there's traces of blood and hair on it."

"Bag it and give it to the ETs. Good work, Charley."

For years Charley Picket had been the only African American deputy on the force. His job, before Ike's election, was to patrol what was euphemistically referred to in the bad old days as the *colored section* of town. Times had changed and Charley, like Dilsey Gibson, had endured. He now enjoyed the privileges granted to a deputy with senior tenure and, more importantly, patrolled wherever he was needed.

Ike lingered at the crime scene until he felt sure everything that needed doing had been done. He drove away from town toward the countryside. His father and his stepmother, Miss Dolly, lived on the family farm several miles from Picketsville. Abe Schwartz did not farm. No one in the line of Schwartzes who traced their immediate ancestry back to East Prussia and an earlier century, had ever farmed. Abe's forbearers arrived in the United States from Europe in advance of the then-current pogrom. They joined the thousands who had left their "mother country" in the mid to late nineteenth century. The Schwartzes settled in Richmond, Virginia. Several generations of tailors-turned-haberdashers ended when Abe took up politics. At one time or another he'd held most offices in the state government except governor. During his career span, the thought of a Southern Jewish governor had been unthinkable. Times and demographics had changed, but not in time to benefit Abe. That didn't mean he didn't still harbor hopes for his son. Ike, he felt, wasted his talents as a small-town sheriff and said so—often.

Abe's barn sat twenty feet back from the road. It had been built as a hay barn and its double doors faced the road. Tractors, or teams of horses in the old days, could pull the wagons filled with hay more easily along the road. Before the advent of automobiles and time-sensitive lifestyles, that arrangement made perfect sense. The barn had been empty for years. People rushing by would not know that, but kids forced by their parents to put their X-Boxes on pause and go outside, discovered it and, during daylight, it became a place for relatively innocent mischief. At night it appealed to a different sort of activity and prompted the expression, made by hormonally imbalanced teenaged boys, accompanied with sniggers and orthodontically augmented leers: "She's got straw on her back."

Ike pulled off to the shoulder and stepped out. He breathed in the humid air and the scent of newly mown hay and honeysuckle. Abe rented his fields to a local horse breeder. The arrangement kept the scenery picturesque, saved the breeder significant money in feed bills, and Abe the trouble of maintaining his property. Definitely a win-win.

The barn doors were ajar. Ike wrenched one open and stepped in. Abe was correct: Someone had dumped an armful of things onto the floor. The sheriff poked at it with the remains of a pitchfork and wondered idly how the thing had lasted so long. Something like a pitchfork, even one with a bent and broken tine, would normally have disappeared years ago. The clothing sat in an untidy pile to one side of the barn floor. It did seem to be mostly baby apparel, worn Oshkosh by Gosh pajamas, a raggedy stuffed animal—things like that. Ike did not know much about babies or their clothing needs, but the condition and the general appearance suggested they were from another decade at least.

Further sifting revealed papers, some handwritten and some typed, and yellowing photographs. Someone had dumped trash, but why in this place? Why not dump it on the roadside like every other litterbug? Or, if they were fastidious, there were dumpsters aplenty in the area. And why wait ten, fifteen, twenty years to do the dumping? He stared at the scattered materials for several minutes, then turned and left.

Ike kept a variety of things in the trunk of his cruiser—a pump shot gun with a shortened stock and barrel, a Kevlar vest, a crime scene kit, and a change of clothing. In a separate box he stored tools ranging from a five-pound maul to a set of lock picks (entering a building in the pursuit of evidence as opposed to making an arrest often required different approaches), flashlights, and padlocks. He grabbed one of the latter and a spool of crime-scene tape. He shoved the barn doors closed, threw the rusty hasp over, and locked them shut. He reconsidered stringing the tape. Yellow tape without some sort of supervision of this remote building would be an invitation to the curious to break and enter.

He would send someone out in the morning to collect the stuff—if he could. Right now they had enough to do with two fresh murder investigations. The paperwork alone would take hours.

He felt good. He was back at work.

Chapter Four

Except at work when they had no choice, Ike and Ruth had made a decision to avoid people in general. Socializing prompted questions. Questions about their vacation in Maine, for example. Questions about their brief stay in "Sin City." Questions from family—that would be Ruth's mother, Eden Saint Clare, and Abe and Dolly Schwartz. Questions about future plans—specifically marital. So, for the last three days, they had been eating their meals at either Ruth's house or Ike's apartment. On the weekend they planned to retreat to Ike's A-frame in the mountains. Buried in maples and laurel, they were guaranteed a modicum of privacy. Tonight, however, they risked a public meal at Frank's Restaurant and Grill. Frank stayed in business as a restaurateur chiefly because in a down economy, no major chain wanted to risk the start-up costs involved in opening a competitive location. That had to change soon. Rumors of a Denny's had been circulating for months. The fact that a Denny's would be considered a better choice as a place to dine than Frank's tells you everything you needed to know about Frank's culinary skill.

Thus, Ike and Ruth felt moderately safe at Frank's because, aside from the roast beef, Frank served truly mediocre food. Chances were slim that anyone they knew would eat there on a Tuesday night. Ike picked a roll out of the bread basket and searched for butter.

"We have a problem," he said and waved to their waiter.

"Just one?" Ruth asked. "From where I'm sitting we have… well, *I* have multitudinous problems. If I had a really good option, I'd be out of here in a New York minute."

The waiter arrived and Ike asked for butter. The server stared at the table for a moment hoping, Ike supposed, to find the missing butter hiding under the napery. He nodded and left.

"You say that every summer and fall, Ruth. New faculty and new students on their way in, old faculty and students who can't behave, on their way out, and the paperwork attached to all of the above sits like the Himalayas on your desk. Yes, I know and you know it will all smooth out by Halloween, and then you'll be fine. The problem we have at the moment is about us and how we announce to the world we're getting married when, in fact, we already are."

Ruth pushed back from the table and sighed. "You'd think Frank could at least have a restaurant that smelled good. A restaurant should be filled with the aromas of fresh bread, roasting meat, garlic, something. This place smells like Pine-Sol."

"Are you sure you want to sniff at Frank's cooking?"

"Frank should put an onion or two in the oven. I had a friend who did that. She couldn't cook a lick—ordered catering brought in when she had a party, but the house smelled like she'd done it all herself."

"You think Frank ships this *dreck* in from outside?"

"This? Don't be silly."

"Maybe we should drop in on the Reverend Blake Fisher and see if he'd oblige us by putting on a show wedding."

"Do you think he would?"

"Who would…Frank and the onion or…?"

"Fisher and the ceremony, of course."

"I have no idea. My experience with any sort of clergy, and Blake Fisher in particular, is limited to solving a felony murder and a theft involving the contents of his safe. But, why wouldn't he? He likes you, Ruth. Didn't you almost offer him a faculty position? I bet he would if he thought you might start attending on Sundays."

"But I didn't and I won't and he knows it. Maybe you should instead. You could sing in the choir, be an altar boy or something."

"I don't think they're called altar boys in the Episcopal church and aside from being Jewish and not baptized, a status I assume to be a precondition for membership, I can't carry a tune in a basket."

"I've heard that choir. You'd fit right in. Is there a reason we are planning this now? I mean we've only been back a few days and the craziness we got ourselves into up in Maine has leaked into the grapevine. People are full of that, not what our plans are."

"Two reasons. Abe and Dolly want us out for Sunday dinner. That would be lunch anywhere else, but the traditional, big heart attack meal of the week is always served around noon on Sunday at *Chez* Schwartz. We have not been invited for our company. They will ask, they will probe, and they will have it out of us unless we have something else to discuss. Also, my people are pestering me. We need to stop the questions."

"Then I guess we should meet with Fisher before Sunday so we will have something to report."

"I'll call him and set up a time. Send me your 'can't make it' times and I'll see what we can do."

"What about tonight?" Ruth said.

"Tonight? Sorry, tonight what?"

"I am getting the stink eye from some of my more traditional faculty and one or two board members. They find the sight of the town's top cop slouching in my house after dark for what they fantasize as unbridled sex unacceptable."

"I don't slouch and they wouldn't if you hadn't refused to be bridled for so long."

"You know what I mean. And if I stay over at your poor excuse for an apartment, I have to sneak back home like a naughty school girl hoping her parents didn't notice she'd been out all night with a boy. Can sex with a bride be considered anything but bridled?"

"Good question. Do horses have unbridled sex, do you suppose?"

"Enough already. What about it? Where do we go tonight?"

"I think tonight, I don't slouch and you don't sneak. We go our separate ways and live chastely, at least in public, until we get the Reverend Fisher to sanctify our union."

"How long can you manage celibacy?"

"Two or three days ought to do it. Over the weekend we can go to the A-frame and shed our bridles to our hearts' content."

"You're sure about that, because I have that desk full of paperwork to tackle and having you off the premises would make it go more quickly."

"You have my assurance that I am fine with it. Maybe we could do a little heavy necking on the way to your house, though."

"When was the last time you *made it* in the backseat of a car?"

"Before your time."

"You mean you did? With who? Never mind, I don't want to know."

"A lifetime ago and it was all about teenaged hormones, both hers and mine, that prompted it. The question is, do I really want to invite a leg cramp and pulled muscles wrestling with my wife in the backseat of a Buick?"

"And?"

"Just think what we can tell our grandchildren."

"Now you are getting ahead of yourself. So, changing the subject—how was your day? Murder and mayhem?"

"Murder, yes. Andy Lieux's dog found a woman taking a dirt nap out in the woods and then when she was lifted out we found another corpse sharing the same twelve square feet of parkland. Two dead people separated by perhaps a decade and stacked, you could say, like cord wood. Not something you generally run across."

"Two? Holy cow, Ike you are back on the job less than a week and people start dropping like flies. You are worse than the plague."

"Worse than?"

"Okay, not worse. So, who are they?"

"I don't know much except the ME says the woman has been dead less than a week, the other corpse is male and has been there at least ten years. I doubt they're connected but it did seem odd digging up one body and discovering it nestled on top of another."

"Two dead people spooning in a grave but buried ten years apart?"

"About ten, yes."

"Maybe they were husband and wife and she outlived him and her last wish was to be buried with the love of her life."

"Her head was bashed in. I doubt her killer had her last wishes in mind when he whacked her with a tree limb."

"You never know. Okay, I will send my available dates and times to you, and you will set up something with The Reverend Fisher ASAP. We will go to Abe and Dolly's for Sunday gorging and…Oh, I have it, we'll invite my mother to join us and kill two birds with one turkey dinner."

"Don't say kill. I've had a day full of that. Are you finished?"

"Done. Pay the bill, Handsome, and then I'll race you to the car. Where shall we park to play teenagers? The quarry or the dark end of the parking lot at Callend?"

"It's Tuesday and a school night. The quarry will have fewer teenagers than the parking lot will have students."

"The quarry it is. Wow, I really am behaving like a naughty school girl."

"Maybe you could put on a uniform. You know, plaid skirt, white blouse, bobby socks—"

"Bobby socks? What the hell are bobby socks?"

"Sorry, wrong century. It comes from watching too many old movies on TV. Short white socks."

"Sorry, I left my school uniform at the cleaners. You'll have to make do with my power suit and sensible flats. I'll ditch my pantyhose in the ladies' room on the way out."

Chapter Five

Ike plunked down in the only comfortable chair in his rented apartment. The two of them had driven to the quarry as planned and, like the teenagers they weren't, had attempted some heavy petting in the front seat, not the back. It didn't work. It didn't work because, in fact, neither of them were teenagers anymore and hadn't been for much too long. It didn't work because the press of real work and duty distracted them from the moment, and because…hell, all those adult concerns push in and stifle whatever spontaneity they might have enjoyed. Ruth took care of him in a less athletic manner and he had driven her home. He had the sense that Ruth had more on her mind than just work, but Ruth was Ruth and she would work through it.

He let his gaze wander around his apartment. Ruth had said "poor excuse of an apartment." She was right, of course. He'd rented it when he had been elected sheriff. The drive into town from the mountains where he had his A-frame took too long to be convenient and was too tricky when the snow fell and iced the roads. The apartment's two rooms, kitchenette, and bath had come furnished. In the intervening years he'd added little to the décor. He had a bookcase of his favorites. Ike did not collect books. He figured if he had no plans to ever read the thing a second time, he'd pass it on to someone who might. His bookcase contained, then, a couple of dozen volumes, mostly nonfiction and two-thirds of them biographies of leaders, famous and infamous. He'd purchased a flat-screen TV which had not yet been connected to cable. He used it to watch old movies he streamed from Netflix and rented DVDs. Also he had some plates, pots and pans, and a second small freezer he kept stocked with frozen dinners, and that was pretty much it. So, aside from the books, there was precious little to move over to the president's cottage. Actually, "cottage" diminished the building. "Mansion" more nearly covered it. Downstairs was largely given over to receptions and meetings. Ruth occupied an apartment carved out of the upstairs. It was barely larger than his, although there were guest rooms for visiting dignitaries. Fitting in the bookcase might be a challenge.

The larger question resonated around the minutia of marriage and cohabitation. Did he really want to share a bathroom? Was he ready for things like loofahs and body wash on the tub's sill? He was a bar soap man and things that came out of squeeze bottles made him nervous. Was she the sort who would use his razor in places and for purposes it was not designed? The truth about marriage and its many failures, he thought had more to do with the everyday frictions over trivia, than any lack of passion, love, or communication.

He sat back and ran the thought through his head once again and laughed. Bullshit. You adjusted or you installed a second bath—problem solved. Marriage was a state he'd only tasted, never completely devoured. He'd leave heavy analysis to Abigail Van Buren.

Charlie Garland called Ike around midnight.

"So, you have done the deed."

"Which deed would that be, Charlie?"

"Las Vegas, the Budding Rose Wedding Chapel. That deed."

"Is there anything about me you do not know? Charlie, if I didn't know you better, I'd swear you're having a bromance with me and that thought is really scary. Why in hell were you snooping into my time in the west?"

"I am your guardian angel, your Clarence. I wanted to get my wings. Your wedding bells secured them for me."

"What?"

"*It's a Wonderful Life,* don't you remember? Jimmy Stewart, or rather George Bailey thinks all is lost, his career as the town do-gooder finished and—"

"I got it. You as Clarence Odbody, the postulant angel, is way too much of a stretch, Charlie. You are the villainous Henry Potter, if you are anybody."

"I am wounded. I have to ask, are you ready for this move?"

"Ready? How do you mean?"

"You were a single guy for a long time. Then, you married Eloise after what…a twenty-minute romance?"

"It wasn't twenty minutes."

"Close. Eloise died and Ruth helped you heal. Are you sure that isn't all there is to this latest move?"

"Charlie, you are not my mother, you are not even a good psychologist. Stop prying."

"Very well, if you insist. Moving along, the director wants to know if your nuptials will temper Ruth's chronic enmity toward the nation's select service. If so, does this raise the possibility that you could be tempted to help us out on, say, a consultant basis from time to time?"

"The contrary, my friend. At her request and my concurrence, you have been removed from my speed dial. Your name may not be spoken in her presence. You are permanently banned from the premises. Before you ask, that is because she dislikes being caught in a cross fire especially when the bullets are real. She wishes never to be so again. And so say I. Done and done, Charlie."

"You two are annoyed. I understand and I am sorry about that. I will take it, then, that you are temporarily out of the loop."

"Not temporarily."

"We'll see." Charlie hung up. Ike sighed and thought of Bruce Willis and Helen Mirren and *RED* and wondered if there was ever an ending to a career foolishly begun in the darker reaches of the CIA.

More importantly, now that Charlie had resurrected it, had Ike finally said goodbye to Eloise's ghost?

◇◇◇

Ruth believed she handled stress about as well as anyone she knew, except Ike. Her cure was to do more. That is, if work stressed her out, she'd just work harder. If something in her private life, her not work life, caused her to pause, she simply pushed on through. Truth be told, that part of her life had been anything but stressful. Her relationship with Ike, which had started out about as oddly as any, had over time found a comfortable place, a rhythm. It could have gone on forever just as it was. But it wasn't going to—not now. Las Vegas and tequila had seen to that. So, a new game. Until now, the faculty, confronted with their coupling had, as a whole, managed with varying success to look the other way. Long before Ike appeared on their doorstep, they had bought into the *de rigueur* notion of "celebrating diversity." Most of them had done so as a knee-jerk response to the then-fashionable idea. None had actually considered what it meant beyond recruiting the occasional minority student—Latino, African American, gay, and so on— whatever the social imperative suggested to be important at any moment in time. All agreed that it was a good thing they did and so they "celebrated."

Having their PhD, DLitt president sleeping with the town sheriff, however, forced some of them to rethink their early subscription to the concept. Somehow, Ike and Ruth as a couple, a sexually active couple, didn't fit the broader intent. Yet, objecting to Ruth's choice exposed in them a level of hypocrisy which they found difficult to internalize. So, they looked the other way and hoped in time the whole affair would just go away. It hadn't. Ruth had dealt with this as with everything else. She soldiered on, daring anyone to say something. No one had.

That was then and this is now. It was one thing to be perceived as having a fling with a "townie," as one or two of her students did each year, and more than one faculty member did as well. But those flings were considered anomalies and not to be taken seriously. For Ruth to flaunt the norms of her "class" by actually marrying the man created a wholly different problem. She had not found an easy way to work through that. Her relationship with Ike could no longer be allowed to be viewed as a mere trifle, a whim, or a peccadillo, on her part, even when in fact it never really was. She'd permitted that camouflage to exist when she knew in her heart it was essentially disingenuous. Now it would no longer disguise anything. She had stepped over the line and the man many of her people viewed as "the hick" would soon be moving into the president's cottage permanently.

And for this, she felt stress. Even an old divorce years before did not leave her in such a state. Sometimes while in the shower or lying in bed late at night when sleep eluded her, she thought about what it would be like when the two of them reached this place in their relationship. At those times she had difficulty catching her breath. She knew she wanted Ike more than anything—didn't she? She did, but…

"What's wrong with me?" she'd mutter to the shower head or the ceiling. "I told Ike I've wanted this since…" Then she would recall the night up in the mountains. He'd just finished telling her about Eloise, his bride of a hundred days, accidently killed by an assassin in Switzerland. She'd heard the pain in his voice and his plea for understanding and wondered at the man who in spite of her bitchy behavior had been supportive during an extremely difficult time in her life.

"I don't know if I should cry or be angry" she'd said to him at the time, "and here's something else for you to think about, I think you are the most irritating, engaging, infuriating, attractive man I have ever met." And, that said, she'd stepped up and kissed him. "Smooched" him, she'd described it in their Las Vegas hotel room, wearing nothing but an overlarge bath towel. My God, how far they'd come. She smiled at the image. Not much had really changed since that early beginning. Nothing about Ike, that is. He could still be irritating and engaging, infuriating and attractive. And lately, she found him to be the coolest man in a tight spot she'd ever known or imagined.

Now, things had to change. They were no longer playmates. Their sandbox days were over. No more necking out at the quarry…well actually, that hadn't worked out too well. The two superannuated teenagers would have to settle into adulthood. And when they went public, there could be no turning back. She took a deep breath. They'd manage it, somehow.

Second thoughts? No, none. They'd figure it out.

Chapter Six

Essie looked up from her dispatch desk and raised one eyebrow. The clock read 7:45, early for Ike under any circumstance. He backed in the door, a box under each arm.

"An improvement of which everyone will approve," Ike said in response to her unasked question. "Clear the stuff off the table in the corner."

"That's the coffee corner, Ike. What kind of improvement comes from dumping the coffee pot?"

"A great deal, trust me. Just do it." He put the boxes on the floor next to the table while Essie began moving the coffeemaker, jars containing sweeteners and lightener.

"Where do these go?"

"The pot in the trash, the other stuff on the empty desk. That reminds me. Did you post the job opening on the town website?"

"I did and in the journals and all the other places you wrote down. Why are you chucking the coffeepot? Have the food police finally arrived?"

"In the first place, it's not a pot exactly. It's a very tired old urn. It is going because I am no longer willing to risk life, limb, and tooth enamel on the stuff that pours out of its spout. I am replacing it with modern technology."

"Like what?"

"K-Cups."

"Whose cups?"

Ike unpacked the two boxes and placed a K-Cup coffee brewer on the table and handed Essie a plastic container he detached from its side. "Here, fill this tank with water, then watch and learn."

He opened the second box and pulled out one of the cups.

Once the tank had been filled and the brewer plugged in, he loaded the small covered cup into the receiver, tapped the start button, and the machine groaned, gurgled, and hissed out a single cup of coffee. He added his creamer and a half package of sweetener and took a sip.

"Every cup fresh and, even better, making coffee will no longer be on your job description."

"It never was. I just did it because the department is full up with out-of-date macho guys who can't or won't, and I got tired of the whining. Makes me wonder how you manage to catch the bad guys. "

"A pungent observation. Score one for you. And you're welcome. Now all you need to do is teach those macho whiners how to do this and make sure the last one to empty the tank refills it. So, no more liquid asphalt, burned, or industrial-strength coffee. Now ditch that piece of crap that used to be an unhealthy part of our lives."

Frank Sutherlin, who served as acting sheriff when Ike was off duty, had entered the room and listened to this last exchange. "Can it make tea too?"

"Indeed. I had you in mind, Frank, and bought these little cup things. You can dump your teabag in them, substitute them for a K-Cup, and you have nice fresh-brewed tea, or prefilled cups with a variety of teas are available. I didn't want to risk picking the wrong kind. Tea drinkers can be tiresome about things like that…green, black, chai—whatever that is, no offense meant."

"None taken."

"Any news on our victims in the woods?"

"Some usable information on the latest, nada on the other. We were able to lift prints from the dead woman's body. It turns out she has a jacket three inches thick. Her prints practically jump off AFIS. Her name is Ethyl Smut, if you can believe it, AKA a number of aliases—none particularly original—Jones, Smith, Franco—and a history of drug busts for using, distributing, and abuse, meth mostly but had an occasional fling with heroin, also prostitution, and petty larceny."

"A busy lady and now she's dead. Good Lord, with a history like that there must be dozens of people who might have killed her."

"The drug culture is not a nice group of people to hang with, that's for sure. Some of those meth heads would kill for a stick of gum."

"They'd kill for something trivial, Frank, but probably not gum. Their teeth couldn't survive a stick of Juicy Fruit. Where does, or where did, she live?"

"Still working on that. Last known address according to her rap sheet was over in that mobile home park out past Bolton. You know where we send a cruiser or two most weekends?"

"Okay, let's confirm it and get out there and toss her place. Then, find who she's working with, associates and all that stuff. Put Billy on it and make sure he has backup."

"Right."

"Who's manning the computer since Grace White left?"

"I got a kid on loan from the Police Academy who knows electronics. He was due to intern somewhere so I asked Captain Rodriguez for him, and he said okay. Rodriguez owed me a favor. We have the kid for two weeks and then we have to send him back."

"With any luck, we'll have our new geek cop in by then."

"I miss Sam," Essie chimed in.

"So do I, but our former deputy and first official geek cop, Miss Ryder, now Mrs. Hedrick, is firmly ensconced in Washington, D.C., at NSA. She's busily listening to our cell phone calls and reading our mail, and isn't available."

"She isn't doing that, is she? Don't answer. You could spring her."

"Not likely. What's the attraction of the Picketsville Sheriff's Department compared to international snooping in the capital of the universe?"

"More friends and fewer Congressional investigations?"

"Good point. Frank, get Billy up to speed on Miz Smut and send him out to her digs. He can take the kid from the Academy along. Reward for finding her in the first place and to keep your Captain Rodriguez happy."

"On it."

Ike left Essie to sort out the new coffee equipment. His office, the "fishbowl" as the deputies called it, had windows for walls. It had been built to the specifications of his predecessor who, the old-timers said, didn't trust his deputies and felt he needed to keep an eye on them. All but a handful of them had since died or landed in jail, including him, so it seemed he'd been correct.

Frank dropped the two new murder books on Ike's desk. One he'd labeled "John Doe" and the other, "Ethyl Smut." The Doe file didn't have much in it—a few pictures and measurements. Ethyl's was fatter and included the downloaded materials—her record and a series of mug shots. Ike shuffled through the sequence of mug shots and marveled at the changes in her appearance over time. When she'd first been arrested on a minor drug charge, the picture in the file showed a moderately attractive young woman. Then, as the years passed, he face seemed to collapse as the ravages of methamphetamine tore at her. Her latest photo could have been that of any of a thousand women addicted to the drug. Sunken cheeks, popped and frantic eyes, scraggly hair, bad and missing teeth—meth face.

According to the file, she had a daughter, Darla or Darlene. An occasional mention of abuse, child abuse, allegations concerning the child were noted here and there, but the charges had been dismissed. The hearing judge had tossed them because of shoddy police work, mostly a failure to Mirandize Smut in a timely manner. Interestingly, that judge had also followed some of the town's former deputies into jail. The child had refused to testify. Most victims won't. A penciled note in the margin suggested that the girl was too frightened of either her mother or the current live-in boyfriend to say anything.

Or too ashamed.

There had never been a Mr. Smut, but the child—a young woman now—had to have had a father. Ike jotted a note to search him out. He also wanted to read the complete abuse record, but it would be filed and most likely sealed in Child Protective Services, and he'd need a court order to get it. It would be easier to find the girl and ask her directly. He scribbled another note.

He called his father and accepted the dinner invitation for Sunday, and then put in a call to The Reverend Blake Fisher. He listened to the church's answering machine, waited for the beep, and left a message.

A call to the medical examiner produced one important new wrinkle to the Smut case. She'd been stabbed in the side before someone bashed her head in. The wound was not lethal, but serious enough to warrant medical treatment, which had not been administered. The ME said he'd need more time to establish the interval between the two incidents, but Ike might want to start looking for a blood trail. He also stated that he had no idea who the other body was or even where it had come from. The only clue so far related to the man's clothes.

"What about the clothes?" Ike asked.

"Well, they are not local. The suit he had on when he was killed came from New York and was not off-the-rack cheap either. It has a label from a tailoring outfit, A. M. Rosenblatt and Sons, New York. Also, he'd been shot in the head and chest and one bullet had lodged in his spinal column. I retrieved it and sent it to the state ballistics lab. I also have his dental chart, and it's also on the wire, as we used to say. We should hear something in a week or so. I'll put copies of the photos in the report and shoot it over to you."

Ike thanked him and hung up. Then he remembered his father's hay barn. He sent for Charley Picket. Ike gave him the padlock key and directed him to go out to his father's barn and collect and bag anything that didn't belong there.

Last, he asked that the evidence the deputies had collected at the crime scene be brought to him. He would go through it on his return. His morning briefings would not be complete until he'd dropped in the Cross Roads Diner for breakfast and gossip. He left the office and headed the short block to Flora Blevins' diner, which was, after the university up on the hill, the town's most enduring institution.

Chapter Seven

Flora Blevins' middle initial was said to be *S*. No one knew what the *S* stood for but all agreed it was not Subtle or Saintly—Stubborn, maybe. As Ike entered the diner, she fixed him with a fierce eye.

"I hear you got Ethyl Smut on a slab at the morgue," she announced. Ike couldn't tell if the news had come to her as a surprise, an expectation, or simply as bad.

"I do, Miz Blevins." No one called Flora by her first name before ten o'clock. As with her middle name, the reasons for that rule remained buried in Picketsville folklore. "Did you know the woman?"

"Another lifetime, maybe I did."

"Right. Okay, would you know where her daughter is?"

"Why would I know that?"

"You said you knew the woman, I thought it possible you might know the daughter's whereabouts. We are looking for her in connection with her mother's death. So, you don't have a suggestion where we might start?"

"That ain't in my job description, Sheriff. What I can tell you is she ran away from home at sixteen or so. She could be anywhere or nowhere."

"And you know her because...?"

"I was her godmother and so I still care about her, that's how, not that it's any business of yours. She was a darling little girl when she were little, Darla was. Ethyl ruined her and I don't blame that girl for booking out of that trailer as soon as she had a chance. Been, what, two, three years now."

"Her godmother?"

"Don't you go and give me that look. You heard me. Now eat 'fore the hash browns get all cold. And try Facebook."

"Facebook? Flora…Miz Blevins, you look at Facebook?"

"Me? Not a chance. I don't own one of those computer things and don't ever aim to. I heard about it from old Colonel Bob Twelvetrees before he up and died on me. He used to do all that whatever they do on them things."

"Facebook. I'll keep that in mind. You said she was a nice girl back in the day?"

"I said she was a darlin' little girl. That didn't last long. Not past her seventh or eighth birthday, it didn't. No, sir. That Ethyl, she ruined the little girl."

"How?"

"Ain't proper talking about it here, or anywhere else either as a matter of fact. I'll just say this, if I'da had the opportunity and felt pretty sure you wouldn't find me out, I'da snuffed the Smut bitch my own self. And that's the truth."

"Listen to you, Miz Blevins. I declare. I am making progress. I have my first suspect."

"I didn't say I did it and I ain't the murdering kind. I only said *if.*"

"I heard you. Would you be willing to drop in the office and fill me in on why, *if* you were the murdering kind, you would have done in Ethyl Smut?"

"Why? How is knowing what I woulda done *if,* gonna help you catch the person who did?"

"Because, if you feel that strongly about a woman whose daughter you agreed to sponsor at baptism—have I got that right?—it's reasonable to assume that some others, many others in fact, might share those feelings. And I need to know why, to find out the who."

"That's too many words in one mouthful there, Ike, but sure, I'll drop by. I only know what I saw. No, make that only what

I was allowed to see, if you follow my meaning. There's more to it than that."

"I am sure the girl could tell us a great deal, but as you can't help me find her, I am stuck with you. Is there anyone else in town who might know where she is?"

"That's all I can say. You read Ethyl's arrest file. You'll see. Lordy, I don't know how many times me and the neighbors called to complain about what was going on in that trailer. Then, of course, she moved away with that bum, Angelo somebody."

"Angelo was the girl's father or Ethyl's boyfriend?"

"Not the father and just one of God-only-knows how many men. She jumped from one to the other depending who would feed her habit. It was the flavor of the month, you could say. Franco."

"What?"

"Angelo Franco was one of them that she lived with for a spell. He was probably in on it too."

"In on what?'

"Misusing that little girl is what. I ain't saying anything more."

"Okay for now, but later you will need to talk to me. And now, don't *you* go giving me the look. So, she lived in your neighborhood for a while and then left. Is that right?"

"Yep. Now eat."

"Yessum."

◇◇◇

Ike returned to the office, his mind on Flora. He believed she had information that could open the investigation so, why did she only offer gossip? Usually she would be forthcoming. Today he would swear she had something she did not want to share. What was she not telling him? He stepped through the sheriff's office door. Something was missing. He couldn't put his finger on it, but the office had somehow changed. He felt as if he'd somehow walked into a parallel universe configured exactly like his own but different. He stepped into the squad room and looked around. Essie stared back at him.

"What?" she said.

"Something's wrong."

"You think?"

"Yes, definitely. I can't figure out what it is."

"Probably 'cause you don't smell coffee. That's what's missing. Good or bad, fresh or burned, this place always smelled like coffee brewing. Now we don't brew except one cup at a time in that thing you brought. The office has lost its coffee personality."

"Ah. Gone, but not forgotten."

Ike retreated to his desk and picked up Ethyl Smut's file. He caught the Police Academy intern out of the corner of his eye as he exited the office. Ike called out to him.

"You managed to find a recent address for the Smuts. Good work."

He grinned, pulled himself up, and tried to look police professional. Ike said that when he returned he should search through Facebook and find the girl, if he could. The kid said he would. If she had a wall, he'd find it. Ike didn't ask him what the hell a wall was. TMI.

Charley Picket arrived with a large evidence bag filled with things he'd found in the hay barn. Actually the evidence bag was a garbage bag with an official-looking tag, but nobody needed to know that. Ike retrieved his key and padlock and dumped the contents of the bag on the floor. He began to pick through it, then thought better of it. His father's mystery intruders could wait. He had two murders on his desk, one old, one recent, and he needed to concentrate on the job at hand. He could sort through all this stuff later. He gathered the pile on the floor together and shoved it back in the bag. He paused over a faded photograph. It could have been an early Polaroid. It wasn't, obviously, but the degree of yellowing and the serrated edge made it seem so. He put it aside rather than returning it to the bag.

Essie was right, there was no coffee personality. Funny how you get to expect something like that. It wasn't as if it held any great attraction, the opposite actually, but change, even change that improves, isn't always easily accommodated. He swiveled back to his desk and directed his attention to the meager gleanings from the crime scene in the woods.

In addition to Charley Picket's apparent murder weapon find, the deputies had uncovered a few odds and ends. One plastic bag held an old shell casing—nine millimeter—corroded. It wasn't clear if it had come out of or lay on the ground, but in either case it had done so for some time. Ike wondered if it might be connected to the older case. Certainly a possibility.

A second bag held a faded ragged one dollar bill with a phone number scrawled in pencil on it. Who used a pencil nowadays? The United States Treasury printed bills on expensive and special paper. The formula changed from time to time as counterfeiters grew increasingly more sophisticated, and there was a very readable serial number on it. There was a better-than-even chance he could date the bill by the paper's composition and serial number. Then, if it connected to the dead guy, he'd at least have a rough time frame and a phone number from the time to look up. He'd have it tested. No area code with the phone number, so it could be for anybody and from anywhere. Still, it was worth a try. The dead man's clothes, the ME said, had been purchased in New York. That narrowed the search area somewhat. He'd have someone look for the phone number in the Connecticut, New York, Long Island, and New Jersey directories for the years the bill had been in circulation. Maybe something would jump out.

Then there were the dental records the ME was cooking up. He should have an ID soon enough. There was no way all or any of this could be linked to either killing with certainty, but the fact they were found at the scene might lead to something. One hoped so.

The techs had made a plaster cast of a footprint, boot print actually. It could be either that of a child or a woman and the tread indicated the boot had been recently purchased. He'd need to identify the maker and survey the local stores for a recent sale of that particular boot. So, progress. As soon as Billy and the intern returned, he'd get them cracking on this stuff.

He stared at the yellowed photo, leaning back in his ancient oak desk chair which, mercifully, had responded to oil and lost its squeal.

Chapter Eight

In mid-June the scent of hundreds of flowers and shrubs compete with each other for attention, particularly in the morning when the air is cooler and the dew still adorns the petals. In a few weeks or perhaps days and, if you haven't planned your plantings carefully, only honeysuckle will be in bloom and by July, that will be the only relaxing scent anywhere. Aromatherapy is not a New Age invention. Gardeners have known about it for millennia.

Ike and Ruth sat in his car on the parking lot of Stonewall Jackson Memorial Episcopal Church with the windows rolled down. They'd had their hour with The Reverend Blake Fisher and now stared through the windscreen seeing, but otherwise not appreciating, the flowers that bordered the graveled lot.

"He said 'No.' Do you believe that?" Ruth asked.

"He did, and I do."

"I can't believe it. I mean, we have known him since he arrived as a wet-behind-the ears vicar with enough baggage to keep a shrink busy for a year. You solved a murder that practically shut his church down and could have sent him packing. And, as you pointed out, I very nearly made him a faculty member. Well, thank God that didn't happen.'

"Slight exaggeration on the baggage quotient there, Harris, and it's his church. I guess he can do anything he wants. Maybe if you had given him an appointment of some sort, he'd have to have accommodated. Hell, you're the president."

"Nuts. How could he not marry us?"

"Listen, he does have a point."

"Which was? Remind me."

"He said a church wedding is a sacrament and not to be taken lightly. In his line of work I guess that's important. He said he loved us both but he also knew that the wedding would be just for show and to cover our asses—actually he didn't say asses—embarrassment at the circumstances of our foray into matrimony in Vegas. But doing it for us certainly did not represent a commitment by either of us to a religious point of view, lifestyle, or the sacrament involved."

"I don't care. He could have done us a favor and ignored his scruples."

"He could have, but let's face it, he knew neither of us would ever darken his door again except for an occasional drop-in for someone else's wedding or funeral. We are not members of his congregation, never will be, and I guess he didn't want to turn his church into an East Coast version of the Budding Rose Wedding Chapel."

"He didn't say that."

"Not in so many words, no, but that was the gist."

"I don't care, he could have."

"If he'd asked you to put on a mock graduation ceremony and award him an honorary degree to help him be elected bishop, would you have done it?"

"Don't be ridiculous. Honorary doctorates are earned by a lifetime of scholarship or…Oh, crap. I get it. Okay, now what do we do?"

"We have two choices. We can try other churches—Rabbi Shusterman will give us the same lecture, by the way—or we can cowboy up, tell the truth, and throw the town a party."

"Cowboy up?"

"Okay, cowgirl up, bite the bullet, face the music, be the man—"

"I get it. Right. This weekend, we will go up to the A-frame and start writing guest lists. Call your dad and ask if he can delay lunch an hour or so. Sunday, we'll drive back here at noon, pick up my mother, cow-person up, and bite the music."

"Nicely put. How about some lunch?"

"As long as you really mean lunch and are not angling for something more physical. I have work to do. The board meets this afternoon and my spies tell me one or two of them have issues."

"Issues? What kind of issues? And I did mean lunch as in eating food and drinking liquids."

"Good, find us a place where we can sit, bitch about the sanctimoniousness of The Reverend Fisher, repent of it, eat a sandwich or a salad, and discuss the board's issues."

"I know just the place."

Blake Fisher, the object of Ike and Ruth's annoyance, did not think of himself as particularly sanctimonious nor did he believe he could be fairly described as either rigid or unsympathetic. But he had lately begun to resent and then react to the increasing secularization of society in general and the church in particular. It was one thing to minimize the forms of worship as "seeker churches" did in order to help younger people find a comfortable, if shallow, spirituality. You had to start them off somewhere. But, it was another thing entirely to jettison the substance with the forms in order to be politically correct or make people comfortable in their disbelief. Add to that, this business that Ike and Ruth wanted. Why do people who have no religious grounding or interest think they need a church wedding? Every May he turned away at least four couples who asked to "rent his church." He really did like Ike and Ruth, respected their position, and he wished them well, but if he bent the rules for them, he'd have to do it for everyone and he did not want to be known as the "Marrying Sam" of the Shenandoah Valley.

His thoughts were interrupted by a soft knock on his door. His secretary poked her head in and said there was a young woman waiting in the church who wanted to speak to him.

"In the church? Why there and not in the office?"

"She didn't say. Shall I call someone…ask the sheriff to come back?"

"Ask the— Why would I need the sheriff?"

"She looks sort of scruffy. I think she's a homeless person here to hit you up for money. You know how those people are."

"No, Dolores, I don't know anything of the sort."

Dolores Manfred was a temp. Happily so. A church needed a secretary who shared at least some basic Christian qualities, and bigotry wasn't one of them.

"I'll talk to her. If she tries to attack me, you'll be the first to hear me scream."

Dolores huffed back to her office.

Blake's office gave way to a small room that served as the sacristy and then to the church nave. He stepped through the oak door and glanced around. A figure in a faded hoodie sat slumped over in the front pew. She was only twenty feet away and the hood nearly covered her face, but Blake could see she'd been crying.

"Mrs. Manfred said you wanted to see me?"

The girl started. Blake would have sworn she'd cringed at the sound of his voice.

"I don't know. See, I don't, you know, go to church much. Is this a Catholic church? I saw the little statues on the walls with the numbers and figured it had to be."

"You saw the Stations of the Cross. They are not necessarily Catholic with a capital C. Other denominations use the stations on occasion as well."

"Oh. So you're not, like, Catholic."

"I am catholic with a lower case C, not Roman, if I take your meaning."

"What?"

Blake realized a lecture on catholicity and its many inter-pretations would not be useful at the moment. "I assume you are not a Roman Catholic, Miss. Why did you ask? Do you want to go to a Catholic church, or is there something else?"

"A guy I used to know…see, one time he tried to fix me, but couldn't or something. He said I should confess to a priest and then I would be okay with God."

"You want to make a confession?"

"I guess. Will I be okay with God if I do? I've been in some pretty bad shit…sorry, I forgot. There, you see what I mean? I can't even talk to a preacher without pissing off God. Sorry."

"God has heard it all before. If you wish, I can hear your confession. Or, if you'd rather, I can tell you how to find a Catholic church, or you can sit here as long as you like and talk to God yourself."

"I tried that. It don't work, somehow I can't, like, get connected. That's why I came here. You're allowed to do that stuff? I mean you're a priest and all?"

"If by 'stuff' you mean hear your confession, I can, and if you want me to, I will. Does anybody know you're here?"

The girl started again and gave him a look he would have described as frightened—except why would that question scare her? Unless she was on the run.

"Yeah. I told my…I told the people I am staying with about it, sort of."

"Sort of?"

"They're not, like, church people. I don't think they'd get it, so I said I wanted to take a little walk."

"Okay. I don't want to be accused of misleading anybody. So, yes, I can hear your confession."

The girl frowned and scrunched up her face. "I don't know. Aren't there rules or something about that?"

"Probably, but that would be someone else's problem. Here's the deal. I will listen to you. Anything you say will be confidential. You know what the 'Seal of the Confessional' is?"

"You can't tell the cops?"

"Pretty much, yeah."

"You know I'm crazy?"

"Pardon?"

"Like if I let go for even a minute, I lose it. Like, I am hanging on to being normal by my fingernails."

Blake glanced at the girl's hands and saw little evidence of nails. She had chewed them to the quick.

"Why is that?"

"It's like the shit…the life I was into back in the day. One doc who saw me said I'm 'chemically imbalanced' from back then, like when I was born or something. Hey, if it's not something you can do, you know—"

"It's okay. Do you have a name?"

"Yeah, but not today. Maybe I can say it later, but I better not yet. Is that part of the confessing? I gotta tell you my name?'

"No, not a part. God knows you. That's enough for now."

The girl scratched her arm and studied the carpet. Blake noted that there did not seem to be any needle marks on it. A good sign.

"Okay. What do I do now?"

Blake handed her a prayer book. "Read the pages I've marked with a ribbon. When you're ready, just tell me what's going on."

Blake watched as the girl read the pages he'd indicated. Her lips moved as she tracked the words. She looked up, her expression a question mark. Blake motioned her to kneel at the altar rail. He sat in a chair on the other side at a right angle, facing away from her and staring at the wall to her left. Twenty minutes later, when she'd finished, he gave her absolution. He assured her he would not talk to the police. He understood why she might not want to, but that she should. She mumbled something about it being part of her problem, shook her head and left. He didn't know if she felt better. He knew he didn't. He returned to his office furious at a society that allowed people to do terrible things to their children. He still did not know her name.

He wanted to weep.

Chapter Nine

Tom Wexler had been hired as the county's newest medical examiner a little over two months earlier. He had not yet had a chance to assess the various actors in the area. Ike Schwartz especially seemed a puzzle to him. Half the time Ike sounded like one of the good ole boys, and the rest of the time he could pass for a faculty member from the local university. Tom preferred his cops to be slow and respectful and uncomplicated. Schwartz was certainly not slow and the respectful part was still up for grabs. He'd think about the complicated bit. He knew Schwartz had a story, but beyond that, little else. He'd had heard rumors but discounted them. Why would an ex-CIA agent become a small-town sheriff? He couldn't think of any reason, and with big-city wisdom on his side, he'd dismissed the thought.

Before moving to the Shenandoah Valley, Tom had served as assistant ME in Detroit, which at one time held the dubious title of Murder Capital of the World. That honor now rested with Juarez, Mexico, or Honduras. The honor seemed to have become a moving target. Tom believed the correct answer to the question of what city should bear the dubious title is Cabot Cove, but he received only a blank stare when he said so. How soon they forget. He also found that the rural pace of western Virginia took some getting used to. His desk, when he'd arrived, faced a window. He'd had it turned one hundred and eighty degrees after two days on the job. The valley's lush scenery and the view of the Blue Ridge Mountains had become a major distraction. Now he sat facing an orange-yellow-glazed brick wall adorned with official-looking paper Scotch-taped to its surface.

He rifled through the papers on his reoriented desk and stared at a blue computer screen. He pulled up the newly digitalized dental record he'd constructed of the dead man found in the woods who now occupied a drawer in his morgue. He would send the chart to the registry. If he were lucky, he might have an ID back in a few days.

It would be the first time he'd tried this—for him—relatively new technology, and he had no idea how well it would work, if at all. But he'd been assured at the recent forensic conference that if the subject had a dental record on file with the National Dental Imaging/Information Repository, an ID could be made. All this assumed that he'd correctly translated the dental information into the computer and that the dead man's record had found his way into the system at some time—a missing person, a perp. At the very least, the chart could confirm an identity. He compared the chart with the X-rays made. Satisfied that the chart correctly represented the teeth and that he'd done what he could; he punched the "send" button and sent the data sailing off through cyberspace to the NDI/IR and the FBI.

Next, he turned his attention to the toxicology screen made on the dead woman. No surprises there. Her bloodstream could have been distilled and sold as a one hundred-proof methamphetamine-alcohol tonic. He shook his head. Whoever clonked the old woman on the head after stabbing her could have saved time and a murder charge if he or she had waited another week. No one could survive much longer with titers of drugs and booze as high as those found in Ethyl Smut. Of course, druggies did have an amazing resilience to things that would kill an ordinary person. Somehow Darwin's theory of natural selection didn't work in the drug world. First-timers and the chronically stupid would frequently succumb on their first or second foray into that dark world, but hard-core stoners seemed indestructible. Then, just when it appeared they had super powers, their personal Kryptonite locked on and they imploded.

He closed the toxicology file and sorted through the rest of the tech's findings—fibers, clothing, estimates of the weapon used to stab her. Not much to work with. Most of what he had would confirm a killer, or method, but not lead to him or her. He envied those TV characters that could identify pollen from Patagonia with a click of the mouse, or clinch the ID of a killer by running a DNA test in twenty minutes on a sample of gummy bears taken from a garbage can. With that thought in mind, he remembered he wanted to order a DNA screen on the tissue scrap from the skeletal remains. It would be a long shot at best. Schwartz hadn't asked for it, and although it would put a dent in his budget that he might have difficulty justifying later, his gut told him it would be needed. He didn't know why. He claimed no extrasensory powers, but when his intuition spoke, he listened. Today it was nagging him to order the test.

Ike returned to his office alternately annoyed at Blake Fisher and admiring him for standing by his convictions. In a world committed to the homogenization forced on it by political correctness, the mediocrity of celebrity worship, and the cult of self-empowerment, a person standing on principle was a welcome rarity. He would not have objected if the good vicar had bent the rules this one time, however. A problem he believed solved now owlishly stared at him, daring him to find a quick and easy solution. There did not seem to be one.

He placed a notepad in front of him. Pen in hand he considered who and how many people he should include on his guest list. If there is one thing a man hates to do, party-planning would be near the top of the list. Party-planning, reading Christmas letters, pets wearing clothes, and drinks made with crème de menthe. He was okay with quiche.

The intern, who by now had acquired the label "TAK," The Academy Kid, walked past his door. Ike called him in.

"How good are you with computer stuff?" Ike was not a Luddite, but his skill set in most things electronic was pretty much limited to pushing the I/O button and double-clicking icons.

"I get around the web," TAK said.

"Our original geek installed some sophisticated software on our system and I want to know if you're good enough to run it."

"Yeah, I scanned through some of your programs. 'Sophisticated' isn't the half of it. You have enough stuff jammed into your box to start World War III."

"To end it, maybe, but we'd never start it. Here—" Ike picked up the yellowed photo on his desk. "See if you can scan this in and run it through the facial recognition program. If this child ever entered the system, we may get a hit. I want know who left their antique trash in my father's barn. Also, run it through the program that ages people. How old would you say this picture is?"

TAK took the photo from Ike and turned it over. "Eleven years more or less. There's a date on the back."

"Okay, I'm guessing the girl in the photo is five or six, so age her eleven years."

"I don't know, Sheriff. I know computers as good as the next guy, but running that software might be beyond me."

"TAK, do you know the first rule of police work?"

"Umm…which first rule would that be? The instructor who teaches forensics said the first rule was 'Never screw up a crime scene until the ME clears it.' The range officer said the first rule is 'Always use two hands.' The traffic instructor said—"

"Okay, I got it. So here's the first rule that trumps all previous first rules: 'Fake it 'til you make it.'"

"What?"

"When you are faced with something new and unexpected, you can't wait for the experts to arrive. If you do that you will never get anything done and you may end up with some bullet holes in places you'd rather they weren't. You live by your wits on the streets, son. Do something. What's the worst thing that can happen here?"

"I could fail."

"Fear failure and you flunk life. There, you can write that down and put it on your refrigerator or your Facebook—what did you call it?"

"Wall."

"Exactly. Post it on your wall thing. Now go see what you can do."

"Yes, sir."

The intern wandered back to the converted cell where the Picketsville Sheriff's Office had assembled its electronic presence. Ike returned to the consideration of his guest list. The phone rang. With any luck, he thought, this will be a massive catastrophe of some sort that will require my undivided attention for the next twenty-four hours. After that, the list-making could be addressed with ample amounts of bourbon to make it doable. It was Ruth with a request. Close enough.

"Before we go this weekend, you need a haircut."

"Thank you for that."

"Thank me for…? Never mind, get a haircut."

"Just one? Wouldn't it be better to get them all cut?"

"Don't be a smartass. Call Lee Henry and move your uniformed butt down the street."

"I do not wear my uniform except on special occasions."

"I stand corrected. Move your non-uniformed butt and get a haircut."

Chapter Ten

Hannibal Colfax worked at the FBI as a career agent. He had survived the tag end of the Hoover years, not Hoover himself— he wasn't that old—but the residue, you could say. And he'd endured the succession of directors since. He understood the ramifications the politicization of the agency. Furthermore, he was old...well, getting old. His arthritis plagued him no matter how many Percocets he popped. His wife of forty years left him for a classmate from grammar school, and the children took her side in the divorce procedures. His coworkers knew all this and wondered why the kids chose their mother over him and consequently looked sideways at him. Hannibal was not a happy man. He walked toward the meeting room with a gait that signaled his aches and wore an expression that confirmed them.

The Dental Information/Imaging Repository isn't so much a place as it was an elaborate software program. It requires a few people to manage calls and to sort new submissions into the proper categories or to send them back to the submitting agency for clarification and correction. For Hannibal, it was the dead end that came before unceremonious retirement and a move to a rented apartment in a middling neighborhood and a bleak old age.

When the system worked, it provided a smooth, efficient, and cost-effective addition to the FBI's many services. Who could argue with an easily accessible system to help trace missing persons, identify victims, or even their killers? But it had its critics. While inexpensive, it still cost money to operate, and politicians, Hannibal knew, find expenditures they don't think are vote-getters easy targets for public displays of fiscal outrage. By the same token, and often it's the same politicians, they find enthusiastic support for the same program or service in times when a tragedy is avoided or a life is secured. The nature of politics in the twenty-first century, Hannibal thought, is that expediency trumps principle. With these dark, cynical thoughts in mind, he pushed through the door of the conference room to hear the latest from his section chief, a man half his age who commanded a quarter of his abilities.

"Congressman Trangant is annoyed at us again," the section chief was saying. "Apparently the agency's Fraud Division has stepped on a few toes in a corporation that contributes large sums to his campaign. Accordingly, he will be bringing a sub-committee of the Appropriations Committee through here on Monday. He believes he will find waste and inefficiency." He shot a veiled glance in Hannibal's direction. "Well, if he knew where to look, he probably would. However, he doesn't know, so he and his fellow political hacks are on a fishing expedition. He has decided the cost-benefit ratio of some of our newer services is demonstrably poor. So all of you, especially your group, Hannibal, make sure you look busy when the sharks swim into view."

Hannibal returned to his section and instructed his team to take the rest of the day off. He would see them bright and early Monday, he said, and they were to prepare for an inspection by a panel of Congressional poo-bahs. They were not to touch any of the materials currently stacking up in their electronic in-boxes but should wait until the politicians arrived. When these good gentlemen and ladies entered, the staff was to tackle them then and look terrifically busy. Satisfied his group could stand the scrutiny of even the most persistent prober, he joined his group by vacating the premises. Monday was a long weekend away.

◇◇◇

Lee Henry used to cut hair in her home where she acquired a substantial client list and some small savings. She was an early subscriber to the lemons-to-lemonade philosophy and had parlayed hard times into an entrepreneurial success. Instead of hunkering down when things got tight, she plowed her small savings into what she believed would be a successful business plan. She took over an abandoned commercial site on Main Street, installed several specialty chairs, and opened a salon. The extra chairs she rented to women like herself who thought a place in town would be more profitable than cutting and shampooing in their basements or kitchens, even after paying rent to Lee. Some were forced by hard times to return to haircutting to make ends meet.

Leasing chairs to women did not quite cover it. Bob Blankenship, Flora Blevins' retired cousin twice removed, rented one of her chairs every Wednesday and Friday afternoon. "Bob the Barber" worked those times because, he declared, men, if they planned ahead, usually had their hair cut late on Wednesday and, if they didn't, had it done on Friday. The rest of the week's business wouldn't pay him enough to lure him all the way out of retirement. When he worked, Lee assigned Bob the first chair. She didn't think his clientele mixed well with hers or the other girls'.

When questioned by one of Callend's faculty members at the term *girls*, Lee had brushed it off with a succinct—one might say rude—remark about folks giving up the joy in language usage for fear of offending, and she didn't give a rat's rear end for that. Actually she had not said "rear end," but used a somewhat earthier term. The faculty member had never returned. One look at her hair was enough to confirm the truth of that, Lee had remarked later.

Lee said if Ike got his handsome Semitic self over right away, she'd fit him in; she'd had a cancellation. He stepped into the shop's unmistakable aroma of wet hair, conditioner, Lysol, and whatever the rest was. He could never quite determine what, but guessed it had something to do with permanents.

"Well, you got here pretty quick, Handsome. How you been, how was your vacation with the beautiful Miz Harris? I been hearing stories."

"Stories? The vacation had its moments. Maine is beautiful in late May. Just trim me up the way you do. What's the latest joke? I've been away and have missed your naughtiness, Lee."

A young woman entered. Ike scanned her as she walked past. Cop habit. He did not notice anything out of the ordinary except her clothes. They were new, all of them, blouse, jeans, shoes, everything new. How often does a young woman wear everything brand spanking new? And if he guessed right, everything wholly out of style. Most young people wore jeans that were past redemption—torn, worn, and ragged either from wear or were made to look old and decrepit with a belt sander and bleach. This young woman's jeans were new and very blue. The copper rivets gleamed. He couldn't quite guess how old she was. She had old eyes. That he did see. Her face had a familiar look, but he would have said that about half the women her age. The familiarity could be a generational thing.

"You go see Grace," Lee said to her. Grace Chimes rented the third chair today and apparently Lee had handed this client off to her.

"Lordy," Grace said, "we need to get that mop of yours washed before we do any cutting. How long has it been, Sweetheart, since it saw a dab of shampoo?"

Ike didn't hear the reply.

"Okay, Mr. Sheriff, sit back while I spritz you." Lee said. Ike could no longer see the girl but he could have sworn she jumped when Lee spoke just then.

"Whoa there, Honey, you okay? I didn't get soap in your eye, did I?" Grace asked.

"No. I'm okay. Just a little jumpy I guess."

"So," Lee began, "a rabbi, a monsignor—that's one of them Catholic preachers, you know—a Baptist, a Muslim, and an atheist all come into this bar together, okay? And the bartender says, 'Is this going to be some kind of a joke?'…Get it? It's like—"

"I got it, Lee. That's funny."

"I don't get it," Grace said. "What's the joke the bartender thought was coming?"

"Aw, come on Grace," Lee said, "all them jokes start that way. You know: a this, and a that, and the other go fishing or come into a bar or whatever and one says something. It's a whatchacallit."

"Cliché," Ike added.

"I still don't get it."

"Well, shoot, Grace. You just ain't been around this salon long enough or you woulda. Okay, Ike, you ain't answered my questions about you and the beautiful Doctor Miz Harris. What's up with that?"

"I expect you'll know soon enough, Lee." He nodded his head fractionally toward the girl.

In a lower voice Lee said, "Flora Blevins' niece or grandniece, I think. She said something like that anyway. Flora called and set up the appointment. Luckily, Grace was in today. The kid's here on a visit or something. What do you mean, 'soon enough'?"

"Ask me that next week sometime."

"That don't qualify as encouraging, Ike."

Chapter Eleven

The ballistics test from the bullet imbedded in the man's spinal column lay on Ike's desk when he returned from his trip to Lee Henry's salon. The lab verified it as a nine millimeter with no important or distinguishing marks. It had been photographed and the images transmitted to the national registry. It would be checked for matches against other samples from around the country. If the gun that produced it had been used in the commission of a crime anywhere and had been entered into the system, they would soon know.

It was progress, of a sort, especially for a cold case like this one. Not much, to be sure, but crimes were not solved in the hour television devoted to the art, forty minutes if you discounted the time spent on commercials. The woman's death was a different story. She'd been identified and had next of kin lurking around somewhere. She also had a record. She had acquaintances; Flora Blevins knew her, for example. Surely one had either to be the killer or lead Ike to the killer. It would take some time but not as much as the dead-a-decade guy.

TAK rapped on his door.

"What have you got for me, Son?"

"I found the girl on Facebook. Not too much there—no photo, just an avatar." Ike's eyebrows shot up. "Um…it's like a cartoon face only not always. See—"

"Never mind, I got it. Go on."

"Anyway, I'm sure it's her. She uses the name Darlene Dellinger instead of Darla." Ike started to speak and thought better of it. Give the kid his moment. "And here's the good part. When I tracked her through the juvenile justice system, I discovered she'd had a name change right after that entry. You'll never guess to what."

"Darla Smut."

TAK's face fell. "How'd you know?"

"Since you nearly wet your pants waiting for me to guess, it had to be one of our latest problems and a female child meant the Smut woman's daughter. Why the name change?"

"Okay, here's the rest. The mother's name changed, like, monthly as she jumped from one alias to another. Most of them were scams—ID thefts to collect welfare or food stamps she could sell. Dellinger was the father's name, according to her birth certificate in the file—Mark Dellinger, and she decided to use it. I guess she thought she could hit him up for support money. Anyway, he took off for parts unknown about the time the kid was born, did a dime for assault and public drunkenness, and disappeared for good after his release."

"Did she ever catch up with the father?"

"Guess not. So, the girl had a history of having been abused. The arresting officers thought that the mother might be complicit. I guess she thought a name change would get her off the radar, so to speak."

"Thank you. You've done good, kid. Any luck with the program that ages a face?"

"No, sorry. Running that program is way beyond my pay grade. I'll keep trying, but don't hold your breath."

"Fine. Before you give up on computer work, see if you can find a picture of Dellinger for me and anything else that's available."

"Yes, sir. You want his arrest record and—"

"There ought to be a mug shot in the system somewhere and maybe a dental record."

"Yes, sir." TAK drifted back to his temporary desk and began his next assault on the computer's keyboard.

Ike leaned back in his chair, put his feet up on his desk, castled his fingers, and began running through the few facts he had and wished he had. All he knew for certain was that Smut had a long history of drug and child abuse and that she changed her child's name at least once. What were the chances she'd done it multiple times? Pretty good, probably, if she wanted to stay ahead of Child Protective Services and the police. But there was the business of her rarely spending any real time in jail and the fact that serious charges were almost never brought. Why was that? Finding the daughter, whatever her name was now, would help. But to do that depended on someone stepping up with an address, a phone number, or a sighting. Unfortunately, the streets of America's cities were filled with waifs and strays most of whom looked too much alike. You've seen one runaway, you've seen them all—like meth-faced women. That girl in the salon for example, Flora's niece or whatever she was, in other circumstances, could easily be one of America's lost children.

Finally, he had to concede that, farfetched or not, the woman's murder and the other body could be related. That is, if the other body in the grave turned out to be Mark Dellinger. Maybe it was he who did the molesting and the Smut woman popped him for doing the girl one time too many. It made sense, but only if the person who killed Smut also knew about the father. Perhaps he had a brother or close relative who decided to even things up. That would explain going to all the trouble of having them share a grave.

Likely or not, he'd post the connection as a possibility on the tack board he'd set up in the outer office.

◇◇◇

Charley Picket stood on the sidewalk outside the Cross Roads Diner and stared at its glass door. It was that time of the year when the humidity level caught up with the temperature. He mopped his forehead with a red bandanna. He could smell the food cooking inside and his stomach started to growl. He had not eaten anything since five o'clock and he'd missed lunch because he had to chase some redneck in a pickup for miles before the boy finally gave up and pulled over. The truck was a mess, the kid not much better. Charley had given him a ticket for failure to stop at a four-way and another for not yielding to an order to stop. He called in the plates and turned the kid loose.

Charley was close to sixty, which side and how close were not clear. He had never eaten a meal or even had a cup of coffee in the Cross Roads Diner. Growing up, it had been forbidden territory. "Coloreds" were expected to eat in their own restaurants. All that had changed a good while back, of course. It had taken a long time, but the changes came. Still, he hesitated. Laws can change what people do and where they can do it, but not how people feel. Until this moment he had never had any desire to find out if the attitudes of local white folk had changed since *Brown v. The Board of Education* out there in Topeka, at least as it related to the Cross Roads Diner. But he was hungry and Jack's Lunchroom was located over on the other side of town.

"Whatcha waiting for, Charley?" Billy Sutherlin had somehow snuck up behind him. "Flora can be mean as a snake, but she's an equal opportunity mean snake. She'll as likely yell at me as you."

"Yeah, I guess so. It's just I never been in this place."

"You're kidding? Hell, Charley, you must be the only man in town that ain't."

"Well, it's just that—"

"Charley…hey, all that stuff was a lifetime ago. Ain't nobody in there going to come at you and I ain't just saying that 'cause I'm white. So come on."

Billy shoved open the door and held it aside for Charley. Flora Blevins glared at the two of them.

"Get in or get out, but either way, shut the door. I am not in the fly farming business. You must be Deputy Picket. How come you never eat here? Jack's food can't be that much better. I do reckon I'll never match his ribs, though. Billy, shut the damned door."

Charley grinned an apology and took a booth with Billy in the corner. Flora plunked down a slice of apple pie with a wedge of cheddar and a cup of coffee in front of him.

"Excuse me, Ms. Blevins, but I didn't order anything yet."

"You will and that is what it'll be. Billy, your chili is on the way."

"But—"

"It don't do any good to complain, Charley. Flora decides what you need and you get it. After you've eaten here a while you might be able to change it, but for now, your afternoon between-meals eating at the diner will be coffee and pie. It's good pie, by the way. Flora, what's the hold up on my chili?"

"I told you once already, it's on the way."

Chapter Twelve

Friday finally arrived and with it the prospect of an uninterrupted weekend. However, Ruth and Ike had work to do. Not work related to their professions, but tasks connected to their behaviorally rash evening in Nevada. They had to decide the means by which their hasty and irregular marriage should be announced to the public. For ordinary folk, the problem would not loom so large, but for a popular public servant and the respectable president of an emerging university, the situation had facets ordinary people could not appreciate. Or so they thought.

Ike signed out early that afternoon at four. He could be reached at his A-frame, he'd announced, but short of a national emergency approaching Hurricane Sandy proportions, he would prefer to be left alone. Ruth managed to sneak out of the Administration Building at Callend University by a side door and thereby missed an unscheduled meeting with a very irate chairman of the Biology Department who'd just discovered an FTE had been cut from his budget. The fact that he hadn't filled the slot in three years, and clearly did not need it whereas others did, meant nothing. Turf and pride were in play. To lose so valuable an asset, even if not needed, constituted a blow to the department's prestige and, more importantly, to his ego. The fact that the creative writing division of the English Department got the faculty slot didn't help either. Ruth's surreptitious exit meant his complaint would go unheard until Monday.

Ruth did leave a phone number where she could be reached. Agnes Ewalt, her secretary—administrative assistant—knew it and she would screen how and when and by whom it should be and could be utilized. That would be any and all attempts to reach her. On the whole, Ike thought, Ruth had a better avoidance system than he did.

They ate an early dinner of leftover pizza salvaged from an office birthday party, which they supplemented with a bottle of red wine. Neither could identify it as to vintage or year as the label had mysteriously disappeared.

"Mice?" Ruth asked.

"Cheap glue most likely. Does anyone ever use the word mucilage for glue anymore?"

"It may be the ugliest word in the English language, Anglo-Saxonisms excluded. Language aside, and stop stalling, Schwartz, where," Ruth said as she simultaneously sipped and grimaced at her wine glass, "do we begin?"

"No idea. Parties and generating guest lists are not in the male skill set. They are in the category that includes thank-you letters, Christmas cards, and the excessive affection for cats that often borders on the obsessive. I think those traits are on the X chromosome and apparently require two of them to be expressed or, in this case, to generate such a list."

"Bullshit, Schwartz, you don't get off that easy. This is your town and these are your people. You pick up your BIC and start writing."

"Let's think this thing through. Do we really need a party? How about a mass mailing of a nice engraved announcement? I can run down to Roanoke tomorrow and have the whole thing done in an hour."

"And what? You will order an 'All in ZIP Code' mailer?"

"It's a thought. How about I find us a bottle of wine with a label still attached while you mull over the idea?"

"Yes to the wine, no to mulling. There is another possibility, you know. The Reverend Fisher might reconsider and anyway, he's not the only game in town."

"We've been through this once already. I told you Rabbi Schusterman would likely say the same thing as Blake, and showing up at the Baptists or the Methodists begs the question."

"I'm not thinking about trying another church. Why not a Justice of the Peace?"

"It would require we apply for a marriage license which could take some time to acquire and an affidavit that there are no impediments and/or previous marriages. Since it is a legal document, that might entail a bit of perjury on our part. Jail time or probation isn't a good way to start a marriage, do you think? It's a stretch, but it could happen, and then our embarrassment would triple."

"Crap. So, what do we do?"

"We have three options. We beg Fisher to reconsider, we proceed with the party and admit to our rash behavior, or we do nothing and hope lighting strikes—metaphorically speaking."

"You are hoping someone or something else solves this for us?"

"In a word, yes."

"That is a trait found exclusively on the Y chromosome, I believe. Doing nothing only puts off the inevitable. Our relationship, as jolly as we seem to think it is, has produced major heartburn among the faculty, your deputies, and our respective parents. Doing nothing will only promote more of the same and perhaps irrational behavior by the people we need in order to maintain our professional positions."

"Wow! All that? Who knew? In the first place, you know what I think about my professional position, as you call it. I have been elected sheriff of the town twice, which is one more time than I had planned for. So, if the job goes away, it will be a mercy. You, on the other hand, can pick just about any academic post you want. If it's in the northeast or the People's Republic of California, our relationship would be celebrated as an exercise in diversity and broad-mindedness. Political correctness would elevate us to star status. So, no big deal."

"Don't be a horse's gazunka, Schwartz. You know what I mean. We are here, will be for the near future, and at the moment I have no desire to move north, east, or in any direction, and for all your fake disdain for your job, you love it and you know you do. So, get the wine and let's get serious."

Ike uncorked a bottle of Merlot with an odd year, which he'd been assured by the bald guy at the liquor store was a good thing. Ike did not know or wish to learn the niceties of wine appreciation. Red was red, white was white, and pink was pink. What more did anyone need to know about wine?

Ruth tasted the new batch and nodded. "Better. Plans?"

"How about this? You know the mayor…"

"Of course I know the mayor. Everybody knows the Town Dope. Why?"

"We'll ask him to do the honors."

"You want "the Mayor from the Dark Lagoon" to perform our wedding? Ike, he hates your guts."

"He does and that's the best part. He hates me, but he owes me for saving his cookies in the last election, remember? So, he'll be glad to even things up a bit." Ike grinned at the idea of putting the mayor front-and-center. "Oh, and let's have your guy who teaches comparative religion…you know, the Presbyterian-pastor-turned professor to be the co—whatever you call them when they tag-team a wedding. Think of it. Town and gown together, a celebration of unity."

"I know you think you are being cute and funny, but you may have hit on something. Do you think the mayor would do it?"

"We have but to call and ask."

"You think?" Ruth did not sound convinced.

"No, but on the other hand I really do not want to make a party list tonight."

"No? No, you're right. We need to think this through and neither of us is acting particularly sensible at the moment. Remember you've slept at your apartment for the last three nights and if you're over the leg cramps you developed in your Buick, not to mention the endgame, shall we say, coming up less than what you expected—"

"I have no complaints about the end game. You may end the game that way anytime you wish."

"Be happy to, but it is a bit one-sided. Anyway, with that thought in mind, I have a better idea where we might polish off this mediocre red. Different ending, however."

"I like the way you problem-solve."

Chapter Thirteen

Sunday dinner at Abe Schwartz's farm was variously described as a heart attack-about-to-happen or the tryptophan two-step. Either way, the time that might have been devoted to discussing—or rather avoiding a discussion of—a forthcoming wedding, devolved into desultory murmurings and, in Abe's case, snoring. The dinner and its sequelae would have no long-term effect on the life and times of the citizenry of Picketsville, nor on Ike and Ruth. After all, plans are made to be modified or, in this instance, remain unspoken.

While the family attempted to stay on task, four miles away, two people, who should have known better, sat across the table from one another and downed the first of what would be many sidecars. By the end of the next week, one more body would be added to the count. It would not be discovered for several hours and its significance for several more.

One of the two was George LeBrun, convicted felon, arsonist, and local terror. He had been put away for life-plus-twenty for murder, attempted murder, and assault on a police officer among other things. But a judge, at the cajoling of a member of the Richmond ACLU and backed up by the considerable talent of one of the country's more prominent jurists and former member of the previous presidential administration, had been persuaded there were, or might reasonably be, certain technical irregularities with the evidence presented at George's first trial and ordered a new one. The Rockbridge County prosecutor would assure local police and Ike's office that re-conviction on all counts was a slam dunk. That was all well and good, but in the meantime, George posted bond and God only knew where he disappeared to. The betting was on Picketsville with revenge in his heart. Essie Sutherlin, nee Falco, would hear of his release on Monday and, unlike George, would really disappear. She would take her child and remain invisible until her husband, Billy, found her in a cheap motel in Bristol, Tennessee. He would consider and then reject the sensible possibility of joining her there.

Meanwhile, back in the nation's capital, Hannibal Colfax's cynicism, combined with his superior's ambition and the threat of a Congressional Oversight Committee visit to his small corner of the FBI, had resulted in one of those classic bureaucratic moments when progress and accountability cross paths and efficiency flies out the window. By late Friday, his section had, as he'd ordered, ground to a complete halt. All requests for information, some even vital to the solution of serious crimes in several parts of the country, piled up in in-boxes. Police departments from Albany, New York, to Albany, Georgia, from Bangor, Maine, to Bangor, Washington, waited while suspected perps with dental records on file roamed free. Within the remoteness of the alabaster-lined halls in the nation's capital, the possibility that a Congressional committee might create as many problems as it solves is a topic rarely, if ever, discussed.

At any rate, the dental chart belonging to the unidentified remains found in the woods outside Picketsville, Virginia, arrived, was logged in, and then sank deeper and deeper in a pile of similar requests forwarded hourly to the NDI/IR, all newly dispatched to it from all parts of the country and nearly all marked URGENT. They had continued to pile up on Saturday and Sunday. For all intents and purposes, on this weekend the National Dental Information/Imaging Repository did not exist. Thus, it would be days before a tentative ID would be forthcoming and a few more days before Ike would hear anything. And, when he did hear, it would not be what he'd hoped or expected.

As Hannibal had expected, the arrival on Monday of the Congressional Oversight Committee turned out to be all "show and no go." An array of politicians and their sycophant aides, following an unacknowledged but familiar choreography, pranced through Hannibal's area poking into cabinets and asking questions about privacy and the potential breech of Fourth Amendment guarantees. He guessed they'd lifted the queries from the morning's *New York Times*. An Op-Ed columnist, possibly tipped off by one of the members of the committee, had devoted three column-inches to the topic and the impending visit, and wondered editorially if storing dental records of criminals was somehow another blatant example of governmental over-reach infringing once again on the right to privacy guaranteed by the Constitution. It was followed by a brief and quite inaccurate recap of the leaks that had dominated the news sometime in the recent past.

Hannibal bit his tongue and resisted the temptation to quote the amendment to them and point out that the word *privacy* does not appear in the text at all, and in any case, what his group did was not technically a search, and was most certainly warranted. The staff stayed busy and the piles of requests for matches slowly diminished. The group from across town finished their posturing and was on its way back to the halls of Congress and an early lunch, not to mention the evening news deadline, when a worker signaled to Hannibal that he had a problem.

"There's a flag on this one," he said.

"A flag? What sort of flag?"

"This guy is dead."

"Of course he's dead. That's why the…" Hannibal glanced at the sheet of paper that accompanied the chart, "…why the coroner for the Picketsville police requested the search."

"No, that's not what I mean. Look, the FBI investigated this murder a bunch of years ago. They filed this chart with a notation that the case was closed, the body accounted for."

"Wait a minute. If the case was closed, why did they send the chart over to us?"

"It came in a batch. When we set up the NDI/IR they just sent everything they had, old, stuff, new stuff…everything with notations of each case's status. I guess they figured they didn't want to waste time culling through them and figured if the case was closed it wouldn't get a hit and, anyway, it would be our problem."

"They punted it to us and now we have a dental chart of a man who's supposed to have been identified and accounted for eleven years ago. That would mean either we have a dental twin or somebody screwed up over in the big house."

"I guess."

"Find out who closed the case and ask them to check in with us. It's probably just a foul-up or a wrong label on the file."

"Probably."

Chapter Fourteen

Karl Hedrick had been assigned desk duty for more than a month. He wasn't complaining, but he found shuffling through the old cases of a recently retired agent bordered on the boring. Still, he could catch a quick nap now and then, which he counted as a blessing. With a new baby, sleep in his eight hundred-square-foot apartment had become a rarity. More importantly, Samantha, his wife, was on maternity leave and, between the baby and the gift of free time, she'd discovered just how small their apartment really was. Every Sunday she dragged out the real-estate ads from the paper. The words "Here's a nice place in Fairfax we could afford" had induced a cold sweat on Karl's forehead. He greeted Mondays and the need to drive downtown to his office at the FBI with relief, desk job or no desk job.

His morning had been quiet and, except for inventing excuses for why he couldn't possibly go look at some properties during lunch, uneventful. As it happened, he had been assigned all the old cases left by retired special agent Tom Phillips. Most of them needed no attention, but he had been instructed to be keep them as active/solved until all parties involved were deceased. Karl had only a quick look at most of them. Some were still on microfiche, waiting to be digitalized. Newer ones had already been processed into the latest technological format which, given the rapidity of technological innovation, would be obsolete in six months. Someday, he thought, he would find the time to sort through them, but not today. The live bad guys and open cases owned his time.

His phone rang and the person on the other end asked for Phillips.

"Not here, Special Agent Phillips retired a year ago."

"Oh, sorry. I was told the Barbarini file was his and was given this number."

"You got half of that right. I am Special Agent Hedrick and Phillips' files were dumped in my lap. What can I do for you?"

"I don't really know. This is Al Sampson at the NDI/IR and—"

"The what?"

"The National Dental Imaging/Information Repository. We have a problem with an ID."

"What kind of problem?"

"We had a request to match a dental record with anything we might have on file and we made it but it can't be right. What can you tell me about Anthony Barbarini?"

"Who?"

"Anthony Barbarini. The notation on the file says he is dead and the case closed ten or eleven years ago, but we have a newly unearthed stiff down in Virginia whose dental records match his. I need to reconcile this somehow."

"I'll have to pull the file and call you back."

Karl made a note and went back to sorting through the stack of papers on his desk. One dead guy more or less could wait. He'd take the file to lunch and see what's up with Anthony whoever he is, or was. He'd told Sam he was too busy at lunch to house hunt. Now it was true.

His phone rang again.

"Hedrick? This is Tom Phillips. I'm—"

"You're a retired Special Agent. I have your cold files."

"I know. That's why I'm calling. Listen, you will be getting a call from those dental guys about—"

"I already have. Something about a guy named Barbarini."

"Tony Barbarini. He was known as Barbie back in the day."

"Barbie as in Barbie and Ken?"

"Maybe, I don't know where the nickname came from. Anyway, they think they have his body but that can't be."

"Okay…you might want to fill me in a little here."

"Do you have some time? This could take a while."

Karl looked at his watch and sighed. "Shoot."

"Barbarini was a made man in the New York crime scene and a wannabe big-time wise guy. The word on the street back then said he had plans to take over one of the New York families. Next thing you know, he disappeared and then the word got out that Alphonse Damato and Johnny Murphy iced Barbarini. It turns out it was Damato's family he was trying muscle into. Both of them were arrested, charged, and convicted of murder, racketeering, and witness tampering a dozen years ago, okay? The federal prosecutor believed that Barbarini had been dumped in the ocean off Atlantic City."

"In the Atlantic Ocean?"

"Yeah. A snitch said that Murphy and Damato took Barbie out in Murphy's boat one night, wrapped an anchor and chain around the guy's ankles, and dumped him overboard. There was surveillance film of Murphy dragging something in a bag, that could have been a body, onto his boat which backed up the prosecutor's assertion. It was a weak case, but juries don't like organized crime and will happily convict anybody of anything if you can show they're mobbed up."

"Okay. So, he was drowned, but no body was recovered?"

"You're kidding, right? It's a big ocean with lots of hungry fish. Unless you had GPS coordinates and got on it within days, the chances of finding anything other than the anchor and a pair of five hundred-dollar shoes would be slim to none."

"Maybe he slipped his chains and swam away. Made it to shore and—"

"You don't really think he was awake when he went in, do you? Houdini he wasn't. No, they would have made sure he was dead."

"So, if he's in the ocean, how come the dental records people are getting a request to ID a body from someplace in Virginia?"

"See, there's the problem. If it turns out that guy is Barbarini, we have a couple of goons in Sing Sing who might get sprung or, best case, get a new trial. That would create a problem because the snitch who was obviously lying back then, turned up dead a few weeks after the trial, and the evidence trail, you could say, is very, very cold. The Federal Prosecutor's Office is going to get egg on its face. The goons could walk. You see where this is going? If that's Barbie down there, nobody's going to be happy."

"What are you telling me, Phillips?"

"I'm not telling you anything, Hedrick. Consider me the messenger, okay? I am passing on a heads-up from some folks who worked the case a dozen years ago who hope, if you follow my drift, that you will declare that this new dead guy is definitely not Barbarini."

"So, I should do what?"

"Can't say, Hedrick. The dental records got sent over to that identity facility, so it's too late to lose them. You might go down to wherever they found the stiff and make sure it can't be Barbie."

"And how would I do that?"

"He had other identifying marks, like a missing pinky finger. You'll say it's a dental clone or twin or something. I don't know. You figure that part out. Best case, if this new body has all his fingers, you're in the clear."

"I'm in the clear? Excuse me, Phillips, but it's not my out-of-wedlock baby we have here. If there was a screw-up in the original investigation, it's someone else's problem."

"Hedrick, you haven't been listening."

"I haven't been…Wait, are you asking me to 'take one for the team'? A couple of our guys go for a quick close on the basis of a snitch's chatter, and the prosecutor is…is what, running for office and needs some good ink? Sorry, not my game."

"Listen, Hedrick, you're right, it's not your game, mine either, but the trouble is, there's some guys who worked this case then who are still active now and who are in positions that could affect your career. I don't like this any more than you do. Just know what's at stake here."

The line went dead.

Chapter Fifteen

Essie Sutherlin had every right to flee from an at-large George LeBrun. It had not been that long since he'd dragged her and her then-to-be husband to a local park and attempted to kill them both. As soon as she heard the news, she'd packed up the baby and left for Bristol. She told no one, not even Billy, where she was going. Once there, she checked in to a motel owned by an old high school friend who would not register her name in the computer. George LeBrun would have his work cut out if he wanted to find her.

◇◇◇

A year and a half in prison, denied the crystal meth that previously had been LeBrun's daily diet created for him a clearer state of mind, and a set of government-issue dentures had restored his face to near normality. Before his surprising and—for practically no one else—welcome release from the maximum security facility, he'd used this relative clarity to assess his business opportunities, past and future. His cousin had made a botch of the meth cooking operation in his garage, and his brother likewise the importing of weed and South American glass from Norfolk. As both were no longer in play, he'd managed to assemble another, tighter network from his prison cell. Everything seemed to be going well and he'd intended to focus his attention on his retrial when the news that Ethyl Smut had been found dead in a shallow grave in the woods threw a small wrench into his not-yet-well-oiled machinery.

At this particular moment the object of his anger was not Essie Sutherlin, but whoever killed the Smut bitch. The man across the beer stained-table shook his head.

"I got nothin', George. I asked around, you know, but nobody out there has a line on her or anybody who might have snuffed her."

"Nothing?"

Ethyl Smut meant very little to George in the big scheme of things, so her death did not disturb him that much. What did cause him to overdo his first hit since coming outside was the possibility that her death signaled the entrance of a rival drug dealer into what he considered his territory. Ethyl, for all her obvious faults, had served him well enough as an informant and dealer. Her irregular visits to the prison had enabled him to put together his current group and keep track of it, not to mention the considerable cash it generated, cash he needed to keep lawyers on retainer.

In her younger days, before the effects of her addiction had ravaged her face and melted her mind, Ethyl had served him in other ways as well. But then she'd stooped to taking on anyone, anything , any way, to support her habit. It was too bad her kid had run off like she did. He preferred younger women—hell, everybody did. He licked his lips and fumbled in his shirt pocket for his cigarettes.

"What about her kid?"

His companion looked away and mumbled something George couldn't make out. He cleared his throat and said he had put out feelers but did not get much in the way of information. The girl was in the wind, maybe dead, maybe in a foster home Back East. He didn't know.

"You don't know or don't want to say?"

"I asked around, spent some money, and dealt some smack, but no one knew anything about the old woman's killing or where the kid went."

"Listen, Dellinger, you disappear for a million years. Then you pop up on the radar screen looking to make some money.

So, okay, we can do business, like, maybe for old time's sake. But if you're not being straight with me, if you're hiding something, it could go hard on you."

"George, you got more important things to do than worry about the girl. Your lawyer said—"

"I know what that snake said."

"All I know is that the kid has dropped out of sight. Someone said she went to live in a foster home in Virginia Beach, but I can't find her nowhere. Some said they heard she OD'ed up in Baltimore. It's a big user town now so, that makes sense. Jesus, leave it. Is it that important? I could, maybe, put somebody on it, but it would cost you."

As far as George was concerned, she could stay out of sight in Virginia Beach or Timbuktu. If she did come back and refused to get back in the game, though, she'd have to be taken out of circulation. She knew too much and, more than that, she could send people to jail—important people. That is, if she decided to talk to the cops. So there could be no talking.

"There's rumors that she's come back to town," he said.

"I ain't heard that."

"If they're true, it could complicate my day." George polished off his third beer and a shot. "See, it could be good if she's on the game, but not so good if she's clean and chatty. Either way it's a good bet she'll turn up in time. Stoners and junkies always do. They need their lift. Keep your eyes open just in case."

For the moment, he needed to sort out who bumped off the old lady and deal with the guy on the other side of the table who, George was convinced, had an agenda that had put them on opposite sides, so to speak. Some people, like this guy, were too sentimental about things like family and friends. He leaned back in his chair, finished his beer, and realized he liked the way this was working out. It's a lot easier working on the outside than in.

"Where's Essie?" Ike asked. The main office seemed unnaturally quiet. The few deputies who were on their way out, shrugged.

"She called in and said she needed a few personal days and asked me to fill in," Rita, the night dispatcher, said. "I've fixed it up so Darcie Billingsley will sub for me tonight. Things are quieter at night and her kids are old enough and smart enough to go to bed and stay there. Besides, Ike, she needs the work."

"Okay, I'm good with that, but why did Essie go off? Did she say?"

"You haven't heard?"

"Apparently not. What should I have heard?"

"George LeBrun. He's out of jail. Some smarty pants lawyer from Richmond got him a re-trial hearing and he's out on bond, or something."

"Ah, that would explain it. I have seven text messages on my phone. One of them must be about that."

"You have seven texts and you haven't responded?"

"I don't like text messages. You want to contact me, call, write, drop in and chat. Nobody's time is so damned important that they have to resort to misspellings and ridiculous contractions just because it will save thirty seconds of their precious time. So, no, I haven't responded. I am sure there is an official announcement on my computer or in the mail. What has that to do with Essie…? Oh, crap, I almost forgot. It's George LeBrun who's on the loose. Where'd she go?"

"She didn't say. She was just scared of what LeBrun would do to her if he found her."

"How about Billy?"

"He's off duty for two days anyway. I guess they've both bolted."

"Billy knows better. See if you can find either of them and let me know. And, thanks, Rita."

"No probs, Boss."

Ike slipped into his office and nearly tripped over the bag of miscellany from his father's barn. He gave it a kick and sent it into the corner. Two dead guys and George LeBrun on the loose trumped a bag of trash. He paused and stared at the bag again.

"Might it have been left in that particular barn because whoever left it there wanted it found by someone who would tell me? But who's that clever and if they are, wouldn't it be simpler to drop it off here? Maybe they didn't realize what they were doing as a conscious thing. Maybe it was one of those Freudian worms Ruth was talking about."

"You talking to me?" Rita called from the outer office.

"Nope, just consulting with my inner cop."

"If you say so. While you have his attention, ask if he can get some more of those coffee thingies. The night crew went through the whole box. That's what you get when you serve up drinkable coffee."

"On it. By the way, Rita, you've lived here all your life. What can you tell me about Ethyl Smut and her daughter?"

"You have enough overtime in the budget to cover the hours it will take to tell you? I mean there's a thick book on the old lady and another, thinner one, on the girl. Neither one of them is pretty reading, you could say."

"Check with me before you go home and, yeah, I can cover it."

"Just kidding about the money, but hey, if you got it…"

"I do, and I will."

Ike turned back to the papers on his desk, booted up his computer, cursed at three error messages and wished Samantha Ryder had never been shanghaied by NSA. And why did that girl in Lee Henry's Hair Cuttery seem familiar, and where the hell was the kid from the academy, TAK?

Chapter Sixteen

Leota Blevins had lived in Virginia Beach since her thirtieth birthday—after the breakup of a disastrous affair with an ex-Marine. The affair had invoked the disapproval of her cousins and grandmother, and the upshot had not been pleasant. She'd returned to Old Dominion University after a five-year lapse and received her Bachelor of Library Science degree. She moved to the shore and took her first—and so far only— job as an assistant librarian in Little Creek, a position she'd filled for almost two decades. Any chance of promotion was blocked because her immediate superior was eight years younger than she. And as Leota's inquiries about openings elsewhere evinced no interest from any other library, and because her boss did not seem interested in leaving, she'd settled in to making a career in eastern Virginia. After her fiftieth birthday she had abandoned all hope of an alternative venue and started to count the days until she had accumulated enough time and age to start drawing a modest pension. Social Security would come soon after—that is if the system didn't collapse from years of being raided by a Congress eager to spend other people's money.

She also had cousins in Picketsville—Flora and Arlene, who ran a diner. They rarely spoke and never exchanged Christmas or birthday cards or, indeed, correspondence of any sort. The coolness in their relationship stemmed from two unrelated occurrences that happened at about the same time. One had to do with a dispute over a set of Spode china each claimed their mutual grandmother had wanted them to have and a misunderstanding about funeral arrangements. Then, of course, there was the problem of the ex-Marine. They never spoke of that either. As all these events are intertwined in that part of their collective consciousness where emotion and often-rash decisions are made, there would be no resolution. Leota turned her back on her family and settled in the east, as far from them as she could manage.

On this particular Monday afternoon, Leota sat in her pickup, its motor idling, as she wondered if she had made the right decision about the girl and if she ought to retrace her route westward again. Perhaps she should have given Flora more of a heads-up. Dumping the girl on her without any warning would not sit well with the eldest of the cousins. Then, had she thought through what she'd done? Should she have taken her back to Picketsville at all? Of course, the child needed to be told about what happened to her, but in the end, what good could come from that? She had not bothered the caseworker, since that person had not been any help before.

The girl, Darla, had not come to live with Leota of her own free will, exactly. A representative of the commonwealth's Child Protective Services office had offered the child an either/or choice. Go to jail or be placed in one of the foster homes known to service incorrigible children. Leota knew the girl's history, and knew that she had been the victim for most of it, and therefore had done nothing to warrant the label incorrigible. But, like it or not, her checkered past landed her there. As luck would have it, Leota heard that the case was in process and knew the remanding official. She persuaded the official to place Darla with her, with the promise that Leota would provide both the care and the security the child required. So, Darla had not been sent to the stringently regulated home she was destined for, to join those like her with similar and nearly always misunderstood histories. In a very real way, Leota thought of the girl as the daughter she might have had.

Leota became distressed after she'd coerced a summer intern into hacking into the court's sealed records and discovered Ethyl Smut had petitioned the court to re-hear her custody claims. The thought of the girl falling back into that woman's hands was unthinkable. What kind of society would ever entertain that possibility for even a minute?

Well, Leota's promise to provide security had been breached. The girl was gone, so Leota dutifully reported her as missing to the caseworker. So sorry. Now what?

Ike did a double take at the entrance. Darcie Billingsly had settled into the dispatcher's desk. For years he had always glanced to his right, waved to Essie or Rita and walked to his office. Not Essie—Darcie. She had the headset on and was busy chatting with one of the patrolling deputies. If Ike had to guess who, it would be Chester Franklin. The year before, Chester's wife had emptied the joint bank account and run off, they said, with a twenty-five-year-old fitness guru. Chester was left alone with two teenagers, payments on a new Chevy Silverado which also went missing, and a mortgage. Darcie, on the other hand, had finally put the death of her husband, Whaite, behind her, and she and Chester had connected at the office Christmas party. Shortly thereafter, Chester had stopped making payments on the truck.

Romance.

Ike shook his head. Maybe he and Ruth could share whoever they could persuade to do the honors and have a double wedding. What had he and Ruth been thinking? They hadn't been thinking, that's what.

Rita, now officially off duty and on overtime, she hoped, plunked down in Ike's only other chair.

"Okay, what do you want to know about Ethyl Smut?"

"What do I need to know, Rita? The woman is dead. I have the impression she was disliked by any and all, and that no one who knew her is surprised or even cares that she's dead. There is also the daughter and her troubles. I don't know why I don't know either of their stories, but I don't."

"You probably don't know because most of her sorry crap went down while you were away doing whatever it was that nobody around here talks about but everybody knows was for the government. And then she dropped out of sight for a while. Her daughter is a different story and one I can only guess at, on account of nobody talks about that either. So, we're dealing with rumors and outright lies."

"Wow. Okay, start where you want. I need as much as I can get and for now I'll even take the lies with the truth."

"Okay, let's start with the girl. Remember, a lot of this is hearsay. People don't like to talk about stuff like this."

"What kind of stuff?'

"Child sexual abuse kind of stuff. Remember, Ike, this isn't the big city and we are not so calloused about things as those folk are. We still hold onto old values and standards—is that what I want to say? You know what I mean. We haven't caught up to Hollywood yet. Some things are just plain evil and that's that."

"I hear you. So the 'abuse' mentioned in the files wasn't just assault and battery of someone, the child?"

"Not even close. I'll get to that in a second. So, okay, Ethyl lived hard and fast even before she started doing drugs. Once she discovered methamphetamine the world changed for her and everyone around her. She got mixed up with that ex-Marine, Mark somebody, and the next thing you know, she had a baby, a daughter. That is when it really got bad. I mean it's one thing to sell yourself for a hit or two, another to pimp out your daughter."

"She traded her daughter for smack?"

"Smack, glass, whatever you call it now and anything else that was moving down the highway from Baltimore and Washington or up from Norfolk. If it blew your mind, Ethyl smoked it, snorted it, shot it, or drank it. Back then I swear she'd shoot up with diesel fuel or talcum powder if she thought it would get her high. So, yeah, from the time the kid was seven or eight, Ethyl allowed as how the girl was available for the right price. Do you have any idea how many men lust after little girls?"

"Yes, and I wish I didn't."

"Whatever number you may have heard it's probably on the low side. Hell, even one is too many. They say that the poor kid was raped for most of her young life just to keep Ethyl on a perpetual high."

"What happened to the girl?"

"Darla? She up and disappeared a few years ago. Some say she got picked up by the children's bureau, some say she died. Some say she ran away to Chicago or D.C. I don't know. All I know is Ethyl was mad as hell that her meal ticket, you could say, had vanished."

"So, nobody knows where the kid is?"

"If she's alive, somebody knows. If they're a friend of hers, they won't be telling, though. I sure wouldn't. She's been through bloody hell. And on the other hand, if they're one of the legions of abusers, rapists, and perverts who went after her, then she's probably dead. There is no way they would want her around to testify against them. As for the girl, there's a limit to how much of that crap a body can stand before it just shuts down."

"Voice of experience?"

"I had to bury a second cousin last year, and her life before taking up residence in the cemetery, was a hayride compared to Darla Smut's, believe me."

"I'm sorry. And the old lady…what's her story? The part not covered by the awfulness she perpetrated on her child."

"Like I said, she got mixed up with drugs early on. Like most druggies, her brains were scrambled so you could argue she didn't really know what she was doing to the kid. I don't buy that, of course, but some lawyer in a thousand-dollar suit, like the one who sprung George LeBrun, might make a case for it. That's the other thing. Ethyl was one of his customers and paid for some of her drugs by being a distributor."

"She hustled drugs?"

"She hustled drugs, her kid, and her own ass to stay afloat, pardon my French. George, they say, had a thing with her before her face fell apart, then he started raping the kid instead."

"Lovely man. And he's out of the slammer."

"With his taxpayer-supplied new teeth and waiting for a new trial, yep."

"And Essie is in hiding. Anything else I should know about any of the players in this sordid drama?"

"I'll let you know if I think of anything...and sordid don't cover the half of it."

"Are there any pictures of the girl?"

"I don't have any, but I can ask around. There should be one or two somewhere. Check your mug shots. The girl had to come across the desk here once or twice. You could also check with the child welfare folks. If she wandered into their system, they might know where she landed. Oh, and check with Flora Blevins at the diner. She used to be tight with Smuts. She might have a snap or two."

"She told me she's the girl's godmother."

"There you go."

"She's not talking."

"That's Flora."

Ike thanked Rita and waved her out the door. What an awful story. Could a mother really do such a thing to her child? He knew of a few fathers who might, but a mother? He needed to talk to Flora again.

A quick check in the files failed to produce a picture of any sort. Curious, that. Did someone just fail to file them, fail to take them, or were they removed for some reason, perhaps because she was a juvenile? Ike shook his head. Things were not getting easier.

Chapter Seventeen

"We're going to Picketsville. Pack for a couple of days and don't forget to lock up your piece."

Samantha Hedrick looked up from her real estate brochures and stared at her husband. The baby slept in her lap having pretty well drained both sides, so to speak. "Picketsville? Piece? What on earth are you talking about, Karl?"

"I'll explain later. Let's just say I stepped into a pile of organic fertilizer left for me a decade ago by a couple of hot-shot agents with more ambition than patience."

"I guess that makes sense in some language. Next time could you try English?"

"A body found in the woods outside Picketsville should have been in the Atlantic Ocean and is causing a major case of the vapors for some of my senior colleagues. I am tasked to make it all better."

"Well, okay, I think. Where will we stay?"

"Stay?"

"Um…yeah, stay. We are travelling to the Shenandoah Valley and you did say I should pack. So where will we sleep, eat, bathe, you know live temporarily?"

"I guess we could find a motel."

"Karl, you guess we could find a…You want me and the baby to hole up in a motel for, what did you say, a couple of days? And you will be doing something which sounds like a major clusterfudge and then all will be fine? Sorry, but as my dad used to say, 'That dog don't hunt.' How about this? Martin and I stay in here D.C. while you travel south to Picketsville for a few days and do whatever it is you're going to do. Say hello to all the gang for me while you're there."

"I thought you'd want to see Essie and Ike and the rest."

"I would, I do, but not operating out of a motel room that you guess we might find. We have a baby to manage here, Karl. Diapers, baby food, and bags of things that he needs plus all the stuff you and I will need. Unless there is a meteorite headed this way, and this is an emergency evacuation from the D.C. area, we can do better than guessing we might find a motel room."

Karl had a suitcase open on the living room couch and was staring at it the way a kitten will stare at its own image the first time it encounters a mirror—not quite sure what to do next. Sam watched as she imagined he made a mental list of items that should go into the case. At least that is what she hoped he had in mind. With Karl, you could never be sure.

"What? Karl, you pack a suitcase in the bedroom. That's where the clothes are."

"I know, I know, it's just that I thought that you would…"

"I would what? Want to visit our friends in Picketsville? Of course I do. But Karl…oh, never mind." Sam picked up her smartphone and scrolled through her directory. She punched the call icon and waited. "No answer at Billy and Essie's. They must be at work. I'll try Dorothy."

"Dorothy?"

"Yes, Dorothy. Dorothy Sutherlin…Billy's mom. We could stay with her if she'll have us. She has a huge house and she'll want to see the baby anyway."

"Dorothy Sutherlin?"

"Men!"

◇◇◇

Dorothy Sutherlin's next-to-youngest, Billy, picked up Ike's call on his way to the drugstore. Ike told him what he already knew: that George LeBrun had somehow finagled a new trial and had made bond. He also knew that Essie had more than likely lit out, and he told Ike that he would either join her or bring her back. He also said he had a pretty good idea where she might be holed up. But he needed to stop at a drugstore first.

"Yeah, whatever, Billy, but—"

"Not to worry, Ike. I know the drill. I'm on it."

"Okay. Do you want TAK to run a check on Essie's credit cards to see where she might be headed?"

"She won't be using them. As far as she's concerned, LeBrun can track them too. It ain't true, but where it comes to that guy, Essie is, like, super paranoid. No, she won't touch them."

"How will you find her?"

"She has a friend who runs a place outside of Bristol. That's where she's going."

"You're sure?"

"Back before we were married, you know, when she was, you could say, more of a free spirit, and things with her old lady were sometimes not so hot—or maybe just to get away from whatever was eating at her—she always went to ground down there."

"Okay, you're the boss on this one, but you know she's better off up here where we can all keep an eye out rather than tucked away someplace where we can't possibly get help to her in time. I can tell you, and this is from personal experience, that hiding where no one can find you—including your friends—while bad guys are looking for you is definitely not a good idea."

"Ike, I'll bring her back if I can, but it'll take some doing. I reckon she's pretty well spooked. Actually I reckon I am too." Billy hung up and went into the drugstore.

There were simple survival things the two of them needed no matter where they rode out the storm that the release of George LeBrun had roiled up. And the drugstore was next door to the hardware store and the hardware store sold shotgun shells.

The sun had set by the time he knocked on the door of unit fourteen of the Wayside Motel, a stopover favored by truckers and salesmen traveling on per diem and short of cash, or with tapped out credit cards. He heard a stirring inside.

"Essie, honey, it's me. Open up."

Essie's voice was muffled but he heard her ask if he was alone. The window curtain twitched and he caught a glimpse of the blue-gray barrel of his old service revolver flick it back.

"It's just me, Babe, open up."

The door opened a crack and one large blue eye peered out.

"See, it's just me. No gun on my back. No George LeBrun fixing to kill us both. Not anymore."

Essie swung the door open just wide enough to grab his shirtfront and pull him in. She slammed it shut and locked it in one continuous motion.

"What are we going to do?" The panic in Essie's voice could have etched glass.

"We're going back to Picketsville. We are not going to let that sumbitch LeBrun run our lives. Get your things, Babe. We're bigger than this."

"He wants to kill us, Billy. He said if he ever had the chance, he would find me and kill me."

"Well, in the first place, he ain't found you. In the second place there is going to be so much security around you he won't get within ten miles 'fore he's looking down the barrel of Ike's .357 Magnum. So, we will be just fine."

"He has people."

"And we have more. Listen, who do you think is the scariest dude in a situation like this, Ike or LeBrun? If I'm LeBrun, I don't get in Ike's crosshairs ever. And don't forget, Danny is home on a two-week pass. He's even worse news for LeBrun than Ike. He's family."

"Danny is a SEAL. He could be off on a mission inside five minutes of getting to the house."

"Until our bad guy is back in the jailhouse, he ain't going nowhere."

"You don't know that."

"Essie, nobody, not LeBrun or any of his brain-dead friends, is going to get within shouting distance of you or me. He'll be back on death row before the week is out."

Billy took her by the shoulder. "Look at me, Essie. Everybody thinks we're hiding out down here, shaking in our boots. It ain't true, but that's what they think. Hell, back awhile, maybe they'd be right. I thought about it all the way down here. But not now. Nobody's going to make me live like a rat in a hole. You neither. The way it sits now, you're covered."

"You promise?"

"Cross my heart."

Essie stared wide-eyed at her husband. She blinked twice, grabbed her as-yet-unpacked bag, and took his arm.

"Let's go, then. I feel safe here only when I am sure nobody knows I'm here. I mean Cindy didn't even register me, you know. But the thought of days without you, and then things like how do I shop for the baby had me in a bind. You're sure we're okay back home?"

"Between me, Danny, Frank, Ike, and Henry—"

"Henry?"

"Well, maybe not Henry. He's more of a lover than a fighter. But you'd be surprised at that boy and what he'd do in a pinch."

Chapter Eighteen

Daylight savings time means that the sun, while low on the horizon, still shines at six in the evening in southwestern Virginia. Ike had promised Ruth they would meet for dinner somewhere and plot and scheme their wedding into place. Rita's narrative about Ethyl Smut's sordid life made clear to him he needed to have a sit-down with Flora Blevins. He called Ruth and asked for an hour's delay.

"No problem. I have paperwork up the wazoo, Ike." Ruth said, "So, okay fine, see you around seven-thirty."

Ike clocked out of the office and walked the half block or so to the Cross Roads Diner. Whether she wanted to be quizzed or not, Ike needed to have his talk with Flora. He doubted she would be eager to have it, but it needed to be done. Irrespective of what people thought of Ethyl, she'd been murdered and whether she deserved it or not, the murderer had to be caught, tried, and put away.

The diner had regulars for each of its three mealtimes. Ike counted as a breakfast regular as did most of the patrons, although many ate breakfast at noon. Dinner regulars were sparser and even then, most preferred the breakfast menu. Only the brave or those suffering from a significant loss of gustatory acuity ordered off the dinner menu, but a few hardy souls were willing to risk gravy out of a can and yellow-brown mounds of flesh which Flora insisted were chicken fried steak. Ike pushed his way in through the glass doors and scanned the area. Diners sat in booths and at tables urging their mashed potatoes into pools of congealing gravy or sawed at the substance Flora insisted was meat with their dinner knives. Flora did not believe in steak knives.

"Too dangerous if a crazy man came in," she'd said.

Ike refrained from asking her how often that happened.

Flora was not positioned behind the cash register or circulating between the tables giving advice on good eating and generally bullying the patrons. Ike asked Bob, the counterman, where she had gone. Bob might not have been his real name. All of Flora's countermen wore shirts supplied by Flora and they all were the same size and identified their wearer as *Bob*. This current Bob, his shirt a size too large, tilted his head toward the rear and door leading to the pantry and the cramped office Flora used to do her paperwork. Another rarity. Flora usually left the paperwork to her cousin, Arlene, who stood the night shift and filled the empty predawn hours sorting through orders, bills, and mail.

Ike eased around a fifty-pound bag of red potatoes. "Evening, Flora. Have your ears been burning?"

"Why would they?"

"I've been having conversations about you on and off most of the day. Can you guess what about?"

"Nope."

"Just 'nope'? Aren't you just a little bit curious?"

"Nope."

"Okay. Well, how about you tell me about Ethyl Smut and her daughter."

"I already done that, Ike. We had that confab yesterday, or was it the day before? I don't know. Either way, I got nothing to say to you. So there. Are you going to get out of my office?"

"Nope."

"Whataya mean?"

"Flora, your former neighbor and mother to your goddaughter has been murdered. It is my job to find her killer. It seems this is the place to start."

"I got nothing to say. Nobody gives a hoot in hell about that evil woman's death. Neither should you."

"Doesn't work that way. Whether she deserved to die or not, murder is still frowned on in my town. Talk to me."

"If I don't?"

"We could go down to the office and chat there. You're my only lead, maybe a person of interest, as they say on the eleven o'clock news."

"So, arrest me."

"Maybe I will. Maybe I will have to. Listen, Flora, I can get as snarky as you and since I wear the badge, I have an advantage. So, talk to me now, here, or later down at the station and under arrest for obstruction of justice. Your choice."

"I thought you were my friend."

"I am. That is why I am talking to you in the middle of sacks of potatoes and crates of canned vegetables and not through the bars of a cell. I need to know everything you can tell me about Ethyl Smut or Dellinger, her daughter, and where I might find the latter."

"Why do you want Darla?"

"Several reasons. First, how about she has the strongest motive to kill her mother?"

"Not good enough. What's another?"

"George LeBrun is out of jail and headed this way."

"No. How'd he do that?"

"Money and friends on the outside. He's drugs, Flora—drugs, murder, and worse, if anything can be. Drug money can buy a lot of friends in high places. Ethyl was about drugs. Ethyl is dead, but Ethyl had a daughter when he was loose before. Does this daughter know anything that might get in the way of his continued freedom? Something her mother knew and took to her grave? Do you want her to take the chance?"

"That ain't fair, Ike."

"What's not fair?"

"That little girl has suffered enough at the hand of them people. You gotta keep her safe, you hear?"

"How am I going to keep her safe when I don't know where she is, Flora?"

Flora sighed. She swiveled around in her chair and faced Ike. "I'll tell you a couple of things, but I ain't ready to tell you where the girl is at."

"Then you do know."

"Maybe yes, maybe no."

"Not good enough. If the girl knows anything—not *if*, I'm thinking—she can identify men who were involved in her abuse, Flora. She is in deep trouble. If those people get even a hint she might talk about what she knows, she's in the same place only deeper. And, as much as I am sure you don't want to hear it, she has to be considered a suspect in her mother's murder. Talk to me, Flora."

◇◇◇

Essie sat slumped low in the seat of the cruiser as if she were afraid she might be seen and recognized and perhaps attacked as she and Billy drove northeast from Bristol. She jumped when Billy's cell phone went off.

Billy tapped his earpiece. "Sutherlin," he said. "What...who? You're kidding, right?" Billy's grin almost reached each ear. He tapped off and turned briefly to Essie. "Guess who's coming for a visit?"

"Who?"

"Sam and Karl. Old Karl has some kind of FBI business in town and them two is coming down. Ma says they'll be staying with us. What do you think about that?"

"Sam and Karl?" Essie sat up straight. "They're going to be at the house?"

"That's what she said."

"It'll be like old times."

"Well, not exactly. I mean Sam, she works up in Washington for the NSA and Karl is still FBI. But for a little while, yeah, it'll be the good old days."

"But maybe they can stay permanent."

"How do you figure that?"

"Well, for one thing, there's that position that is empty now that Grace White has went back to Maine. Sam could just fall right back in and take over all that computer stuff, and…umm."

"Umm is right. We only got one slot and what are the chances the town council with the mayor on Ike's case, giving us another? And if they don't, then where you going to put Karl?"

"I was thinking that maybe Charley Picket was getting ready to retire and Karl could have his spot."

"Retire? Who said Charley was fixing to retire?"

"Well, nobody, I guess. But he could. He should, you know. He's been on the force for, like, forever and it's time for him to think about letting someone else have a chance. He'd still get his pension and all."

"Don't you go there, Essie. Charley ain't about to step down, if I know him, and neither is anybody else on the staff."

"Maybe someone will get hurt or, God forbid, there'd be a fatality or—"

"Hold it right there, Missy. We ain't about to wish for anything like that. You know what they say about wishing for a thing too much. You just get them crazy ideas out of your head, you hear? Wishing for something like that…You do understand that a wish like that one, if you were to make it, could end up it being me that's the fatality? You want me dead?"

"Not you, no, not anybody, and it's not a wish. I'm just saying."

"Well, you can stop it right now."

Chapter Nineteen

Ike entered Frank's restaurant, acknowledged Ruth's presence in a booth in the back with a wave, and went directly into the men's room. Ruth signaled for Frank to bring her another martini and Ike's old-fashioned. The drinks arrived with Ike.

"You look like hell," she said.

"I feel like hell. I feel like I've been dragged backwards through a pile of garbage…wait, make that something worse, a pile of sh—"

"I got it. So, who or what prompted that journey?"

"You know the woman we found dead in the woods last week?"

"Know her? No, I don't. I know that you found a body, yes, Ethyl Somebody. What about her?"

"Ethyl Smut. I just spent an hour discussing the lady's lifestyle with Rita, the night dispatcher, and another hour with a longtime friend of hers, if friend is the right word, and I feel like I need a shower—two showers and a long soak in bleach or something."

"Care to share?"

"Not before we eat, no. It would spoil your appetite."

"Afterwards, then, and we can take the shower together."

"You are incorrigible, but I like your style."

"And hungry. Drink up, Schwartz. I already ordered us the roast beef and a side salad. The shower can be dessert. By the way, did you know that if you want to order a martini nowadays you have to say what kind?"

"You mean vodka or gin, on the rocks or straight up?"

"No. Today, anything served in what is generally regarded as a martini glass is some kind of a martini. So, there are apple-tinis—don't ask, I have no idea—someone sent me a recipe for a s'mores martini last week. She said saw it on Facebook. And then there are chocolate martinis, seafood martinis—"

"What?"

"You heard me. A seafood martini would be a bed of shredded lettuce with shrimp or tuna or, I don't know, maybe whale, in it."

"Lord love a duck. I was just getting used to 'comfort dogs' and now—"

"Comfort dogs?"

"Pooch in a purse. Psychologists prescribe them to anxious patients to relieve their stress, aid in grieving, and so on."

"Like a hook-up bag only it barks."

"Hook-up bag? What the…? Wait, let me guess. Young women, who should know better, carry around a change of clothes, toothbrush, and other necessaries, in case they hook up, spend the night with a man, and don't make it home by morning?"

"You are being judgmental but, yes, that's the idea."

"I am not being judgmental, I am showing my age."

"I like your age."

"I'm beginning to think I don't."

Frank placed their dinners in front of them and bid them "bone appa-tit."

Ruth rolled her eyes. "It's *bon appétit*, Frank. It's French."

"That's what I said, bone appatit."

"Right."

He wandered back to the entrance and positioned himself in the doorway as if to will another customer or two off the sidewalk and into the building.

Ike twirled his napkin into his lap. "There's a new one. Who knew there was an app for that?"

"What?"

"App a tit."

"Shut up. Do you ever think we'll have a restaurant that serves decent food in this berg?"

"Someday. Maybe we should quit our jobs and start one. Anything would be better than being law-and-order in Picketsville. We could serve the state's only comfort martini—a pooch-tini."

"Hook-up burgers."

Ike shoved back from the table, eyes closed. "Thanks for the attempts at hilarity but…"

"Your conversations with whomever…your sources, must have been really bad."

"You have no idea."

"Tell me."

"Finish your dinner first."

They ate in silence. Ruth pushed her plate away and shook her head at the dessert cart Frank wheeled to their table.

"Just coffee, Frank," she said.

"You finished eating?"

"As much as I care or dare to, yes. So, what did you hear?"

"Do you know anything about meth babies?"

"Only what I read. Is that what this is all about? Babies or a baby addicted to methamphetamine?"

"That is only page one of a very thick book. The woman— the one we found dead in the woods, was a heavy user. She supported her habit by dealing, stealing, and selling herself. Then, not surprisingly, she got pregnant and had a baby, a meth baby with all the potential deficits and problems that go with that status."

"So, what happened to the child?"

"Patience…When the baby was eight or nine, maybe younger, we can't be sure, her mother pimped her out as well."

"She turned her daughter, her child, into a prostitute?"

"Yep. The kid, according to the woman I spoke to, had been serially raped so many times that by the time she turned fifteen her reproductive organs were effectively destroyed. Her mind was so scattered by doses of meth, heroin, and booze forced on her that she is, or was, borderline schizoid. If there was ever a prime suspect in the mother's murder, she's it."

"Did she do it?"

"I'm guessing not. I can't say why, but no, I don't think so. Furthermore she ran away a couple of years back and, if she got—and then stayed—clean, she should be more or less stable by now. That is good news and bad."

"Explain. I mean clean is good, right?"

"That part, yes, but if she's rational, she can point her finger at more than one abuser, and that could spell big trouble for some. They will attempt to stop her."

"My God, Ike that is terrible. I can't imagine what that must be like. To have endured the abuse would be bad enough, but now to be in danger for her life because of it? She's the victim all over again. And you say the mother really…men really…?"

"Really. It must have been a whole lot worse than anything you or I could possibly imagine. Think of what that child must have been forced to do. I have seen a lot of really bad crap in my day, Ruth. Suicide bombings that blew up people at random, kids, moms, grandparents, body parts scattered all over and mixed up so that you couldn't tell where one body began and another ended. I've witnessed assassinations, mass murders, and God only knows what other horrors here and abroad, but the thought of a girl spending her childhood and early adolescence—the time when she should be playing with Barbie dolls, or talking for hours on the telephone, or having a small life crisis at the appearance of her first zit, or menstrual cycle, and pursuing boys when the hormones kicked in…Instead of that, she is subjected to a string of pushers, perverts, and men who should have known better forcing themselves on her and all with her mother's connivance. Hell, I could have killed the lady myself…."

Ike's voice trailed off. He stared at the gravy congealing on his plate and drained the rest of his old-fashioned.

Ruth did the same with her martini. "For what it's worth, if I had known about it, Ike, I would have happily killed the woman too."

"And that goes for most of the people I've talked to who knew even a few of the details. We'd have to get in line, like the gang on *The Orient Express,* and take turns. And that's the problem. I have too many suspects and, therefore, none at all."

"Whoever killed her did the community a service, Ike. Let it go. Concentrate on rehabbing the kid. What about her father, or is that asking too much?"

"Her father is…damn, I can't remember the name. That's annoying. I never forgot stuff like that before. It'll come to me. I said I was having problems with my age. Anyway, he is also missing, possibly dead, maybe even the other body we found, although that's a stretch, so, no place to go there. And I can't do anything about rehabilitation—that's for the child services people and assumes we can find the girl. As for doing the community a service, I understand, but, as I said to my source, 'It doesn't work that way.' Murder is murder and the people who kill bad guys go to jail just like the ones who kill good guys."

"They shouldn't have to."

"To do otherwise creates much too great a risk for the rest of us, believe me."

"Yeah, yeah, vigilantes can get out of control and all that, but just this once I'd be in favor of looking the other way."

"I hear you."

"I think I'm ready for that bath now. Jesus, her own daughter. Nine you said? Jesus."

"Eight or nine, maybe seven, yeah. I will put a call into the welfare wonks and see if they happened to have run across her. Flora Blevins knows where she is but she refuses to tell me. I could arrest her for obstruction of a criminal investigation, but she can be stubborn as hell and wouldn't talk anyway. I think the fact that George LeBrun is on the loose shook her cage a little, though. Anyway, until I find the kid, sit her down, and get names, dates, and places, I'm stuck. You know what really frosts me?"

"There's more?"

"Nobody was able to stop it, Ruth. Presumably, the cops were called, but except for a disturbing the peace or a drunk-and-disorderly citation, nobody would come forward with the proof of any wrongdoing. The mother was never arraigned on the abuse charges. When push got to shove, either the authorities were too inept or the people who could say something were too scared to step up."

"You don't know that. I read that the number of sex abuse cases that ever go to trial is, like, twenty-five percent, that prosecutors say they never have a tight enough case to pursue it and get a conviction."

"And they let them walk. You would think they would at least try. Even if they can't nail the bastards, they could put them on notice and in the public eye."

"Prosecutors are public officials with an eye to reelection. They don't like to lose cases, especially ones that carry the emotional baggage child sex abuse crimes do."

"I guess. Then there is the drug culture that spawns it, and the people involved in the traffic who have power and reputations. Celebrities shove that crap up their noses while they thumb them at society. Glamour is cocaine. You remember the t-shirt we saw in Vegas…it had 'Caviar and Cocaine' emblazoned across the front and the moron who wore it seemed convinced that trendy justifies stupidity. Then there is the idolization of gangsters on TV. It might have been great acting, but to make a hero of a man who murders, sells drugs in his own son's school, and keeps a prostitute as a mistress? We have a culture that glorifies crime and refuses to understand that by so doing we are aiding and abetting."

"Wait. What about murder mysteries, books—Agatha Christie, Ian Rankin, Donis Casey?"

"Donis who?"

"Never mind. What about books with crime as the theme?"

"If the bad guys get caught, I'm on it. If the protagonist is the murderer, no way."

"You don't read a lot, do you?"

"I live this stuff twenty-four seven. If I read anything, it will be nonfiction or classics. There are stacks of them I haven't gotten to yet. When I'm done with them, there are plays and poetry."

"Okay, okay, I take your point, but I will say methinks the sheriff doth protest too much. I think you have a secret cache of pulp fiction under your bed and late at night you sneak-read it under the covers with a flashlight."

"You peeked under my bed?"

"You were asleep and I was restless—had a look around. Self-preservation, you could say. If I have to be married to you, I want to know what dark secrets you are hiding."

"And you thought you'd find them under the bed?"

"Where else?"

"In the freezer is where I'd look."

"Right. Getting back to your rant…aiding and abetting what?"

"Murder, for one. The murders committed by gangbangers who shoot up rival dealers in the streets every day. If you are paying some low level dealer for cocaine and shoving it up your nose because it is—or you think you are—cool, you must assume some responsibility for the acts your money bought along with the drugs."

"Wow, a cop speaks his mind. A society that trivializes evil will eventually succumb to it."

"I guess. Who said that?"

"No idea. Must have read it somewhere."

"The point is, we have a badly used child and if that weren't enough, the worst of this whole rotten mess, inherent evil notwithstanding, is that she and abused children everywhere don't make very compelling witnesses. Half the time they're too young and cannot articulate what's happened to them or even know what is wrong. They don't know what has happened to them isn't normal. If they're older and able to, they are afraid to say anything and dummy up."

"What do you do?"

"What we can, I suppose. And you know what really frosts my buns? For some reason, this girl's mother avoided any real jail time, or she pleads out to lesser charges, and nothing changes for the kid. How can that be?"

"Life sucks, Ike."

"For some folks, it does indeed."

"Okay, on your feet. Time for a long hot bath which may include some therapeutic options."

"Works for me."

"One more thing."

"What?"

"My system can't take this in. I can't help but think of the women, the students, who are nominally in my charge and I am scared for them. How many, do you suppose, had to endure something like this in their growing up?"

"More than you or I might imagine."

Chapter Twenty

Dorothy Sutherlin owned her house outright. Thirty years before, when she married her husband, she declared she wanted a large family and room for all the kids. He did not have the money to purchase that kind of house, but managed to put a down payment on a modest bungalow outside the Picketsville town limits where prices were lower. As the youngest of a string of first-generation sons and daughters of Great Depression parents, he'd been encouraged to learn a variety of skills as part of his growing up. His parents, like others who managed to outlast the dark days of the nineteen thirties and early forties, insisted that anyone who could do many things, from manual labor to bookkeeping, could always find work even in the worst of times. He took up carpentry as one of those ancillary skills. Thus, as his family grew, so did the bungalow. Each successive child meant an addition to the house—another room, an enlarged kitchen, a second story and so on, all of which he built himself. In the end when his youngest, Henry, bawled his way into the world, the house had grown to be the largest in the area and, in appearance, the most architecturally challenging. The neighbors sometimes said it would be a dwelling more suitable for a Dr. Seuss story. Nevertheless, it served its purpose by providing a warm and safe haven for his family and that, after all, is the only reason to own a home in the first place.

Billy and Essie now lived across town in a starter home, but Dorothy's eldest, Frank, and youngest were still with her. The other boys, except the one KIA in the first Gulf War, were in the service—SEALs, Army, and so on. So, there was more than enough room for Essie and Billy and their new baby and Karl and Sam and theirs to move in temporarily. And Danny, on leave from Little Creek, rounded out what for Dorothy had evolved into a near perfect week.

It is an axiom that bad news will sometime bring good times. The several murders, old and recent, and the incomprehensible release of George. LeBrun from prison had many worrisome aspects, but it had also created a reunion of sorts. And for that, Dorothy had a celebratory feast laid out for her guests.

"There's enough food here to feed the Eighty-second Airborne," Billy said when he eyed the stacks of sliced thick home-made bread, sticks of real butter, a dark Smithfield ham, two whole rounds of cheese, slaw, a huge bowl of German potato salad, and four pies—one of which he could see was pumpkin, the others' contents hidden by golden crusts. There were four different vegetables and a whole turkey complete with stuffing.

"There's coffee and ice cream for later," his mother said, obviously pleased with the display she'd been working at all afternoon. "Ya'll just dig in. We can just catch up, and later you can unpack." New mothers and new babies will always divert the start of any other undertaking for at least twenty-four hours. After which there is at least a slim chance that more serious activities might be attempted.

"I have died and gone to heaven," Karl said and sat in the chair nearest the pies.

"You eat too much of this meal and you won't be speaking in metaphors," Sam said and moved the pies out of his reach.

"Good Lord, Ma," Frank said. "What were you thinking?"

"Well, look here. We got friends we ain't seen in racketycoon's age and their little one, too. Billy and Essie and Junior are here for a few days and Danny's back from wherever they send them Navy SEALs all the time.

"Key West," said Danny.

"Is that what they call Afghanistan now?"

Danny grinned but said nothing. His mother frowned. She knew her son spent time, too much time, in harm's way and one death in the line of duty was one too many.

"You're going to be here a while this time right, Danny?" she said.

"Yes, ma'am, long as Uncle Sam lets me."

"Sit and eat your supper. Ya'll must be starving."

Ruth settled into the most comfortable of the two recliners in her upstairs office. She was wrapped in the hotel robe that bore the emblem she insisted made her Mrs. Sheraton. She had another towel wrapped turban-like around her wet hair.

"Now, I'm hungry. Next time I press you for the gory details of your latest case before we eat, you remind me of this evening, Ike."

"I could scramble us some eggs. That is, I could if you have any eggs to scramble."

"I don't remember if I do or if I don't. Anyway, don't bother. I can make it 'til morning. Sit down and tell me something cheerful."

"Well, let's see…great shower, by the way."

"You do know that there is a risk in what we did?"

"Risk? Dare I ask?"

"Soap film under foot. If only one of us had slipped, the way we were…ah, positioned, both of us would have fallen in the tub, risked broken bones, and dislocations, not to mention the possibility of having to call 9-1-1 to be extricated. Picture the Picketsville Fire Department or some of your deputies appearing tubside to lift us out."

"We would become part of the local folklore and our story passed on for generations to come."

"We'd have to leave town."

"There are days when that is a very attractive option. Okay, first, no more gore with dinner and, second, we install a no-slip shower."

"What are we going to do, Ike?"

"Do? Well, after skirting ptomaine poisoning at Frank's and risking life and limb in the shower, I think it best if we hide under the covers until morning. We daren't to press our luck."

"Very funny. I mean what are we going to do about us?"

"Us? I thought putting on a wholesale wedding charade with the mayor and your faculty guy was bad and so did you. I thought we dumped the idea. The last idea on the table was to just invite a bunch of locals to a big feed somewhere, confess our rash behavior, and move on."

"The first plan was a stinker, as we decided, and this new one isn't much better."

"It's honest."

"But it ignores family and friends who deserve something after we have teased them for so long.

"I see. Maybe we need to open another bottle of very bad wine and try again."

"We do need to rethink it."

Ike sighed. This was not going to be an early night and he had already prepared himself mentally for a pleasant night ensconced under or flopped out on top of Ruth's new duvet. The two sat in silence for a few minutes. Finally, Ruth stood and went to the bookcase. She rummaged among them for a moment and returned to her chair with one in hand.

"It's in here somewhere, I'm sure of it. My mother and father did it on their twenty-fifth anniversary."

"What is in where and do I really want to know what your parents did on their twenty-fifth anniversary?"

"Hush up while I look. Ah, here it is, the *Book of Common Prayer*."

"You own a prayer book?"

"Every Episcopalian, practicing, lapsed, living, or dead owns a *Book of Common Prayer*. I grant that one or two of them may have disposed of their copy and more the pity for them, but more importantly, there's a lot of good stuff in here, including a service for the renewal of wedding vows. We could probably get Fisher to do that for us."

"Renewal?"

"Right, you know, we stand up and reaffirm the vows. And to be honest, my memory of what we vowed is a little foggy. Crap, it's not in here. Now what?"

"Let me see that wondrous book."

Ruth tossed the book to him and he scanned the index, flipped the book open, and read.

"This ought to do. It will require a touch of honesty and a tad of humility on our part but this will do it."

"What will do what?"

"There is a service—is that what it's called down at the Rev's church? Listen, page 433, 'The Blessing of a Civil Marriage.' We get Fisher to do this bit and if anyone should happen to notice that the service isn't the full monty, so to speak, we will admit our impulsive behavior, but only after the fact and only if necessary, and only to the observant few among the well-wishers who notice the difference. What do you think?"

"Let me see that." Ruth scanned the pages. "Okay, Schwartz, skip calling the mayor, twist The Reverend Fisher's arm, and set this up. For the next twenty-four hours, you are officially a genius."

Chapter Twenty-one

The office still lacked its expected ambience. This time, however, the change had nothing to do with the absent aroma of burnt coffee. Babies. Giggling babies.

"Hey, Ike," Essie called from somewhere nearby, but not from the dispatcher's desk, "look at who's here."

"Look where? And why are you here? I'm happy you are, by the way, but I thought you were holed up somewhere avoiding George LeBrun."

"We're down here on the floor in your office."

"Who's we?"

"Me and Sam. Her and Karl is down here for a visit."

It was true enough. Essie and Sam Hedrick were seated on the floor. A blanket had been spread between them and their children were busy getting acquainted with the less complicated work of police procedure. Each had been given a book of unissued traffic citations which they were gumming into papier-mâché.

"Sam," he said, "it's great to see you. Why didn't you call? And, not that it matters, but why are you here?"

"I sent you a text. Didn't you get it?"

"Oh, right. A text. I'm not up to speed on texting, Sam."

"Okay, noted. We are here because someone in the agency lit a fire under Karl's rear end and he needs to talk to you, your medical examiner, and anyone else who can help stomp it out."

"I see. You are here because of FBI business. Okay, I get that. Where's Karl?"

"He went for coffee."

"We have coffee. We have a snappy K-Cup dispenser."

"I know that now, but when we arrived we didn't smell asphalt in the making so he went to the Cross Roads for carryout. He's been gone for half an hour so I expect Flora's got him buttonholed. And you haven't met Martin, have you?"

"By Martin, I assume you mean the curly haired kid who's on page eight of that citation book?"

"That's him."

"Family name?"

"Dr. King."

"Right. So what's Karl's problem?"

"He'll have to tell you. I can't make sense out of it. It has something to do with a body you found in the woods last week, somebody named Barbie."

"AKA Ethyl Smut?"

"I don't think so unless Ethyl is a mobbed up guy. Apparently he's been dead a decade or so and is supposed to be dead somewhere else besides in your woods."

"I'll wait for Karl on that one. Say, while you're here, I want to introduce you to our intern. Maybe you can show him how to run some of the programs you loaded in that machine you used to drive that no one can figure out how to since you left."

"Sure, which program?"

"For starters, we have an old photograph of a young girl. I want to run it through the process that ages the subject. We're looking for a girl, young woman now, maybe sixteen to eighteen, and I'd like to have an approximation of what she'd look like today. She's maybe twelve in the picture and I'd like to age it four or six or eight years. It would give us something to put into a BOLO."

"I can do that."

"Hey, Ike, you ain't said hi to Junior," Essie said and struggled to her feet. "Woof. I must be getting old."

"Not old, Essie. I know I am approaching the age when I need eyeglasses, but even I can see the bump. You're on your way to number two."

"Well, shoot, Ike, I guess that's why you're such a good detective. Even Billy ain't noticed it and he's got a better view of the crime scene than you do."

"Thank God for that."

"What?"

"Speaking of Billy, where'd he get to?"

"Oh, I reckon he met up with Karl. They got stuff to talk about. Kids and houses and things."

Karl pushed his way into the area carrying a flat of coffees. "Somebody come get these things. They're spilling and burning my hand."

"We don't need them now, Karl. Ike bought a fancy dispenser and we're all good."

"Well, what do I do with this mess?"

Ike lifted the coffees from Karl's outstretched hand and set them on an empty desk. "Who do we have in the cells?" he said.

Charley Picket looked up from the vintage CRT screen he'd been studying. "Two frat boys and a pair of bikers. They had separate parties and then exchanged words last night at Alex's Road House. Anyway, they were too drunk to send home so they're our guests until they are sober enough to stand before the magistrate or be sent on their way."

"Well, somebody take these coffees down to them. Maybe it will speed up the process."

"I'll do it," Charley said. "I love it when those skinheads have to confront this ole black dude."

"Karl, Sam says you have a problem with one of our bodies."

"By one, I take it there are more than the one I am interested in."

Ike described the scene when they unearthed two bodies and the difficulties they were having with sorting out both.

"The decades-old body may be mine now," Karl, said. "You can likely let that one go. I'll need everything you have on it, though."

"Yours? How will it be yours? I am always happy to work with the Bureau, as you know—"

Karl snorted.

"Well, I am always happy to work with you, Karl. But before I give up my dead guy, I need to know why."

"It's a long story, Ike. Show me how to use that space-age coffee machine and we'll talk."

Twenty minutes later Ike sat back and frowned. "So let me get this straight. If the dental records are correct, the guy we found in the woods is a New York hood named Barbarini who was killed ten years ago in that city and then supposedly dumped into the Atlantic."

"Correct."

"And now it appears that he wasn't done in as described and the men who are doing time in Sing Sing may be entitled to a new trial and, since the witness who put them there is dead, the case may never be retried and they could walk?"

"That's part A, yes."

"And Part B is that there are agents in the Bureau whose reputations may be questioned if that were to happen, and subtle pressure has been applied on you to find out that our dead guy is not that dead guy."

"In a nutshell, that's it. If it is Barbarini, then dominos will topple and who knows how many career plans will have to be adjusted."

"Including yours?"

"Including mine."

"Well, not to worry yet. The ME constructed the dental chart from a ten-year-old stiff. One filling or two on the wrong teeth and you are off the hook."

"What are the chances of that?"

"Not too good. This new ME is from the big city and used to getting it right, but we can hope."

"Can I ask you a personal question, Ike?"

"Sure, shoot."

"If it turns out that your body is mine, so to speak, and you were in my place, would you say so or would you let it slide? I mean it's a pretty sure thing those two guys did snuff Barbarini, and even if they didn't, there's enough paper on them to justify the fact they belong in jail. Furthermore, the case is cold and probably could not be retried, especially if it turns out the evidence was tainted which, by the way, it seems it was. In all probability they'll walk. What purpose is served by starting a process that on the best of days can't end up good for anybody?"

"And it could cost you your career—at least slow it down?"

"Yeah, well, there's that too."

"Karl, good or bad, inconvenient, or uncomfortable, in the end, speaking the truth is the only thing that keeps us civilized. It's not a virtue much in evidence in the public sector anymore, but it is still the standard. The system has to work, warts and all, or it's chaos—for ordinary people and for us who have to maintain some sort of order."

"You're saying I should call it as it falls?"

"Exactly."

Karl sighed and nodded. "I'll need to read the ME's report and find out if the body is your problem or mine."

"As much as I'd like to help you out, I could do with one less murder to sort out. I'll get you the report. Let's hope one of the kids hasn't eaten it."

Chapter Twenty-two

It had taken all the willpower she could muster but she'd found him—a phone number for him, that is. After all those years of angry silence, she'd managed to talk to her Marine. The conversation had been awkward, at first. She knew Mark had been through a lot since their time together back then—drugs, jail, and the other—the things her cousins and grandmother had predicted for him, warned her about. Oh, yeah, they'd made a point of letting her know every time he slipped and how they'd been so damned right about him all along. Still, it was she who'd ended the affair. She realized she lacked the courage to shoulder the risks, the burdens, involved in trying to save him from himself. She'd believed at the time that a good Christian woman could bring a man to his senses, even a weak one like Mark. But she'd wavered, given in to her kin and her own lack of conviction. Not quite the Christian woman she imagined she was. She'd turned her back on him and the one love of her life. She never forgave herself for that, for being too weak to stand up to them. Probably that's why she took such an interest in the daughter, the one who might have been hers. Well, too late now.

After a few awkward passes about those missing years, she told him she already knew about most of it and said she understood. That is when he'd told her he'd returned to Picketsville and though he hadn't meant to, he had hooked up again with George LeBrun who, he said, had just been released from jail. She said she knew. He said that before George arrived in town, Ethyl had been after him about Darla, and how she had started the process to restore her custody rights. He'd told Ethyl he wanted to find his daughter and she'd put him off. No way, she'd said, would he get within a mile of her. The phone went quiet and Leota thought she might have been cut off.

"Mark?"

"Look, I don't know how it happened, but I lost my temper and we went at it like the old days. I must have smacked her around a little. She stabbed me, Leota, in the arm. I managed to turn the knife back on her. I heard people coming and I panicked. Listen, I'm sorry but she…what the hell…"

He said he'd shoved her into his truck and took off over the back road to Lexington. He figured they both needed an emergency room, her more than him. Somehow, she got loose near their old picnic spot. Did Leota remember the picnic spot? She said she did. How could she forget? Of course, she did.

"Oh my God, Mark, what have you done? Is that how Ethyl ended up in the woods two weeks ago?"

"You knew she…? Leota, I guess I'd just had enough. She wanted out of the truck. I said, 'Okay, fine,' and dumped her out. Stupid bitch. You know what she wanted Darla for."

She started to tell him everything that had happened to Ethyl when she heard him shout.

"What the hell? Wait…"

She heard a pop and what sounded like a groan and the line went dead. Just like that. One second she heard his voice, his breathing, the next—nothing. Heart racing, she waited through a long pause.

"Mark, Mark, are you still there?"

No answer, then a sound like a bee buzzing and line went completely silent, only the gentle humming of a broken connection. She redialed and listened to a busy signal. She redialed again. The phone rang but no one answered. All afternoon the phone rang but no one answered. Finally, an automated operator announced the line was no longer in service. No longer in service? What did that mean?

She would drive back to Picketsville and talk to him—face to face. He needed to know what happened to his daughter after he left. Then again, he probably already knew most of it, maybe not the part she had. Why would he have gone after Ethyl like that after all this time? Why had he waited so long to come back and why join up with LeBrun? It didn't make any sense. Was the drug culture always so illogical? It must be, or he wouldn't have stumbled into that ditch again. And what was he about to tell her about LeBrun? She locked up her apartment, climbed into her truck, and headed west again. She had to see him at least one last time. She needed to know what he'd done to Ethyl.

Karl had the ME's report in his hand and had been staring at the same paragraph for what seemed like five minutes when Rita announced a call-out from the county fire department.

"I'll take it," Ike said.

"How about I ride along?"

"Sure, Karl, why not? You can tell me what you found in the ME's report that has had you frozen in place for the last five minutes." Ike jotted down the address, collected his gear, and led Karl out to a black-and-white. "So, good news in the report?"

"Not likely, the opposite in fact. According to my predecessor, Barbarini was missing a pinky finger. If your guy was intact, I'd have been home free and all this could be written off as a nice visit to the country."

"I take it the ME reported a finger missing."

"Right little finger missing…well, actually two fingers missing. That's interesting. It's also confusing."

"How so?"

"One finger—the correct one—would confirm the body as Barbarini. Two missing fingers muddies the water. When and where did the other finger go missing?"

"It could have been lost in the dig or maybe an animal found our missing gangster and helped itself to a snack."

"Why would it stop with one finger, then?"

"Good point. Either your report is inaccurate and he lost two fingers, not one, or you have either a reprieve or another problem. But for the moment, that piece of ID data is in the toilet."

"The ME's report is unclear about whether the finger might have been lost in the process of unearthing the body. Whatever evidence there might have been of an animal disturbance would have been obliterated by the activity involved in removing the first body. I can't assume this guy died without his right pinky finger. Maybe he did and maybe he didn't. Why in the toilet?"

"Because you have reasonable doubt on the missing finger and since you cannot explain the second missing digit, you can toss it as an identifier."

"I guess. Could a medical examiner tell from the remains of a hand if a finger had been removed prior to death?"

"I don't know, Karl. They do it all the time on TV. I assume those TV guys do their homework so there must be some validity in the process, but in reality? Who knows? You'll have to ask him to be sure. They can't get DNA done in an hour or two like they'd have you believe, but most of the rest is correct even if the timeline for getting the work done is fiddled to match airtime. Speaking of DNA, what about a match there? I could ask the doc to run one. Wait, the body was almost completely skeletonized. Would the DNA have degraded by now? Would there be any tissue left to test?"

Karl turned the pages and nodded. "There must have been. He already ordered the test."

"Really? Good. That could take a couple of weeks but it could buy you some time. If this is Barbarini, you need to find out how deep the pile of horse manure he has created is before you report back. You should go for at least two out of three—positive on the dental, and/or the digit, and/or the DNA. The 3D trifecta. Anything less than that and you can in good conscience report 'Identity Undetermined.' So far you have ambiguity on the missing digit, so you are down to two."

"I guess."

"We tried tracing the phone number on the bill found on the body."

"And?"

"I think it's a dead end."

"How's that?"

"Lots of people write phone numbers on bills for all kinds of reasons. If they got a bill like that for change, hardly anybody would tidy it up by erasing old numbers away. It could have changed hands a dozen, a hundred times. So, no real hope on the phone number. The bill's age is consistent with the stiff's presumed death time frame."

"Then the dead guy may revert to being your problem."

"We'll take it." They drove in silence for a mile or two. "You really love working for the Bureau, don't you Karl?"

"It's all I've ever wanted to do since I was a kid."

"So, if they don't buy 'undetermined' or if the two-out-of-three trifecta doesn't hit and this business blows up in your face, what then?"

"I don't want to think about it."

"Let's hope the DNA turns out not to match."

"Yeah, let's hope. You remember what brought me to Picketsville in the first place?"

"You had a run-in with your boss. He's gone now and you were cleared."

"True enough, but it's still in my jacket, Ike. There is a sheet in it that says I once had something go wrong with one of my assignments and, even though it's over and done and I was cleared, it still sits in there like a snake in a hen's nest, ready to bite you if you reach for an egg."

"You think that if this job turns out bad—if you have to report the body as the one that's supposed to be somewhere else—higher-ups will take it out on you?"

"If they're embarrassed enough, or if their careers are affected, yes, I do."

"That's tough. What will you do?"

"I don't know, Ike. Wait and see, I guess."

◇◇◇

Fire equipment blocked the narrow entrance to the trailer park. Ike and Karl pulled off onto the side of the road and walked in. Smoke from the fire had thinned out by the time they'd arrived but the acrid smell still lingered. Fires differ in how they reek, and few are pleasant. They grade from comforting to awful— fireplaces, outdoor grills, bonfires, house fires, and near the bottom of anyone's list, a burning trailer. The stench of gutted appliances, chipboard, aluminum, grease, plastic plumbing, and a decade of unsanitary living assaulted their senses. Worse was the unmistakable aroma of burned flesh.

Chief Hake Longanecker strolled over to Ike and pushed his helmet back from his forehead.

"This one looks like it'll end up on your plate, Sheriff. We'll be done here pretty quick except for hot spots, but there's no question you got yourself a stiff in that mess, and unless I'm off my game, the arson boys are going to say this one was deliberately lit."

"Who is it, do you know?"

"The manager of this dump…" Hake looked around with ill-concealed disgust at the collection of ill-kept mobile homes, trash scattered across the open space, and the dead and dying trucks, cars, and ATVs, "…is over under that scraggly crab apple tree. He says the man is named Mark Simpkins. That may not be his real name."

"Why do you say that?'

"Well, you know we always pull burning paper out and away from the flames and some of what we dragged from this mess was mail—envelopes, you know. I just happened to notice that the name on them papers was Dellinger, not Simpkins. Yes, sir, Mark Dellinger, so, either Simpkins didn't live alone—though the manager said there was only one of them in there, the guy was stealing mail—or his name wasn't Simpkins. I'm sticking with that last one."

Dellinger. Ike knew he had heard that name recently. He shook his head. Five years before, a file marked "Dellinger,

Mark" would have been neatly tucked in his brain along with the hundreds, thousands, of similar accumulations. It was the habit he'd acquired over a lifetime of living close to the edge. Bad guys, good guys, allies, enemies all mixed together—the history of his years living in the dark, in the light, and some just there because he liked the person and, well, you never know when you might need a friend in a strange town. Five years ago he had but to hear a name once and he would have it cataloged forever, complete with place and circumstances. Not anymore.

"I'm not that old," he muttered.

Karl glanced at him sideways. "What?"

"I'm losing a step and I don't like it. I heard that name recently and I can't remember when or where."

"Is it important?"

"That's the worst part. I don't know. I think so. Damn!"

"It will come to you."

The chief tipped his helmet forward and went back to directing his crew's mop-up of the scene. "Okay, Sheriff, I'll leave you to it. The area should be cool enough for your medical examiner to look at the body in an hour."

Ike put in a call to the ME's office, frowned and turned back to the chief's retreating bulk.

"Hake, you did say the name on the letters was Dellinger?'

"That's what's on the papers, yep."

"I just remembered who Dellinger was. I need to poke through them if it's okay."

"Help yourself. I'll get one of the crew to rake out as many as we can for you."

Chapter Twenty-three

The medical examiner and his forensics crew arrived while Ike sifted through the dead man's singed and still-smoking scraps of paper. Ordinarily, the ME would have waited for the Arson Squad to make at least a tentative determination before assuming he had a crime scene, but Hake had declared it to be one and that was enough for Tom Wexler. He and his evidence techs eased the burned remains from the ashes and began their routine.

Ike stuffed as many pieces of paper as he could into an evidence bag. "Tom, it would be wonderful if you could lift a fingerprint off this guy. DNA will take too long and I really need an ID."

"I can't promise anything, Sheriff. He's pretty crispy, but he was lying on his side with an arm tucked under, so there is a chance I'll have something for you in a few hours."

"If this is Dellinger, that's one less possibility for the other dead guy we found. Of course, if what Karl here says is true, that went by the boards yesterday anyway."

"What?"

"Sorry. Tom, this is Special Agent Karl Hedrick, FBI. You posted the dental chart and it got a hit. He believes he knows, or may know, the identity of the second body we dug up the other day. If he is correct, he has a problem, and you and I have one less."

Karl looked questioningly at Ike. "Introduction?"

"Right, sorry. Tom Wexler, Karl Hedrick. As I said, Karl is here on FBI business. He needs to have a chat with you about that other set of remains we found with the dead woman last week."

"What do you want to know, Special Agent Hedrick?"

"With all due respect, how accurate is your dental record on the guy? I have to ask because his chart matches a murder victim who is supposed to be at the bottom of the ocean a decade ago."

"Interesting—which ocean? Never mind, I don't need to know. Okay, how accurate? I had a full jaw, both maxilla and mandible. I was able to make a complete set of X-rays, chart the work done, and send it in. There is always a possibility of a dental doppelganger, I suppose, but how likely is that? So, to answer your question, a very accurate record. The wonks in suburban D.C. ID'd him as Anthony Barbarini. Problem?"

"Problem—yes. You sent out a DNA sample. I know it is too early to expect anything yet, but any results back?"

"None, but I didn't expect any. It could be weeks. Now, if the Bureau wants to resubmit on their dime, I expect an 'FBI Urgent' might get a match in a few days."

"Consider it done."

"Umm, Karl," Ike said, "are you sure you want a quick result? I thought you would want to buy some time."

"I know, but to tell the truth, I already know what I have to do, best to get it over with."

"Anything else here, Doc?"

Tom looked at the charred body and shook his head. "You have another one, Ike. This lad, whoever he is, took a bullet to the head before he was burned."

"Great. If you're done here, Karl, I need to get back to the office. What with all the distractions lately, I am losing traction with my original murder investigation. Or, it seems now, investigations."

◇◇◇

The children and their mothers were gone when they returned. Rita waved a stack of pink While You Were Out notes at Ike.

"Ms. Harris called you three times and your father once. Oh, and Billy said he put the report about the search of Ethyl Smut's house on your desk and he's sorry it took so long but he got caught up in the LeBrun thing."

Ike took the reminders, sorted them by their time stamp, and then dropped them in the nearest trash bin. He made his way into his office and opened Billy's report.

"Where the hell is he, Rita?" he yelled.

"Who?"

"Billy. This report is blank. What did he do? Where's the kid, the intern? He rode with Billy. I need both of them in here, pronto."

"I'll find them. Hang on."

The intern arrived on the double in response to Rita's page. "Yes, sir?"

"Okay kid, I sent you out with Billy to scout out the Smut place. I have Billy's report and all that is in it is a list of interviews with neighbors. Not what the people said, but only how many were done. What the hell is this all about?"

"Right. I guess Billy would have said something sooner but, like, there was all the fuss about the man released from prison and Mrs. Sutherlin gone missing and—"

"Yeah, yeah, I got it. Just tell me what happened."

"Yes, sir. Well, we went out to that trailer park where she lived and the pad where her address was? There wasn't anything there."

"There wasn't anything...what do you mean there wasn't anything there?"

"She must have had her unit towed to some other place. So, no mobile home, just tire tracks and trash left behind. We went door-to-door, but those people out there didn't want to talk to us. We asked, like, everybody, but except for the manager, they all dummied up."

"What did the manager have to say? No, let me guess. 'She left while he was not in town and didn't leave a forwarding address' and she was what...two, three months in arrears on her rent,"

"Four months and, yeah, no forwarding address."

"Okay, that is your next assignment, TAK. That unit had a tag on it. It is registered somewhere. If she landed in another park, they will have noted it. You get on the phone or the computer and track her down. I don't want to see your face until you do."

The intern scuttled off.

Karl smiled "My, my, you sounded like a drill sergeant I had, Ike. Is this the new you, or is this kid something special?"

"Neither. He is an intern and I want him to understand that a cop backs up the person he rides with. If Billy was too preoccupied to finish this, he should have jumped right in and covered, not waited for me to tell him what to do."

"Right. So, what do I do while I wait for my DNA?"

"I take it you don't want to go back to D.C."

"We just got here. I'm signed out for the rest of the week."

"You want to make yourself useful? Billy won't be worth a tinker's dam until we put LeBrun back in the slammer. How about you do some TDY in the Picketsville Sheriff's Department?"

"Sure, why not? What do you need doing?"

"There's a trash bag in the corner that is serving as an evidence bag. Go through its contents and, using your keen, FBI-trained intellect, tell me what it means."

"Trash bag? What's in it?"

"Apparently someone's memories—old clothes, baby apparel, scraps of paper, someone's childhood. I would like to know whose and why he or she left it in an abandoned hay barn. More specifically, why they left it in my father's abandoned hay barn. Is that fact important? Did the person who dumped these things want me to find them or was finding them in my dad's place just a coincidence that may or may not play into what we are looking for?"

"You think this relates to one of your murder victims?"

"No idea. I would guess it has nothing to do with the decades-old stiff we currently share, but who can say? The stuff is as old as his murder, so maybe. Then again, there might be a connection to the Smut woman. I don't know whether I hope it does connect or not. There was an old photograph in there, I've asked Sam to show the intern how to run the software that would age it a bunch of years. Where is Sam, by the way?"

"She texted me that she and Essie went shopping. I don't know what for. I guess Essie is feeling safer now. Safe enough to be out and about, in any event."

"Unless they went to Roanoke to shop."

The intern rushed back into Ike's office. "Sheriff, I found it."

"You found what, TAK?"

"The dead woman's new address."

"Do you feel like taking another ride, Karl? TAK, go find an empty cruiser—you're driving."

Chapter Twenty-four

The smoke had abated and the truck and a crew checking for hot spots had left. The eye-watering smells from the fire lingered. There is no odor quite like a burned-out life. Otherwise, the trailer park had not changed in the two hours since they'd last been there.

Karl scanned the area, one eyebrow cocked. "Weren't we just here a couple of hours ago, Ike?"

"This is the place. TAK, are you sure you found the right address?"

"Yes sir, the Lonesome Villas Park. At least that's what the data search said."

"Karl and I were here earlier for that fire over there. They found a dead guy in the ruins." Ike paused. His expression changed marginally. "Dellinger!" he snapped. "You mean to tell me that Ethyl Smut was living in the same trailer park as her ex-husband?"

"Her ex-husband?"

"TAK, you see that smoldering mess over there? That used to be the mobile home of Mark Dellinger, he was—"

"The missing girl's father. Yes, sir, I know. Ms. Smut's unit is three down."

"This case is becoming weirder by the minute. When did you say she moved here?"

"Umm, I'll have to check my notes—not too long ago."

"Karl, go back to the manager and get us some occupancy dates on both these units."

It didn't take long to search Ethyl Smut's living quarters. Druggies don't own anything valuable. If they did it would have been sold, hocked, or traded for the poison of their choice. They usually don't care about the rest of their possessions either. Aside from what looked like a decade of unwashed laundry and dirty dishes, the place was empty.

Except for the blood trail.

Leota noticed the car exiting the mobile home park as she slowed to turn into it. The young man at the wheel, whoever he was, seemed so absorbed in conversation with the others in the car he nearly forced her off the road. Good. Not good for being forced to swerve to one side, but good to have gone unnoticed. The last thing she wanted was to attract attention anywhere near Picketsville, especially now and especially under the circumstances that had brought her back. Until this morning, crime and the people who pursued it, as in either perpetrators or police, did not interest her. But…well, she hoped she hadn't turned paranoid, but she could have sworn the vehicle that nearly hit her was a police car. That begged the question: what were they doing here? Was Mark in trouble again? Is that why the phone line went dead? Worse, did they somehow find out something about Mark and Ethyl? What would they find?

She pulled up in front of an old Airstream near the entrance. It had a handcrafted sign affixed to its side that read *Manager*. She sat and studied the sign on the trailer for a moment, hesitant to make her next move. She could still reverse course and head home. Mark was history, after all, and the passage of time meant that no possibility of any sort of reconciliation existed. Common sense told her to quit now before something bad happened. She had neither the courage nor the skill to sort out whatever was at play here. Common sense notwithstanding, she screwed up a modicum of courage, alit from the car, and knocked on an aluminum door that hung on its hinges by a force that seemed to have no relationship to either the condition of the hinges or the laws of gravity.

A man who stood only inches above her five-feet-two answered the door. She asked for the number of Mark Dellinger's unit. The man looked at her a moment, turned and neatly delivered a brown stream of chewing tobacco spit into a Coke bottle he held in his right hand. Leota noticed that there were several stains on the floor, some undoubtedly very old, which suggested his aim wasn't always that good.

"Dellinger, Mark Dellinger," she repeated, a bit too loudly.

"Ain't no Dellinger staying here, lady." The old man started to swing the door shut. It was then Leota smelled the residual aroma of fire. Not a bonfire, not a barbeque. Something had burned—a house—here? She felt the first signs of panic rise in her stomach.

"Mark Dellinger. He might have used a different name. He used to…" What did he used to do? When he had all those run-ins with the police he'd sometimes used his mother's maiden name. What was it?

"Wait," she said still too loudly. "What happened here?"

"What happened? Are you kidding? Is your nose broke? We had us a fire. Fellow named Simpkins got hisself burned to death here this afternoon."

Simpkins. Madge Simpkins married Robert Dellinger and they had a son, Mark. That was it.

"Cops came, them CSI type of people, lots of excitement, for sure."

"The man said his name was Simpkins?"

"Yep, that's what he put down on the rental form. I didn't check and the coppers got pretty shirty about that, but hell, he paid cash money and seemed okay to me. Anyway, they said his name wasn't Simpkins after all."

"Who did they say he was?"

"Who? Didn't catch it. Makes no never mind now. He's dead, ain't he?"

"Yes, of course. What did they want to know?"

"Know? Well, shoot, they was trying to figure about how the fire got started, I reckon. Then, 'bout an hour ago, they come roaring back. Only this time they're looking for that Smut woman. Seems to me they could have saved themselves some gasoline and time if they asked about her the first time they come. Police...what do you expect? Like to find that woman my own self. She owes me back rent for her place. But she wasn't here. If I ain't heard from her by Tuesday, I'm locking her out, and if I ain't had no contact by October, I'm auctioning off the trailer. Say, who are you?"

"I'm a friend, you could say, of both of them. What did the police want with Ethyl?"

"Want? How the hell would I know what them police wanted? They just barreled in here and tossed her unit looking for God-knows-what. Drugs is my guess. She was one of them users you read about, you know. Looked like hell. I'da warned her about men and parties. I got my rules, but who'd want to party around with someone who looked like that, I ask you?"

"Thank you for your time. By the way, you might as well go ahead and sell the trailer. She isn't coming back. She's dead."

"Dead? You don't say. Well, that'd sure explain the cops and all. Funny how they had to come out twice. Once to find out about this Simpkins fella and then for the woman. Dead, you say?"

"Yes, dead. Did they say what they wanted of the other man...Simpkins?"

"Beats me. Whatever it was went up in the fire, I reckon. I tell you, lady, if you're in the market for a used mobile home, best be careful what you buy. Them old units like the one Simpkins lived in are a problem. Some of them had that aluminum wiring which, you maybe heard about, is a fire hazard and they sometimes go up if there's a short or something like that."

"You're saying it was an accident?"

"I don't rightly know. Now the cops, they think maybe someone set the whole shebang on fire." He paused to make another donation to the Coke bottle, this time with less accuracy.

"See, the man, Simpkins, or whoever, was in it and all, so they're naturally suspicious. But I think it was them aluminum wires. See, I heard this pop like you get when there's a short in the electrics and then, pretty soon, there's smoke. Somebody called the fire department and then the trucks came. The chief, he thinks it's arson, but I ain't so sure. I mean who sets fires to trailers unless they're insured and then it's the owners doing it for the money, right?"

"I suppose so. Thank you." Leota left him muttering on his doorstep and wandered over to the burnt-out ruins of what she now knew to be her Marine's last home.

"Mark, what happened here? What were you doing that got you killed and why the old picnic place? Why did you let her out there of all places?"

She stared at the tangled and charred remains for what seemed like an hour or more. Then, a decision made, she walked back to her truck and turned it toward Picketsville. It was time to settle things with her cousins, Flora and Arlene.

Chapter Twenty-five

Blake Fisher happened to be in his office late in the afternoon and not busy. He greeted Ike and asked him to sit.

"Ike, I feel like I owe you something of an apology for the other day."

"No apology required. I understand your concern, I think. As I am not, strictly speaking, one of the flock—"

"Except in the larger sense. Saint Paul says—"

"It's okay, Rev, I didn't come here to ask you to reconsider, exactly. We had another idea we hope will be more doable. I want to run it by you and then I need to ask you some questions about a girl you spoke to last week."

"I spoke to? Who said I spoke to a girl?"

"Her guardian, godmother, one or the other. I'm not entirely sure what the relationship is, to be frank, but she said she thought the girl staying with her had stopped here to see you before she went to the godmother's place."

"Okay, what about the girl?"

"Let me clear the other thing first. After thinking over what you said to us, Ruth said that in effect 'we were asking you to trivialize a sacrament in order to cover our embarrassment.' Have I got that right?"

"That's pretty much it, yes. But—"

"No buts. On reflection, we finally saw the point. Then, while struggling for a way out of the mess we'd made for ourselves, Ruth dug out her Common Prayer book."

"*Book of Common Prayer.*"

"That one, yes. In it, we discovered what I hope will be a compromise for us both. Is it true every Episcopalian on the planet owns one of those books?"

"I don't know about the planet, but theoretically, yes, most do, or did. Many lapse and leave them at home when they strike out on their own or move and the book ends up in a yard sale. But if they were confirmed, there is nearly a one hundred percent chance they have, or have had one. What's the compromise?"

"Amazing. Okay, we were browsing, I guess you could say, through that book and found something called…" Ike pulled a scrap of paper from a shirt pocket and read,…The Blessing of a Civil Marriage. Could you do that for us?"

While Blake Fisher listened to Ike's request his eyes wandered from Ike to the door that Ike knew led to the sanctuary. Ike sensed he was about to be rejected again and worried how Ruth would take it. And, more importantly, what they would do if Fisher said no.

"Rev, is something the matter?"

"What? No, sorry, my mind wandered a bit. Thinking about the girl and seeing you in a uniform and wondering if there was a connection. You almost never wear one. I won't ask you what the occasion is. Work, I presume. So, yes, I can perform the Blessing of a Civil Marriage for you. I should have thought of it when you and Ruth came to see me last week. Sorry about that. It's just…churches and clergy are bombarded with requests to do weddings about this time of the year. For parishioners it's one thing, but for non-members…"

"If that's a problem, we could—"

"Not a problem. At least in your case it isn't. It's just, I don't know why, but it seems that everyone—irrespective of their faith or lack thereof—thinks they need to be married in a church. I had a couple in here last month who said they wanted to be married here at this little parish. They spent twenty minutes telling me how gorgeous the church was and so perfect…actually, the bride to be said she thought it was 'cute.' As they were not members, I asked them why this church and not their own. By now I should have known the answer. The bride to be said, 'For one, the church is so picturesque,' only she pronounced it picture-skew, 'and would be so cool for the photos and all.' Before I could respond to that bit of inanity, the young man admitted that neither he nor the bride-to-be attended church. I asked him, 'Then why do you want to get married in one?' And he said it was because the bride's mother wanted a church wedding. I asked, 'Well, why don't you get married in your future mother-in-law's church?' and he said—"

"And he said she didn't go to a church either. I am suddenly feeling guilty and forced to confess that neither Ruth nor I can claim much in the way of good intentions in that respect. Ruth and I are asking you to perform a ritual to which neither of us subscribes. You turned us down in the first instance, and rightly so. I am delighted you will accommodate us but am curious to know why you are relenting now."

"Relenting? Is that what you think I am doing? Well, perhaps I am and perhaps not. There are at least two reasons. You are my friends, and you are no longer attempting to bamboozle the public with a bogus wedding to cover your possible embarrassment over a rash decision made in Sin City. What you propose is the correct thing to do—at least in my admittedly narrow view."

"Thank you for that. For the record, what we did in Vegas may have been alcohol-fueled, but it was never rash. The two of us have been dancing around nuptials for a long time. After we ran into some very scary stuff the week before, we both realized in our different ways that we might be pressing our luck and may have put the thing off for too long."

"I won't ask you what 'scary stuff' you experienced. You seem to live an inordinately dangerous life for a small-town sheriff, by the way. Sometimes it feels like we're filming a reality television show around here. So, okay we'll set the thing up. Now, to finish my lecture. Clergy, like me, live in the constant hope that we will find a way to bring people to the Lord, particularly friends and those we care about in special ways. You need to understand that we take this calling seriously and all that it implies. We worry about your soul even if you and the rest of the world do not."

"So this is like a free trial offer. If it takes, all to the good. If not, it's a loss-leader."

"I wouldn't have put it quite like that, but you're close enough, so yeah, I guess you could say that."

"Well, thank you. The two of us are a lot alike, Rev. I worry about the same things, the safety and well being of the people of Picketsville, even if they resent my intrusion into what they perceive as their right to privacy, which they define as doing what they damned well please as long as nobody gets hurt. But, like it or not, I do intrude and I do hope that by providing a permanent police presence, things will get better, or at least no worse. I am a street cop walking a beat, so to speak. In a way, so are you. You walk a different beat, but we're both in the same business—getting people home safe and sound. We have a different definition of home and operate with a different set of commandments is all."

"Not so different. So what do you want to know about the girl, woman?"

"We're looking for her. I know now she's in the area somewhere. Do you happen to know where she is, Rev?"

"I don't know. Why would you think I might?"

"She came to you once. I take it she wasn't forced to do so. It occurred to me she might have again."

"Sorry. She didn't and I haven't seen her since. Why are you after her?"

"She is a person of interest in the death of her mother. Her name is Darla Smut aka Darla Dellinger, by the way."

A frown formed on Blake's face and his gaze drifted to the window.

Ike realized that the clergyman wrestled with something he wanted to tell him but thought he shouldn't. Fisher sighed and turned back to Ike.

"I can tell you this. She asked me to hear her confession. I'm not sure she even knew what that was, but I took it that way. You understand, then, there is not much I can say."

"You know, Rev, that to make a broad generalization, like where I might find her, wouldn't necessarily be breaking the seal of the confessional."

"I said I don't know where she is, Ike. I really don't. She showed up here that afternoon and left. If I had to guess, I agree with you, she is still local, probably hunkered down somewhere she thinks safe, but I really don't know. Okay, this is what I can tell you, but please don't press me for more."

Ike nodded his agreement with the full knowledge that if he thought it would avail him something, he would press the clergyman for more even if it meant threatening him. He had a murderer on the loose and the nicer points of medieval canon law would not sway him from doing what he had to do to catch him.

"Okay, for the record, she did not kill her mother. Lord knows she had every reason to, but I can say categorically that she didn't. I think she knows, or suspects, who did, but she did not tell me. If you know her story, you will understand that if I had been in her shoes, even I would have been tempted to do the woman in myself. Her life has been horrific, Ike. Unbearable, even. Find her, Ike. Talk to her. Get her into some sort of rehab situation, but for the love of God, do not arrest her for something she didn't do."

"I've heard her story. You are right, it is awful and even if you are wrong and she did kill her mother, I don't think a jury would convict her of anything worse than manslaughter. Probably go with self-defense, maybe even acquit. So, is that all you can tell me?"

"That's all I will tell you. If you know her story, as you say, there isn't anything I can say that you haven't already heard."

"Okay, Rev, thank you for that much. I will do my best to find her and get her the help she needs. You, on the other hand, will call me if she turns up again on your radar. If she didn't murder her mother, and I have no reason not to believe you when you say you're sure she didn't, then she may be in danger."

"How so?"

"Whoever killed the mother could have the child in his crosshairs now. If I understand the extent of the trauma inflicted on her over the years, and I am not sure I will ever be able to do that, I am afraid there are people, some of them important people, some from this area, who would be uncomfortable, extremely so, if it were to be public knowledge that she's come back to town and is talking to the police. They will be tempted to do whatever they need to keep that from happening. If I have her data correct, she's not yet eighteen which means the statute of limitations has something over two years left before it runs out on what was done to her by those men and women."

"But, if that is so, wouldn't the last thing she would want is to be in contact with the police? Frankly, if I were the girl, I would hot foot it out of town before anyone could find me."

"I take your point, but here's the thing, she can't run forever. I'm afraid that if she doesn't get help soon, worse things will happen. I don't care how strong a person is, no one can carry a burden like that forever. She's still a child when all is said and done and at least with us, she'd be safe."

"Can you really guarantee her safety, Ike? In the old days, she could throw her arms around the altar in the church and no one would dare touch her—for fear of the law and God. Now days, nobody seems to fear either one."

"You are becoming cynical, Blake. Come on, you don't believe that, do you? If you did, you wouldn't be sitting in this backwash community working like one of the Hebrew slaves trying to making bricks for the pharaoh from straw and clay."

"No, you're right, but I confess I do get discouraged."

"And opportunists like Ruth and me don't exactly enhance your faith."

"Frankly no, you don't, but, as we say in my line of work, we live in hope." Blake Fisher smiled. "So, A Blessing of a Civil Marriage…I can do that for you. When?"

"I know your weekends are busy, how about next early next week?"

"Monday works for me, unless that is too short notice."

"Monday's good. I'll e-mail Ruth and we can get this party together."

"Dorothy Sutherlin is our resident festivities person. You might have a word with her."

Chapter Twenty-six

George LeBrun's lawyers told him to be careful for the next few weeks, until his hearing for a new trial can be held.

"Circumspect," his lawyer had cautioned. "You cannot do anything that would give the law enforcement community an excuse to stop and charge you. One false step, George, and you are back in the slammer. Drive slowly, stay sober, no dope, no fights, and for God's sake, no dealings with your former associates."

Circumspect was not a word in George's lexicon, but had it been, he still might not have subscribed to it in his current circumstances. He did understand the gist of the warning, however. His attorney stared at George as hard as he dared and had made it clear that his behavior while out on bond must be squeaky clean. "Not even a parking ticket, George," he'd said.

Except for the trip to the mobile home park to take care of a potential problem, George had remained open and very public, his every move carefully covered with an iron-clad alibi if one were needed. Someone else drove him when he had to get about. He stayed out of sight in his rented rooms over the Road House. No one would pick up on his brief detour from this regimen at the trailer park. After all, he'd needed to plug a leak, to solve a problem, to end a potential threat. And he had.

He held up his fingers, noticed and then dismissed the obvious need to clean his fingernails, and began to tick off his current situation; the Smut woman, dead; Dellinger, dead; but the girl still in the wind, maybe local, maybe heading to the cops and that Jew sheriff. He'd heard the rumor. Frankie Chimes' sister-in-law said something about a new kid in town she'd worked on at the beauty parlor. The girl, she said, seemed rabbity, all jumpy and scared like, which figured, and she would be the right age. He needed someone to find her, check her out, and if it turned out she was Darla, take care of her. This close to being sprung he didn't need the little bitch to bring that old crap up. A lot of people didn't, in fact. If he got the girl out of the picture, a lot of high muckety-mucks would owe him a favor or two, for sure.

But who would be available to nose her out? He spun the virtual rolodex located in the still functioning portion of his brain and searched for a name. He would follow his legal advisors and stay out of trouble, but he had work that needed doing and he couldn't wait for permission from a suit in Richmond to do it. He needed a pair of hands and some muscle to do it for him, preferably someone who would work cheap or for product. He preferred the latter. He had access to more methamphetamine than cash.

Sam studied her husband. She imagined she could read him like a book. Wives can, as a rule. Husbands think they can do the same with their wives but that notion, along with the one about the efficacy of having sex to settle arguments, is largely delusional. An argument is over when the wife has won it. That fact may not emerge for days, weeks, or even years, but it is the nature of the process and the only thing the sex will do, as enjoyable as it might be, is delay the inevitable.

"So, where are we, Karl? Is the dead man your problem or Ike's?"

"If I had to guess, at this stage he's mine. I won't be able to say for certain until we get a DNA match, but it isn't looking good."

"If it ends up in your lap, what do you do?"

"Do?" Karl buried his face in his hands and rubbed his eyes. "Yeah, what do I do? You know my options. I report it to my boss and he sends it up the ladder and if it doesn't get buried somewhere along the way—which in the present politically charged state at the Bureau isn't likely—it comes back to bite me. And three or four special agents with tenure, reputations, and seniority to protect are going to be in a bind. The upshot of that means, as I said, I will hear about it and my career could be in trouble."

"For telling the truth?"

"No, not for telling the truth, for rocking someone's canoe. Two of the men who worked the case back then are either agents in place or head up regional bureaus in big cities. They have bright futures in the Bureau. If the men convicted of Barbarini's murder get a new trial and/or are released because the evidence that convicted them is too tainted to bring them back to court, careers will be compromised and that means I acquire some important enemies who will be only too happy to see that mine is too."

"That's not fair. You did your job. You didn't screw up the case, they did. I can't believe they'd punish you for that."

"It isn't viewed as punishment, Sam. I would be breaking ranks. The thugs who iced Barbarini belong in jail. In their view the fact that the investigation was a screw-up shouldn't alter that. That would also be the unofficial consensus in the Bureau as well. It follows that since justice was done, however imperfectly, the proverbial dog should be allowed to stay sleeping. And, you are forgetting something...."

"What?"

"Do you remember why I was here in Picketsville and how we met?"

"Of course. You were on administrative leave."

"I was in 'exile.' My section chief fouled the nest and wanted me to take the fall. It didn't happen, of course, but in the end, to keep things quiet, he was allowed to retire without prejudice and I was returned to duty."

"Well then?"

"My exile and the reasons for it are still in my personnel file, Sam. If I have to label this ten-year-old case as a foul up, it will land in there, too, as the second eyebrow-raiser in it. I will be labeled as the guy who torpedoes his superiors."

"So? You did the right thing then and would be doing the right thing now."

"Yeah, yeah. Okay, consider this: Let's say a promotion review board looks at two candidates. They see two identical records except one has these odd inclusions where the agent played a role in bringing a senior agent down. Who do you suppose they will select?"

Sam clamped her jaw and shook her head. "That's just not fair at all. Karl, they can't do that. You could appeal and—"

"Create a third negative entry into my file. No, I couldn't do that."

"What will you do?"

"I will hope the DNA doesn't match. Failing that I will either lie and say the cadaver in the county meat locker is a John Doe and not Barbarini, or I will tell the truth and consider what other options I may have, career-wise."

"You won't lie, will you?"

"No."

The two sat in silence, lost in thought.

"Is the dead guy's nickname really Barbie?"

"That's what it says in his folder."

"The Mob does that, doesn't it?"

"Does what? You mean give their people funny names?"

"Yeah, like No Neck Noonan or Jimmy the Fish, and they're almost always put-downs."

"I expect they are considered a badge of honor or something among the brotherhood."

"Did you have a nickname growing up?"

"Until I outgrew my friends I was called Hedy, like some old-time movie star. Then, when I passed them at six feet-something, they changed it to Stork."

"Me, too, only my short person name was Barbie, like your dead guy. I got it because I was proportioned a little oddly, if you know what I mean, and sort of strawberry blonde. You grow too fast and your legs don't fit your torso and your bumps pop out, and it was awful. The hair darkened to red when the hormones kicked in and I really shot up. Then the peculiar body proportions started to work for me."

"I'm all over that."

They sat in silence again for a while, Sam anxious, Karl, sad.

"Sam, do you like your job at NSA?"

"Well, sure, I mean it has its challenges but the technology I am allowed to use is amazing. NSA is not as much fun as when I worked for Ike, but…oh well, that was then and this is now. You know what happened and I can't complain. Shoot, at least we both work in the same town now. Commuter relationships are for the birds."

"Right. You know that being an FBI agent—"

"I know, it is all you ever wanted to do since you were a kid. Yes, I know. You mustn't let go of that, Karl. If this business with Barbarini turns out badly, you fight through it. You are a good agent. No, you are a great agent and the people in the Bureau who make decisions about who does what and where they do it know you are. You will be fine. Just do what you know is right."

"Yeah, I suppose. Still, this would be a nice place for a kid to grow up, wouldn't it?"

"Picketsville? Yeah, I guess so. But so is the D.C. area. We won't be inside the city limits much longer. We'll get a little house in a suburb with a good school system and…sorry, I'm being a mom before being a wife. Karl, it will be fine."

The problem with living the way he did, LeBrun thought, was it was nearly impossible to make and keep friends. They betrayed you, they went to jail, or they died violently. An hour of heavy thinking had produced not a single name of someone who was both trustworthy and currently available to work for him. Recruiting outside muscle was a possibility but had risks he didn't want to take. It would be too easy to employ someone who turned out to be working for the cops undercover, or someone whose loyalty was with a rival, or someone who could be bought. No, he'd have to do the searching for the girl on his own. The lawyer said to stay clean; he didn't say to do nothing.

Then he thought of Jack. Perfect.

Chapter Twenty-seven

Ike pulled chairs into his office and instructed Rita to call in as many deputies as she could. "Just the ones who would be able to drop whatever they are doing and come in. I don't want to leave Picketsville unattended." Unlike its big-city contemporaries, Picketsville did not have a scheduled roll call before each shift change. The uniforms dispersed to assume the duties posted for them as they arrived and checked in with the dispatcher individually. Ike would talk to them if he needed to and if he happened to be on station at the time. That didn't happen often since he is a determined "night person." He trusted his people and, in turn, they did all they could to confirm it. Ike had been criticized by at least one accrediting agency for this lack of order and his ignorance of conventional procedure, but since his closure rate for major crimes approached one hundred percent, because he was elected, not appointed, and because Picketsville's citizens generally approved of his performance, nothing ever came of it. Today, however, he wished he'd put the roll call practice in place. The murder of Ethyl Smut remained unsolved. Little or no progress had been made in the nearly week since the body had been found. In the meantime, another body had been added to the list of crimes to be solved and even though the recent murder and the Smut case were undoubtedly connected, until he could establish it, his caseload had just doubled.

Movement. He wanted some movement.

Frank Sutherlin, his brother Billy, Charley Picket, and Karl shuffled into the office and sat down. Three other deputies crowded the doorway.

"Okay," Ike began, "so you know, we are borrowing Karl from the FBI and he will help us wherever he can. The body found buried with Ethyl Smut has been tentatively identified as Anthony Barbarini, a New York hood murdered ten years ago by two guys, Alphonse Damato and Johnny Murphy. They are currently serving life without parole in Sing Sing. A DNA test has been ordered to nail down the ID. If the test confirms it, Karl has a problem, but we close a cold case on our books. If not, the problem of the body and making an ID reverts to us—add one more. Until then, we will let that one ride and Karl can be available for whatever we need done here."

Ike stacked and restacked papers on his desk, shifted around in his chair, and sipped his coffee.

"Okay, moving on to Ethyl Smut. If I forget anything, jump in, and if you have something new to add, ditto." He frowned and straightened up in his chair. "We started with a straightforward murder of the lady. Then, we were gifted with a second murder. A fingerprint confirmation IDs the body in the burned out trailer as Mark Dellinger. He also had dental records on file if the prints weren't enough. I believe the two deaths, Smut's and Dellinger's, are connected because not to do so asks me to accept too much in the way of coincidence. I need to review everything we have on Smut and anything else even if it relates only slightly to her death. Then we connect the dots. Somehow, I have a sense we are missing something obvious but it keeps eluding me."

"Excuse me, Ike," interrupted Frank Sutherlin, "but if my sources are correct, George LeBrun had a connection to both the woman and Dellinger and as yet no one has even mentioned him, much less approached him. Given his past, don't you think we should pull him in?"

"Noted. Frank, I want to take this chronologically. We'll get to the town's premier scumbag in a minute. Now, Ethyl had a daughter, Darla or Darlene, whom she abused in ways that seem inconceivable to me and I won't detail here but you check Smut's jacket and you'll get the picture. The daughter is known both as Darla Smut and Darla Dellinger, depending on time and place. She may be calling herself something else by now. She will not be easy to find unless we get some help. More on that later. Anyway, she fled her mother's clutches several years ago and until now, could not be located."

"Until now?" Frank said.

"I have it on reasonably good authority that she is in the area. I don't know for certain, but if not now, recently. That said, and given the nature of her relationship with her mother, she heads up our suspect list. I am not happy about that. My source insists she did not kill her mother and I would like to believe that, but for now, she is a person of interest at the very least….I need more coffee…Rita?"

Ike handed his coffee cup to Frank who passed it to one of the doorway jamming deputies. He, in turn handed it to Rita who filled it at the K-Cup machine and handed it back and the route was repeated in reverse.

"Thank you. Next, is Mark Dellinger. He is the girl's father. He is ex-Marine with a less than honorable discharge and an old rap sheet. He slipped off the radar ten years ago and for a moment we thought he might turn out to be the body unearthed with Smut. He has spent time in the system for a variety of felonies, some serious, some not so. He must have resurfaced recently and ticked off somebody because, as I said, we found his body in a burned out mobile home north of town. That park happens to be the Smut woman's latest address as well. That alone would suggest his death and hers must be connected. The ME confirms he took a nine mil to the head before the trailer was torched. Striations on the slug suggest the weapon had a noise suppressor attached. Dellinger was killed midday yesterday and his unit set on fire to cover the murder. If he had a recent run-in with Smut, we have no evidence of it. We can only guess at what, if anything, transpired between those two, but you can bet your pension they at least had a conversation.

"Finally, when we went back to the Smut woman's trailer on our second trip to the park later the same day, as it happens, we found evidence of a struggle and a blood trail leading out the door. There were two blood types on the floor. One definitely matches hers."

"DNA?"

"Not going to order DNA just yet, Frank. It seems safe enough at this point to assume we're looking at her blood. We know someone stabbed her before dispatching her with the ever-popular 'blunt instrument.' So, now we know where her murder story begins."

"Do we, Ike?" Frank asked. "I mean…okay, we'll accept that the blood is hers but then what in hell was she doing in the park? Charley found the tree branch that launched her into the great beyond out there, not in her trailer. Did the same person who stabbed her conk on the head with the stick? If her killer took her there, why did he wait to finish her off in the woods and not the trailer and, finally, why finish her off with a clubbing? Why didn't he complete the job with his knife?"

"I can't answer the second part, but if I remember correctly," Karl said, "that park is off the back road that leads up to Lexington. There is a hospital and ER there. Maybe she got away from her stabber and was heading to the hospital."

"But why stop and wander into the woods and then get herself hit over the head? What happened to her vehicle, and then… this is the biggie as far as I am concerned…why did her killer go to the trouble to bury her?"

"He didn't want her found?"

"Okay, but why would he care? She's dead and as far as anyone knows, there was no reason to maintain the illusion that she was just missing. She was not an important player in anything, so why go to the trouble of digging a hole and dumping her in?"

"Frank, you have a point. I wish I knew," Ike said.

"None of this makes any sense, Ike, unless…"

"Unless what, Frank?"

"Unless the stabbing and the clubbing are separate events. Look, suppose Smut had an argument with someone, let's say Dellinger, or LeBrun. I like that one better. So, there is an argument and she is stabbed. Whoever did it either doesn't realize what he's done or she flees before he can finish the job."

"Okay, then what?"

"Then she heads to the park and meets someone there and this second person whacks her on the head."

"Possible, Frank, but again, why? Why would she go there with a stab wound and who would know to be there when she showed up? And then again, where's her transportation?"

"No idea, but it is the only way it works, Ike."

"Maybe you're right. Now a quick hit on LeBrun, the boil on the backside of the world. Frank, we don't hassle him because he has his lawyers breathing down the neck of the county attorney who in turn is telling us, telling me, to lay off unless I have something rock solid. The absolute last thing the prosecutor wants to do is explain to a judge why the sheriff of Picketsville is harassing poor Mr. LeBrun. Yeah, I know, it blows, but there it is. If we do nail him, though, he said I could slam him any way I wanted to. So, for now, we wait and watch."

"I don't like it."

"Neither do I but that's the way it is just now. Okay people, let's go to work. Karl, see what you can make of the bag of old clothes and get Sam in here if possible. I need TAK to run the fancy software she installed before she left."

"I'll call."

"By the way, does anybody know TAK's real name?"

Chapter Twenty-eight

Sam arrived after lunch with Karl. Ike introduced her to TAK who looked up at her with eyes that in another generation would have been described as moony. As he stood five-foot-nine and she a few inches over six feet, his only option was to look up. She smiled and he nearly collapsed. The two of them disappeared into the converted jail cell that used to serve as her inner sanctum. Karl dropped the bag of clothing found in Abe Schwartz's barn on the floor next to his temporary desk.

"What did you do with Martin?"

"Essie is babysitting both of the kids. She's in hog heaven. I'm afraid I got next to nothing from this pile, Ike. About all I can tell you from checking the labels in the PJs is that they are for an infant and that they are fifteen or sixteen years old, but you already knew that. The papers are mostly a collection of school stuff, report cards, notes from teachers, things like that. They stop at the third grade, by the way. I don't know if that is important or not."

"Whose?"

"The notes are addressed variously to Mrs. Smut or Smuts, Mrs. Dellinger, and Mrs. Franco. I deduce they were all sent to your dead woman over a three-year time frame as she shifted partners and identities. Equally, I guess the garments once belonged to the daughter. There might be some recoverable DNA on them if you wanted to find out."

"I expect it will be a waste of time just now. Is there any indication why they ended up in my father's hay barn?"

"No clue. My guess is they were dumped in a hurry and maybe as an afterthought. Don't ask me why I think that. It's just that from my limited experience, things like these are more like mementos than practical items, you know. It's like someone collected them to pass along to a family member or as souvenirs. Also, I can tell you that the clothes were recently laundered and the papers sorted chronologically. They seem to have gotten mixed up a bit along the way, but I think that was the idea."

"The photographs?"

"Same thing. I left them with Sam and your intern. She will tackle the head shot first and then enhance the group pictures. You think the stuff was dumped by the missing daughter?"

"I think that is one possibility. What I want to know is how they ended up in the barn. If the girl put them there, where'd she come from and why dump them in the barn?"

"Maybe the mother did it. I can't think why either, but nothing in this case makes a hell of a lot of sense."

"If her mother did it, when and why did she pick that spot? On the other hand, if someone else dumped them, who and why and when?"

"Maybe Sam will come up with something."

"Let's hope."

TAK rounded the corner and stood in front of Ike's desk. "Sir?"

"Do you have something for me, son?"

"Yes, sir. Ms. Hedrick ran that picture you gave me through her program, the one that ages people, and here it is—the girl at sixteen and then at eighteen and also at twenty."

Ike took the pictures and spread them out on his desk. "That's the girl." He pointed at the presumptive eighteen-year-old. "That's the girl from Lee Henry's. I'm sure of it. Come on, Karl, we have a call to make at the Cross Roads Diner."

Leota Blevins' confrontation with her cousins the next day had not gone well. Flora Blevins fixed her with the gaze that had cowed scores of customers over the past two-and-a-half decades and demanded she tell her why. Her cousin, Arlene, sat in the corner trying desperately to look small, which is not easy for someone of her girth. If Arlene, with her generous curves, rosy cheeks, and 'natural insulation,' as her father used to describe her, could be described as a dumpling, Flora was beef jerky—tough, stringy, and definitely an acquired taste. Flora fixed her out-of-town cousin with a glacial eye.

"Why, after all this time did you decide to dump her in my backyard, Leota? I swear some days you don't have the sense of a squirrel. First it's that bum you near-to-married and then years later you up and go promising the girl a new life. Okay? And then you dump her back here. Did you know what this has done? Do you have any idea the spot you put her in?"

"Flora, listen to me. What Mark Dellinger and I had or didn't have back then is done and dusted. There's no reason in the world to drag all that up again. Now about the girl, Darla—"

"Now ain't that just typical of you, Leota? Don't you agree, Arlene? Of course you do. It all started with that loser. Do you realize that if you hadn't of dragged that sorry pup back here to Picketsville, there wouldn't be no Darla Dellinger to get herself messed up? He gets into town, lays eyes on Ethyl Smut, meets up with her drinking buddies and bam, we got us a baby on the way—a baby that ends up living with a monster for a mother."

"If you and Granny hadn't stuck your noses in where they didn't belong, that girl would have be mine, not Ethyl's, and raised up right."

"Leota, for someone who has a college degree, sometimes you can be as dense as a box of hammers. I know you never was no good at math, but that girl was born seven months after you and the Marine broke up. Seven months, Leota. Think a minute. That bun was in the oven while you and the loser were still together."

"No! She was premature because of the dope."

"She was late on account of the dope, Leota. Wake up, woman. I know you thought that if you could get Dellinger to settle down, you could maybe make a solid citizen out of him. But he were a loser, Leota, and instead of you making him a decent citizen, you'd have been ruined instead, and Ethyl Smut woulda been in and out of your life forever."

"No, that isn't true."

"Face it, Leota. I'm right, ain't I Arlene? There, you see? Arlene agrees."

"Arlene hasn't said a word in the last hour. How do you know she agrees?"

"You ain't answered my question. Why'd you dump that poor girl off here?"

"Because…I can't say, Flora. Something happened a while back and I figured that she'd want to be close to where she grew up for a while, and I thought a visit would be helpful. I had things to work through. Then, I figured if she had a look around and saw things were different, she'd begin to open up some. I intended to take her back after that. You are her godmother, after all. I would have thought you'd be pleased."

"I am that, but how do you figure her coming back to Picketsville and being, first, with her ruination of a mother, and second, in the same county that has George LeBrun on the loose, could be a good thing?"

"Her mother wasn't going to be a problem and I didn't know about George. She needed a new start and Virginia Beach wasn't working."

"How do you mean her mother wasn't going to be a problem, for mercy's sake? What else could she possibly be but a problem? Surely you didn't think the girl was strong enough to fend her off?"

"She wouldn't have to fend because…Never mind, you were here and I didn't know about George at the time. How could I? He's supposed to be serving life or something. How'd he get out?"

"One of them lawyer things. Evidence questions. Ike is mad as all get out and he'll put him back in PDQ, but in the meantime, we got to hide the girl so's LeBrun can't find her."

Leota stared at the sacks of potatoes and canned carrots against the wall. "Where is LeBrun, do you know?"

"He's around. Someone said he's rooming over at Alex's Road House out on the highway where all them bikers hang out."

"I have to go."

"What? Where you off to? What about the girl?"

"I said, I have to go. Don't worry, Darla is going to be fine with you and Arlene."

"With me and Arlene? You just wait a minute, Missy."

Leota had slipped out the back door of the Cross Roads the same time Ike and Karl entered through the front. Things might have turned out differently had they used the same door, or perhaps not. People who think a certain way will tell you it's about Karma and what will be will be, and that fate must run its course no matter how we think we can will to change it. They're usually optimistic and usually wrong.

Chapter Twenty-nine

"Would you care to identify this woman for me, Flora?" Ike thrust the picture of eighteen-year-old Darla at Flora Blevins. "Or maybe it's this one you might identify." And he flipped over the twenty-year-old version.

"Don't know what you're talking about," she said. "How am I supposed to know them girls?"

"How about you, Arlene. Ever see this girl?" Arlene studied the two photos as if her life depended on it. She glanced at Flora and shook her head.

"Karl, what do they teach you at the FBI Academy about lying?" Ike asked.

"It's in the eyes, Ike, always it's in the eyes. They dilate, or they shift left and down, or they slip out of focus. That indicates to you that your suspect is lying."

"I ain't no 'suspect,' Ike, and you know it."

"Right, not a suspect. And did you see anything like that in Arlene's eyes, Karl?"

"Oh, yeah."

"How about Flora here? Did you see any evidence of prevarication in those baby blues?"

"Right again."

"Well, Flora, there you have it. It can't just be me. Karl is a certified FBI special agent and he will testify, in court if he has to, that you are, and have been, lying to me for several days now. Why would you do that? Am I not one of your favorite customers? I always clean my plate and leave a generous tip. So, why won't you tell me the truth?"

"You're getting mighty big for your britches, Mr. Sheriff."

"Okay, Flora, cut the crap. Darla Dellinger, or Smut, is in your care. She has been for days. She had her hair cut by Grace Chimes at Lee Henry's. I was there. I saw her. You knew we were looking for her all this while and yet you kept her under wraps. You knew I wanted to talk to her about her mother's murder. By hiding her you are guilty of obstruction of a criminal investigation. Unless you want me to make that charge something more, you will tell me right now where she is."

Flora's eyes, deepened in hue from azure to angry cobalt, the color a sky becomes a before a tornado whirls into town.

"So, go ahead and throw the cuffs on me, Ike. Whatever you got to do, you do it, but I ain't telling you where the girl is at."

Ike sighed and looked at Arlene. "Arlene, help me out here. You and Flora don't really want to go to jail, do you?"

Arlene opened her mouth to say something.

"You shut your trap, Arlene, or I tell the whole town what you done with Hake Longanecker down in Cardwell's Gaseteria on Halloween night in '99 and him being married at the time." Arlene's mouth snapped shut with a click that could have been heard in the next room, had anyone been listening for it. "Arlene ain't got anything to say. So, what's it to be, Mr. Sheriff? Are you going to haul the two of us in?"

Arlene began to whimper.

"Flora, I will not do that, not yet anyway, but understand this, the instant I think I need to, I surer'n hell will. Also, Flora, think about the possible consequences of what you're doing. George LeBrun is out on bond and in town. If he gets wind that the girl is local, he'll be after her before you can ruin another steak. He will not be nice and whatever happens will be on your head."

Flora pursed her lips.

"I can protect her, Flora, in ways that you can't."

"You forget her story, Ike. What she's been through? She's as afraid of the police as she is of George. You'll have to give me some time."

"I don't have any time to give, Flora. If anything happens to that girl...if George finds her...well you think about it. You, too, Arlene. Okay, Karl, we're done here."

◇◇◇

Ike and Karl returned to the office. Jack Feldman lounged in one of the chairs near Ike's office door.

"Feldman, why aren't you on patrol?"

"On my way, Boss, but I needed to ask you something first."

"I've told you before. Don't ever call me boss. Okay, what?"

"I hear you confirmed that the girl, Darla Dellinger, is in town."

"We think so. If she isn't now, she was. She's been posing as Flora Blevins' niece. Why do you ask?"

"Well, I thought I might help you when you get around to doing a sweep. I know the folks pretty well who used to be the Smut woman's friends. I could be useful."

"Right, thank you, Jack. I'll let you know."

Feldman rose and sauntered out the door. "And don't forget, I know George pretty good. I can anticipate what he's up to, if that's a help."

Ike's gaze stayed locked on him until he was out of sight.

"Problem?" Karl said.

"I don't know. It's just that Feldman never volunteers for anything. He may be the laziest cop in town. Also, he's one of the very few holdovers from my predecessor's term. That group included George LeBrun, in fact."

"Why'd you keep him?"

"Cleaned house as best I could. Some of the old-timers seemed pretty straight—Billy and Essie, for example. He seemed okay at the time and the politics suggested I keep some of the old staff. So, unless there was a hue and cry from the people, I did."

"Any reason to suspect trouble now?"

"No...except, as I said, Feldman never volunteers for anything, so why now?"

"Maybe you should give him the benefit of the—"

"Doubt? Karl, I didn't live this long by giving anyone the benefit of the doubt. The justice system can and should do that, but when you chase bad guys for a living, you can't afford the luxury."

"Still, he said he knew the people that grew up with and around the girl. He could be useful in identifying the ones to talk to and, don't forget, he knows or knew LeBrun. He'd realize better than anyone what that sadistic slimeball could do. He might really be concerned about the girl."

"You're right, he might."

"But you're not convinced?"

"I am not anything, right now. All I want to do is find the girl before LeBrun does and if that means trusting Jack Feldman, locking up Flora and Arlene Blevins, or burning down the Town Hall, I'll do it."

"Let's don't burn down Town Hall."

"Couldn't even if I wanted to."

"Why?"

"We're standing in it."

After her confrontation with her cousins, Leota drove without thinking about a destination, preoccupied with thoughts about her past, about what might have been. Could it be true what Flora said about Ethyl Smut's pregnancy? What did that say about all those years she'd spent pining over a lost love, a missed chance at marriage and happiness, and more importantly, what she should do next? Common sense told her to turn the truck eastward and head home to Virginia Beach as fast as she could. Once there, park and forget the whole sorry mess ever happened, the past and the present. She was no more equipped to handle a damaged teenager than fly to the moon. What had she been thinking? She also realized that as much as she disliked her cousin, Flora, she recognized her as a strong woman and one who would know best what to do for the girl. Leota, on the other hand, seemed to have made a botch of everything. No, the best plan would be to leave her with the cousins. Still, she hesitated. What if LeBrun…How was she supposed to know about him being out of jail? He'd been sentenced to life-plus the last she'd heard. Could anyone have even guessed he might get out? Not very damned likely. What if he found out that Darla was staying at Flora's? He might kill all three.

She pulled off to the side of the road and shut down the engine. The whole thing had started out reasonably well. How could it have gone so badly so quickly? She felt a migraine coming on. She rummaged through the glove box in search of her pills and that's when she got lucky. She did not know it was luck until later, after she decided to go felon-hunting. She had her water bottle up and had just popped two zolmitriptan when a car drove by and in its backseat, as big as life, sat George LeBrun. She recognized him at once even though it had been years since she'd seen him. Some people never really change—in appearance or attitude. She didn't know if it was instinct or divine inspiration that caused her to move, but she sat up, turned the key, started her engine, and followed the car and its passenger.

She would spend the remainder of the day staked out at Alex's Road House.

Chapter Thirty

Most small-town criminals ply their trade at night. If they are not caught in the act and/or arrested, they will be in their beds, or someone else's, by dawn. That fact explained why mornings at the sheriff's office do not, as a rule, produce much in the way of excitement. The booking will have been done and processing will not start for another three hours and there was nothing left to do except hit the road. This morning was no exception. The eleven-to-seven shift drifted in, dropped off their paperwork and notes, and headed home. The seven-to-three shift clocked in, picked up their assignments, talked some trash with Rita and each other, and left.

Over the relatively short time that he'd been sheriff, the number of deputies on the force had grown disproportionately to the town's population. It seemed that as Picketsville's population shrank, the need for more police grew. Ike was not prepared to make a generalization about that beyond noting that the same phenomenon could be seen in many of the country's larger cities, particularly those near the southern border. At least twice a week Ike tried to hit the seam as the two shifts changed. It presented a time to chat, to be brought up to date on everything from his deputies' personal lives, kids' schooling, and the things they'd noted while out on the road that might be useful in the future. But all in all, quiet was the norm at seven in the morning.

It came as something of a shock, in the midst of this relative calm, when Flora Blevins exploded through the door yelling at the top of her lungs that she needed to have words with the sheriff. As it happened, Ike had chosen that morning to put in his appearance but was running late. The apparent lack of urgency shown by the deputies who were otherwise occupied and therefore reluctant to drop everything and deal exclusively with her problem caused her to raise her voice a full octave and the volume several decibels beyond comfortable.

Darcie Billingsley, substituting as night dispatcher for Rita who in turn was filling in for Essie and who would not report for another hour, left her desk and met Flora and tried to calm her down.

"Whoa up there, Miss Flora. I'm sure we can get this all sorted out. One of these nice men can handle whatever problem you have. Is something going on at the diner?'

"I need to see Ike Schwartz and I need him right this very damn minute."

As Picketsville rarely heard Flora Blevins swear, everyone within earshot froze in place and stared at her.

"Where's he at, Darcie Billingsley? I need to talk to him now."

"Well, sure you do. I am sure he'll be along any minute now. Why don't you have a seat in his office and I'll fix you a nice cup of tea. How's that sound?"

"Don't you mollycoddle me, girl. Don't want any tea. Can't stand the stuff. Tea is for old women with blue hair and for Nancy boys. You got any coffee? Good, fetch me a cup, black with one sugar, and then you call your boss. Tell him what I said, that I need to talk to him."

Darcie had Ike's cell phone number punched in when he walked in the door, his phone twerping.

"Where you been?" Flora shouted from across the room. "I been here like an hour waiting for you."

"You've only been here five minutes, Miss Flora."

"Darcie, you mind your own business Listen here, Ike—"

Darcie stiffened and glared at Flora. "What I do here is my business, Miss Flora, and you need to know you are not the only person with a problem. You can be a rude as sin if you want to, but these folk are here to serve this town in ways I hope you never know about, and some of them are dead because of it."

"Now, look here, Darcie, I know you're still grieving for your husband and—"

"It ain't about me, don't you understand?"

"It's okay, Darcie," Ike said and put his arm around her shoulder. "Miz Blevins is just wrought up and she's sorry, aren't you Flora? Now, you go brief Rita and then get on home to your kids."

Darcie wiped her eyes and retreated from the room.

"Okay, Flora, what's on your mind that can't wait and makes abusing Darcie so ever-loving important? I take it you did not come in here this morning to turn yourself in for obstruction of justice, so what's up?"

"She's gone."

"Who's gone?'

"Who do you think? The girl is. Arlene went up to her room where we was keeping her safe and it were empty. That piece of garbage, George LeBrun, must have found out where we had her hid and broke in to snatch her."

"Slow down, Flora. Where had she been hiding and why do you think LeBrun found her and took her?"

Flora launched out of her chair which rolled backward and hit a filing cabinet. The collision made a noise like distant thunder. No way Ike would defuse Flora anytime soon.

"Who else would have done it? We fixed up a room for Darla in the attic. Don't look at me that way. It was a nice sunny room, good as any in the house, only harder to find. She was okay up there, maybe even happy. She knew things had to settle down on account of her Ma being killed and LeBrun on the loose. Then this morning, boom, she's gone. Either LeBrun got her or she's off and running."

"Assuming you are wrong about LeBrun, and I am afraid I already know the answer, but do you have any idea where she might have run to?"

"Maybe back to Leota."

"Who's Leota?"

"Leota Blevins, my other cousin. She lives in Virginia Beach and the girl, Darla, had been living with her for the last couple of years."

"Why am I finding out about this now? You do realize that if you had been forthcoming…Oh, the hell with it." Ike turned and called out to his chief deputy. "Frank, I need a new BOLO on the girl, last seen fleeing Picketsville this morning. Also a second one on a Leota Blevins. She's from Virginia Beach—"

"I heard, Ike. I'm on it."

"She can't have gotten far. Flora, think, where might she have gone?"

"Except back to Leota, I don't have a notion. It's gotta be LeBrun."

"If it was LeBrun, I promise you we'd know, and kidnapping would not be his approach in this case."

"Not? You mean…? Oh. What happens now?"

"Now? Now I put extra men on the road and we wait for a call, a sighting, for the girl to return to the attic. There isn't anything else we can do."

"It ain't enough."

"It will have to be. Go back to the Cross Roads and go on about your business. You don't have any reason to suspect LeBrun, but if you start bawling this around town, he will surely hear about it and then he really will be in the game."

"I messed this up a little, didn't I, Ike?"

"Big-time, Flora, big-time. Now get the hell out of here and let us do our job."

◇◇◇

Ten minutes after Ike had dispatched his deputies, the morning shift and half of the previous one was out on the streets, and George LeBrun received a call informing him of this new turn. The caller asked what George wanted him to do.

"Stay close as you can to the search. I need time to think about this. Good work, by the way."

"Always a pleasure. Seems like old times like when old Loyal was running the show."

"Yeah, maybe, if you say so. Loyal Parker was a stupid son-of-a-bitch and now he's dead. If you're smart you'll remember that. Okay, keep your phone on. I may need to talk some more."

George snapped his phone off and sat down for a think. How far could he trust this guy? A lot of time had passed since they worked together. Was this news official or a scrap picked up in the bar last night? People talked all the time. Still, he ought to know. LeBrun realized he should have asked him more questions.

"I'll need to call back, but first I need time to think the thing through," he muttered. He stamped his foot three times which was his signal for Betsy or one of the other girls to crack a pair of Heinekens and bring them upstairs. George, like too many self-indulgent men, believed he did his best thinking with a beer in his hand.

It wasn't true, but he believed it.

Chapter Thirty-one

Leota Blevins spent most of the previous night sitting in the cab of her truck, eyes fixed on the front of Axel's Road House. Trade seemed brisk. Customers—that would be bikers and the bottom echelon of Picketsville society—came and went, but once George LeBrun disappeared inside, he never reappeared. What with the trip from Virginia Beach and the trauma of seeing Mark's burned-out trailer she fought to stay awake and her spirits began to sag. At midnight she could no longer keep her eyes open. She started the truck's engine and drove to a nearby motel whose clientele, judging from the noise that penetrated the cardboard thin walls, were Axel's customers as well. She paid cash and then regretted it. She had not planned an extended stay in Picketsville, just long enough to find Mark and some answers. Consequently she arrived with only her customary sixty dollars in her purse.

"Why sixty?" her friend Florence once asked.

"Because one hundred presents too big a temptation to go off and buy something I don't need. Fifty is sensible and sixty is fifty with a margin for error."

Her friend had raised an eyebrow but hadn't said anything, though by the look of her, she'd come close.

The next morning Leota rose early, purchased two donuts and a second coffee at the local Dunkin' and had resumed her watch by six. The likelihood that LeBrun would be moving so early seemed slim at best, but she didn't want to risk missing him if and when he did. By eight o'clock she began to experience the consequences of her lack of planning when she'd made a decision to stake out a felon. The compounding problem, of course, arose from the coffee, one at the shop and a second, a takeout—extra large.

A sheriff's deputy pulled up beside her and asked for some ID. He studied it, glanced at her through the window over the top of his mirrored sunglasses and pocketed her license and registration. She was about to protest when he requested that she follow him back to the sheriff's office. She had no idea why the sheriff wanted to talk to her but guessed it might have something to do with Darla. Surely he hadn't connected her to either Mark or Ethyl, had he? Not enough time had elapsed to have done that. She'd soon find out, but at that particular moment she had a more pressing problem. For two reasons she agreed to follow the deputy back to town with less reluctance than she might have had otherwise. First, if she made a fuss, the deputy might look in the truck bed and find the twelve-gauge shotgun under the tarp. More immediately, a chat with law enforcement seemed less threatening than venturing into a biker bar to use the ladies' room.

Paper covers rock, rock breaks scissors, scissors cut paper, and a full bladder, sure as all get out, conquers fear of arrest.

Ike slid into the church parking lot and walked the five yards to the office doors. The aroma of honeysuckle still scented the air, but once again, he didn't notice. The Reverend Fisher knew something Ike needed and he would get it from him one way or another. He climbed the stairs and breezed by the secretary who made a feeble effort to stop him.

"Now about the girl…"

"Ike, I told you I won't break the seal of the confessional."

"I understand that, but even you have your exceptions. I heard child abuse was one of them."

"That is correct. But you've already heard everything I can tell you about that."

"Not everything, I'm guessing. The important thing you should know right now is she has run away again."

"Sorry? Again?"

"She fled from her home a few years back and the common-wealth put her in a foster home. Around the time you saw her, she'd moved in with Flora Blevins who owns the Cross Roads Diner. After I discovered that and interviewed Flora, the girl took off. Flora said she was as afraid of me as she was of whoever else is after her."

"Ah, Ike there is something you need to know about that."

"And that would be?"

"Give me a minute. I need to sort out what I can tell you and what I cannot."

Ike tried not to tap his foot. He did not know how much time he was willing to spare on the clergyman, if any, but sitting in the church office waiting for him to rearrange his scruples did not meet his standard of time usefully spent.

"Here is what I can tell you. When all of the really bad abuse, the sexual abuse, happened, your police were involved."

"What!"

"Her words were…I'm paraphrasing…'She'— that would be her mother—'never went to jail because the cops were in on it.' I suppose that when she heard you were asking about her she freaked."

"My department?"

"Before your time, yes. The sheriff then had a funny name, she said."

"Did she offer any other names?"

"Ah, Ike…"

"Okay, okay. I'll say some names and you nod yes or no. A deputy named George LeBrun…Loyal Parker…Billy Sutherlin…Jack Feldman…You're not nodding, Rev. Okay, never mind, you may not want to say anything but your eyes speak volumes. So now I know why the Smut woman never served any real time. She was being covered by my predecessor and his gang of goons in return for making her daughter available." Ike stood and paced. "Rev, if this wasn't a church, I would swear enough to peel the paint off the walls. It is unthinkable, but this is not the first time I've heard reports about my predecessor and his people and their habit of abusing women. Thanks. I don't know if it will help get her back into custody and safe, but at least now I know why she ran."

"I'm sorry I can't be of more help. My heart went out to that girl."

"Maybe you can. If she came to you once, perhaps she will again. If she does, tell her two things. First, I am not Loyal Parker. He's dead. Second, LeBrun is free at the moment and may be looking for her and she should come in before he finds her. Can you do that?"

"Of course. And if she won't?"

"Offer her sanctuary here. And then call me."

"The minute she hears me call you she'll bolt."

"You're right. Call Flora Blevins at the diner instead. She won't react to that. Flora can negotiate for me."

Ike's phone twerped.

"Yes. What do you have for me? Okay, I'm on my way."

"Anything I need to know, Ike?"

"Maybe, Rev. Leota Blevins, the woman the girl lived with before she turned up here, has been picked up out on the highway. I'm hoping she can tell me something and we can bring the girl in."

Chapter Thirty-two

All things considered, Leota, thought, it could have been worse. She'd told the deputies what they wanted to hear and apologized to the sheriff for Flora not being more forthcoming. Had she known the circumstances surrounding the girl's disappearance, of course, she would have come right in, and so on. As much as they might have liked to, they had no real reason to hold her and she had been released. They also gave her strict orders to stick around town until further notice in case the girl contacted her. She said she would. Her plan, which had been forming in her head for a day, now included sticking around anyway. She intended to do so whether the sheriff's department wanted her to or not. She had some serious business to deal with before she'd head back to Virginia Beach. That is, if she ever did.

The cops were serious about finding the girl. "Serious as a heart attack," one of them had said. The threat LeBrun posed seemed to have put the whole sheriff's department on edge, so much so she doubted they could act rationally if and when the girl, LeBrun, or both were to appear. She headed toward the highway to resume her surveillance at the Road House. She hoped her target hadn't stirred. If his car and/or the guy who'd been driving him were still in the area, she'd assume LeBrun remained in place and she'd take up her post again. First she would check out the barn where Darla had hidden her backpack. She might be holed up there. If not, it would draw her in eventually. That backpack contained everything the child valued and, more importantly, everything she needed to travel. Leota could not understand why Darla insisted on lugging those old clothes around. Her childhood, perhaps, the part she still clung to, the part that didn't give her nightmares. In any event, she wouldn't go without it and wouldn't do to have the bag and its contents found by the police if it still happened to be in the barn.

Being on the run was not a new experience for Darla. She'd done it before, several times, in fact. This time would be no different. She regretted leaving her godmother's house, but she'd heard that sheriff talking in the diner and the other guy who somebody said was FBI. Well, she'd had all the Picketsville Sheriff's Department she ever wanted already and wasn't about to hook up with it again. Not in this lifetime anyway. She'd slipped out of the house after Arlene left to go to the diner and Flora had settled in front of the TV to watch some dopey reality show. She'd wandered along Main Street until she was sure no one had followed her. Once certain she was—for all practical purposes—alone, Darla had moved into the service alley behind the street's storefronts. She'd spent the night curled up behind a dumpster near where she'd had her hair cut earlier in the week. The dumpster reeked of discarded salon trash, an aroma she thought a whole lot nicer than the stench of garbage in the dumpster behind the restaurant, which had been her first stop.

The sound of doors slamming and trash cans being emptied had woken her early and she'd scuttled away in the pre-dawn darkness. She intended to make her way to the highway, hitch a ride, or walk if necessary, to the nearest truck stop, tell her "sad story" a few times to some of the over-the-road jocks, and she'd be in a semi on her way west in no time. The routine had worked before. She was sure it would again. But first, she needed to retrieve her backpack with her getaway stuff from the barn where she'd convinced Leota she needed to drop it. It took her an hour to find the barn.

The ramshackle building still retained that old barn smell even though she guessed it had been, like, forever since there were any animals or farm stuff in it, except for, maybe, mice. Evidence of some resident rodents had to be brushed aside as she crawled back under the rafters to where she'd hidden her backpack.

Gone.

Someone had beat her to it? Leota? Probably not. She wouldn't have a reason to fetch it out unless she wanted her to stay put and thought the bag being missing would hold her in place. The old woman didn't know anything about being on the run. Anyway, her stuff was gone. She followed the drag marks where it had been pulled free and out onto the center of the barn floor. She eyed the place where the contents must have been dumped and picked through. So, definitely not Leota. She picked up a single earring the thief missed. She counted several sets of footprints and frowned. She needed to consider what to do next. The possibility of retrieving the bag now was zip, whether Leota or someone else had it. That fact meant she'd be traveling light. Whoever took the bag took her leather jacket, too. That meant she couldn't travel some places without freezing and all. She stamped her foot in frustration. The noise disturbed some of the barn's permanent residents. Darla wasn't afraid of much anymore. Being knocked around by pigs and perverts during your growing up years pretty much toughened you up for anything. Mice, on the other hand, did not work for her. She had a friend in juvie who was allowed to keep a pet mouse. Darla had dumped it out the window one night. She hated mice.

Luckily, she'd managed to lift five twenties from the fancy sugar bowl Flora kept in her kitchen cupboard. Old people were funny. Like, who wouldn't know exactly where to look for a stash of cash in their houses? A hundred bucks wasn't much, but it was a start. A good coat would eat most of it if she went north, but it was summer here, so maybe that could wait. She stamped her foot again, turned and headed for the door. Sticking around this mouse motel wasn't such a good idea and she really needed to figure out what to do next.

She had just cleared the barn door when she heard what she was sure must be Leota's truck approaching. There was no mistaking that crappy-sounding motor. She ducked into the brush next to the barn, hunkered down, and waited. She had no intention of debating with her guardian about next things and all. Leota was a nice lady, but she didn't know shit about what you had to do to survive in the real world. Darla guessed that came from being a library lady. They lived out of books, not on the streets where things were, like, really different.

Leota stared into the vacant space where Darla had stowed her backpack and made the same discovery. Darla must have come, retrieved it, and skipped. God only knew where the girl thought she could go and not be found. Suddenly, and for the first time, the enormity of what Leota had set into motion in the days and weeks before hit her like an ice tsunami, like someone had just punched her in the stomach. She hadn't felt anything so disabling since Timmy O'Donnell had done just that to her in the third grade. She could scarcely catch her breath.

She couldn't pry her eyes from the empty space. A tear ran down one cheek. She had been so sure that she'd done the right thing about Darla and now, instead of making the girl's life safer, she'd made it a hundred times more dangerous. She squeezed her eyes closed and tried to push aside the panic that had started to take over her thoughts. She could just hear what Flora would say when she found out.

"What were you thinking, Leota? Isn't this just like you? I guess they didn't teach you common sense in that fancy college you ran off to, did they? First it's that bum Mark Dellinger and now this."

She heaved a guilty sigh and thought of the girl.

"I didn't think any of this would happen, I promise you, Darla, I thought with your mother out of the picture…How could I have known about George LeBrun? My God, Flora was right all along."

A mouse in search of an exit from what had become an increasingly hostile environment, and emboldened by the preoccupation of the woman talking to herself, darted across the floor and disappeared through a knothole in the wall. Leota was drawn out of her trance an instant later by a shriek. Not a very loud shriek but still audible. She could have sworn someone outside had made the noise. She rushed to the door and searched the road both ways. Nothing. She must have been imagining things. The countryside is full of odd noises. Now what? The Road House of course. Anything else?

What had the deputies been talking about? If she remembered correctly, the sheriff's people had mentioned a BOLO. That meant they were notifying other law enforcement to be on the lookout for Darla, didn't it? They'd had one on her, too, and they'd found her. She had no idea what the acronym stood for but she knew its significance. Would someone find Darla in time? She rocked back on her heels and forced herself to concentrate.

Chapter Thirty-three

Ike had his cell phone clamped to one ear and his land line to the other. Billy Sutherlin had his attention in the former. He waited for Flora to pick up on the latter.

"What's she doing, Billy?"

"She stopped at that hay barn on your dad's property. Went in and five minutes later came back out. Then she jumped in that old One-fifty of hers and took off."

"What was she doing in the hay barn?"

"I got the impression she went in to get something. But she didn't have anything when she came out so, either she didn't find what she was looking for, or there's something else in there she was after."

"She didn't find the pile of old clothes. There was a photograph in that pile. That's the one we ran through the software to identify the girl. So, that's who put the stuff in there. Stay with her, Billy, I want to know where she goes."

"You do know she has a twelve-gauge shotgun in the bed of that truck?"

"Charley found it while you all were questioning her and took the shells out. Before she can do anything rash, she will have to reload. Charley didn't find any reloads in the truck and we searched her purse. I think she's neutralized. If she goes back to the Road House, we can assume she's stalking LeBrun. I don't want…Hold on a second, Flora, okay?…I don't want her messing with that man, especially with a firearm."

"But you would like to know why she's doing it."

"I think I already do, but yes, I'd like to be sure. Out." Ike snapped his phone shut and shifted the land line to his other ear.

"Okay, Flora, we found your cousin, Leota? She had no idea that the girl had disappeared. Why didn't you tell me about her relationship with the girl's father?"

"I didn't?"

"You know you didn't. Listen, your cousin is in town, but you knew that."

"I thought she went home, Ike. Okay, here's the thing, you wouldn't know this on account of it happened when you were off being an international snoop in them days, but Leota, she and Mark Dellinger were an item once, you could say."

"So she said. It gets worse. It looks like she's stalking George LeBrun and on top of that Mark Dellinger is dead, probably murdered. Does any of this mean anything to you, ring any bells?"

"I reckon that'd be good news and bad news."

"There is no good news in this. Flora, what the hell is your cousin up to?"

"With Leota, you can never tell, she's one of them nervous women. Did you just say you thought she's stalking that LeBrun? That ain't like her. She's never showed any spunk in her entire blessed life and you think she's after that piece of trash?"

"I am not a mind reader and I never met the lady until an hour ago. How would I know what she's up to? You're the cousin. You tell me."

"Like I said, she don't have the courage of a rabbit. I can't think, except...that bum Dellinger is dead, maybe murdered?"

"Yes."

"If she thinks LeBrun done him, she'll maybe be after him. I don't know what that flop ears would do if she catches him, though."

"She had a twelve-gauge shotgun hidden in the bed of her truck. Does that suggest anything?"

"Lordy, Lordy. That old scatter gun was her daddy's. He killed hisself with it. You don't think she plans to shoot LeBrun or herself with it, do you?"

"Or both maybe. I don't know."

"Well, I told you, she ain't the brave type. Ike, she's a librarian, for crying out loud. She more likely would throw a book at him."

"I can't take the chance."

"So what will you do?"

"We have her under surveillance. We can only wait and see."

"Whyn't you pick her up and put her away for awhile?"

"And we could do that because…?"

"Vagrancy?"

"She has a hotel room and she hasn't done anything illegal. Not like someone I could name."

"Yeah, yeah. You'd have done the same if you was me."

"Goodbye, Flora. If you hear anything, you let me know."

Ike put both phones down and banged his fist on the desk so loudly Rita looked up from across the room.

"We have a girl on the loose who does not want to be found. We have dozens of people looking for her. Some of them do not wish her well, a half-dozen of them would throw a party if she turns up dead, and one or two would do the killing if they had the chance. On top of that, she is as afraid of the police as her potential killers, so the good guys can't get at her."

Frank who had just walked in from the street, said, "That's the part I don't get."

"Long story short, Frank. Some of her original abusers used to work out of this office."

"What?"

"That's what we're hearing. It puts us in a hell of a bind. She won't come in willingly. If she did, she could have every one of the people who might be after her in, or back in jail in twenty minutes."

"But…"

"But will she risk it? Does she believe we will do that for her? She doesn't. Why should she? And so she's more likely to skip town than allow herself to be drawn back into the godawful life she's had so far."

"What are you going to do, I mean beyond what we're already doing?"

"Hope and pray she stays safe until we can at least isolate her from the bad guys. The worst part of all this is, we still haven't a clue who killed her mother and as much as I dislike the idea, we have to assume she might be the one who did it. At least she has to be on the list of our suspects."

"I think if I were that girl, I'd head west as fast and as soon as I possibly could. Sorry, Ike, but I don't see a good ending here."

"No, neither do I."

The girl in question might have felt her ears burning if she hadn't been so preoccupied with everything going on around her. First a mouse sailed out of a knothole in the wall next to her and ran between her legs. She couldn't help the "yike" that popped out of her mouth. She thought for sure Leota would have heard her and she'd be found out. Sure enough, a second or two later Leota popped out of the barn and looked around. Darla scrunched down as far as she could and made herself smaller. She held her breath. Leota stood there for a moment like she didn't know what to do next and then climbed into her ratty old truck and drove away. Darla rose slightly to watch the vehicle disappear and would have stepped out of the bushes except at that moment she heard another engine rev up. She froze and watched as a sheriff's cruiser sped past.

It must have been sitting down the road watching and waiting, she thought. Why were the cops following Leota? Probably looking for me. She waited a full minute and the black-and-white had cleared the curve down the road a quarter-mile or so before she eased out of the brush and stepped into the sunlight. Cops were looking for her. Leota was looking for her. Probably other people would be too. She daren't risk hitchhiking now or even staying on the road. She couldn't go back to Flora. She'd just call the cops and the nightmare would start all over again. She looked right and then left to get her bearings, then raced across the road and into the woods opposite. If she had it figured right, and if she could maintain a straight line of march, she would be on the north side of Picketsville in half an hour.

Chapter Thirty-four

A tall man with what Leota would describe as "an unpleasant manner" stepped out of the bar she'd been watching and lit a cigarette. She could almost smell the aroma from where she sat hunched down in the cab of her pickup. At least she thought it was a cigarette. It might have been dope. She'd heard about dopers from Darla. Everyone knew that bikers smoked dope and this man looked like one of them although he wasn't wearing a leather jacket with a skull and cross bones on it. Did that matter? she wondered. She'd have to Google it when she got back to Virginia Beach. However there were more immediate things that needed doing that might keep that from happening for a while.

The man glanced casually right and left and then fixed his eyes on her truck. He stared at her for what seemed a lifetime but could not have been more than half a minute. He dropped his smoke on the gravel and without bothering to extinguish it, turned on his heel and reentered the bar. Had he recognized her? Her truck? Had they guessed what she intended? How could they? What to do. Clearly, she was not cut out for this line of work, but she'd made a promise to herself, to Mark, that she would not rest until all of this sordid business was finished. Once one set out on a certain course, its trajectory seemed immutable. It was like fate, like a Greek tragedy. She could almost hear the chorus chanting away in the background, warning of imminent doom. She shuddered. She was not prepared for doom at that precise moment. She imagined George LeBrun, or that dope smoker or even the occupants of the bar, bursting out of the door, racing across the road, and murdering her where she sat. She decided that she wouldn't wait around and find out. She started her engine and headed back to her motel to think.

The prospect of violent death did not frighten her as much as she thought it might. She found that curious. Surely being stabbed or shot or clubbed by drug-crazed monsters should have at least raised her heart rate. But it hadn't. How odd. She was too occupied with these thoughts to notice the black-and-white take up a position a hundred yards behind her.

◇◇◇

Darcie Billingsly pushed her oldest through the door and headed straight for Ike's cubicle.

"You tell him what you done, Junior."

"Darcie, you're back. I thought you had enough of us for one day. Hello there, young Whaite. What is it you're supposed to tell me?"

The boy shuffled his feet and stared at the floor. He tugged at a leather jacket at least a size too large for him and muttered something Ike couldn't hear.

"Sheriff Ike can't hear you, Junior. Now you speak up and tell him what you and Tommy Dewcamp did."

"Umm…"

"It'll be okay, Whaite. Just spit it out and we'll deal with it. It wouldn't have something to do with that jacket, would it?"

A disproportionately large, pre-adolescent Adam's apple bobbed up and down as the boy searched for enough saliva to alleviate the dry mouth a trip to the sheriff's office created.

"Yes, sir, it umm, does. How'd you know?"

"I'm a policeman. I can tell when a crime has been committed. Talk to me."

"And don't forget about that brand new backpack Tommy took," his mother chimed in.

"Okay, Ma, okay. See, Mister Ike, me and Tommy was in the hay barn down on the Franklin Road. You know where that's at?"

"I do. It belongs to my father so, yes, I do. What about it?"

"Oh, shoot, I didn't know it was yours and all."

"My father's. What about the barn?

"Oh, yeah, we were, like, in it. Honest, Sheriff, all the kids go there and even some of the older ones. You should be talking to them because what they do in there is probably against the law a whole lot more than what me and Tommy do."

"Probably, but right now I want to know exactly what you and Tommy Dewcamp were doing in there that has you standing here and your mom so upset."

"Oh, right, sorry. So, me and Tommy was in there exploring, like, and we come across this backpack stuffed up in the rafters."

"And?"

"And so we drug it out and looked at what was in it. Like there was mostly girl's clothes and—"

"Baby clothing, pictures, and papers?"

"Yeah, how'd you know?"

"I told you. I'm a policeman. We know stuff. I'm guessing you dumped the contents on the barn floor, took some of the clothes, including that jacket, and the backpack and…what did you do with the clothes?"

"Tommy…"

"Tommy what?"

"Tommy figured to use them to bribe Francine."

"Tommy was going to bribe Francine…Francine who, and to do what?"

Whaite Billingsly, Jr. blushed and murmured, "DuVal. Francine DuVal. He thought she might…you know, umm, like, that is…"

"I get the picture. I won't ask you if he succeeded. In my experience used clothes that probably wouldn't fit a thirteen-year-old, no matter how snappy they looked would more likely get Tommy a shot to the chops than a carnal moment."

The boy risked a grin. "Yes, sir, and if you mean asking for sex, that's what happened. It was pretty funny."

"So, you stole a bag and clothes from my father's hay barn, solicited an underage girl for sex, and destroyed private property. Is that what you're telling me, son?"

The grin disappeared and the boy gulped and began to sweat. "Well, see…"

"Do you have any idea what that many felonies that could amount to and how many years in jail you could end up serving if convicted?"

The boy stared at Ike in panic. "I didn't have anything to do with Francine Duval. That was all Tommy's idea. And we thought the bag was, like, abandoned or something. We thought we had, like, salvage rights to it."

"Salvage? You think the barn was a ship lost at sea and the bag was cargo?"

"I don't know, honest, Sheriff, we were just…there's something else, sir."

"Something else? What?"

"There was some money in the bag."

"Money? How much and where is it?"

"We counted it and it was, like two hundred dollars. Me and Tommy split it."

"Where is it now?"

"I think Tommy spent his, I got mine in my box."

Ike looked at Darcie.

"He has a tin box with things he collects. I'll bring it in tomorrow."

"Okay, Whaite, you just shuck out of that jacket and hand it over. It's evidence. Rita, call the Dewcamps and have them bring in their son. Whaite, you get off to school now. I'll decide what punishment if any you get later. In the meantime, you need to think about this, suppose that bag had been left there as part of a drug deal and suppose the people who were looking for it found out that it was you who took it? You need to think about what you did and what might have happened to you if the wrong people were involved in this."

The boy and his mother left, he looking pale, she sounding off a mile a minute about what his father would think if he were alive, him once being a deputy sheriff and a town hero. Ike felt a little ashamed of himself for scaring the boy like that. He wondered what he might have said if he had any experience at being a parent. Probably the same thing—maybe worse.

"So now we know how the stuff we found in the barn got there and how it ended up in a pile on the floor. Question, assuming Darla went to the barn this morning and found her bag missing, what will she do next?"

Frank looked up and shrugged. He knew Ike was thinking out loud and didn't expect an answer. He picked up an incoming call.

"Billy said that Leota Blevins also stopped at the barn. I suppose she wanted the bag as well and she didn't find it either. So what is she thinking? That Darla had been there already and is on the loose? Probably."

"Billy just called in. He said after she left the barn the Blevins woman parked outside Alex's for a time and then went to her motel. She hasn't come out."

"So, she's not looking for Darla. She never was. Is she after LeBrun? Lord, I hope not, she'll get herself killed."

Not as long as she stays in the motel."

"Unless she's been spotted and then, she might end up as bait to get to the girl. Why didn't she just stay put in Virginia Beach?"

Chapter Thirty-five

George LeBrun—before he landed in prison for murder, attempted murder, false imprisonment, assault with a deadly weapon and a variety of drug-related charges, and before Ike had put him away for what everyone assumed would be fourteen forevers and before Darla Dellinger was born—had served as one of the more unsavory deputies on the late Loyal Parker's staff. So corrupt had that administration been that the townspeople had finally reared up and persuaded Ike Schwartz to run for sheriff. Ike, with his law school background and government service about which they truly knew nothing, but suspected everything, appeared to be the only person strong enough to challenge an entrenched, corrupt, and potentially dangerous administration. Ike's father, Abe Schwartz, had spent his entire adult life in Virginia politics. Retirement did not sit well with him and when he saw a chance to get back in the game, he pulled out all the stops, called in favors from both sides of the aisle, and steamrollered Ike's opponent—the dirt-bag Loyal Parker. The campaign had been heated. It had been dirty, but in the end and, much to Loyal Parker's dismay, Ike had been swept into office.

The election had not been universally celebrated. Small towns have traditions and hierarchies with ingrained biases which are willing to overlook obvious social pathologies rather than accept change. Within months of Ike's first election, Picketsville's mayor had begun searching for Ike's replacement. He might have been successful in that endeavor had he found a candidate with a modicum of honesty and integrity. As it happened, he'd failed in that as well. Ike's subsequent reelection four years later had not been as easy as his first, and still rankled the incumbent political machine. The difficulty attendant on those who shun ethical paths to exploit the perquisites of power is the inability to develop any semblance of a moral compass, an attribute which would allow them to sense virtues in others. Thus, these empty men and women, hot in the pursuit of power, even small-town power, will routinely gravitate to people like themselves. They never quite realize that people like themselves are the problem to begin with. The mayor had been shocked and then embarrassed when his candidate ran true to form, that is, he narrowly avoided a felony arrest for aiding and abetting and the jail time that would go with it.

When Ike first assumed the title of sheriff, his intention had been simple, to clean house, to send one hundred percent of those associated with the previous regime packing, set up a moderately efficient system of law enforcement, and then retire from public service. But his innate sense of fair play added to the constraints imposed on him by the town's personnel policies meant he had to interview all current members of the office—deputies and administrative staff—and then justify any and all firings using the town's personnel procedures. The exercise had turned out better than he'd anticipated, but was incomplete. He discovered a small core of deputies and staff who were ready and eager to join him in creating a modern and responsive sheriff's department. To date, his trust in the handful he'd retained had been justified. However, Darla Smut's appearance in town and the old wounds her presence evoked could call their newly minted professionalism into question. People could be forgiven if they wondered whether old loyalties and practices had been truly expunged or were merely lying dormant. Ike shared the concern as well. He'd never had to test their loyalty before—not like this.

Like the hum from the high voltage line that skirted the city and carried power west to Covington, old corruption long thought dead and buried, but now front and center, resonated through the minds of the town's old-timers. Ike had to consider whether any of the men, and women—shouldn't forget Essie, as unlikely as that might seem—might be trying to cover skeletons they thought were long buried but which could now resurface like Karl's dead mobster.

He could eliminate Essie and Billy from the list. George had tried to kill them once already and the likelihood either still harbored any residual loyalty to him seemed impossible. Given LeBrun's reputation as a bigot and a racist, Charley Picket could be removed from the list as well. Whaite Billingsly died LOD a few years back and that left only Jack Feldman and Harry Doncaster. Ike realized he would need to watch them both. Doncaster's possible involvement could be set aside for the moment. He had taken vacation time and now lay basking in the sun in the Outer Banks at a place with the unlikely name of Duck. But why had Feldman, quite uncharacteristically, volunteered to help search for the girl? Jack's efficiency reports were like a Dalmatian dog: spotted. Entries stating he showed a "lack of initiative," and "frequent unexcused absences," and "occasionally demonstrates poor judgment." If he'd stayed connected to LeBrun, the answer was obvious. Suddenly, he'd become a cop concerned with the welfare of a girl once mistreated by his coworkers and perhaps even by himself? Ike had assigned Feldman a sector to search that included the park land area around old Route 11 where it led into town. That should have kept him away from the barn and Alex's Road House and hopefully away from what Ike assumed would be the girl's more likely hiding places.

Ike had no idea where Darla had disappeared to, no one did. Worse, he hadn't an inkling which direction she might have bolted. Frank thought the girl would head west as fast as she could. If Frank was correct, she could be out on the highway thumbing rides or halfway to Chicago by now. The state police had a BOLO on her. If she tried the highway now, they would find her and he'd know pretty soon. If she'd caught her ride before the general call-out, he doubted they'd ever find her. If she'd been scared off the highway for some reason, like her bag gone missing, the chances of her being found were better, if only slightly so. Darla had survived in an environment that would have killed a lesser person. Clearly, she was not stupid.

Ike wandered to the shiny new coffee machine and started the thing gurgling and spitting, then promptly forgot it and walked back to his desk. If the girl wasn't already in a semi cab heading out on the turnpike system, she'd gone to ground nearby. But where? The skills she'd learned in the journey that took her out of Picketsville in the first place would be in play again, only this time she was older and smarter. She would stay invisible and remain that way until a window opened and then she'd be gone for good. He wondered whether he'd ever find her. He also wondered if he wanted to find her. It was a fleeting thought, but one with a small measure of merit, at least from the girl's point of view. Of course, the time might come when she would want to be found.

Ike hoped she'd failed in her attempt to catch a ride out. Hoped she would hide somewhere local and wait until things changed. If she lurked in the area she might make her move as early as nightfall when the darkness would allow her to move around more easily. But where would she hide until then? The hay barn? It was just possible Billy missed the significance of the Blevins woman's visit to the barn. What if Leota Blevins had not gone there to search for her at all but to supply her? What if it was the librarian who had been hiding her all along? He told Rita to find Billy and send him back to the barn. When he got there, he was to lay back and wait for backup. Then he had her dispatch Charley Picket to the barn as well. If the girl was in there, they'd have her.

◇◇◇

Darla had misjudged the time it would take to reach her destination. Almost an hour had elapsed before she edged into the trees that bordered the church parking lot. She searched for signs of activity. Two cars were parked near the door that led to the church office. She guessed one must belong to that snotty secretary and the other to the preacher. Low brush lined the edge of the graveled area and she sat cross-legged behind one with the little white flowers that smelled like perfume. Honeysuckle. She remembered that. The moss-covered ground felt damp but soft and comfortable. She waited. The first pangs of hunger arrived about noon. She remembered she had not eaten since the night before. Still, she didn't move. She'd been hungry before, many times. Back in the times her mother had sunk deep into the nuttiness of her meth life, she'd often gone without food for days. She'd subsisted on the meth head's diet—sugary soft drinks and Cheetos. This little bit of going hungry wouldn't amount to much. Somewhere in that church building she would find a refrigerator, a pantry, and something to eat. They probably had a stove in there, too. If she wanted to cook up something, she could. She wouldn't, of course. People in churches were pretty careful about their stoves. Leota had told her that once. She couldn't remember why. They would probably notice it if someone had messed with it. She didn't know why she thought that either. It was more than likely something her mother told her back when they were making the rounds of churches look-ing for handouts. Preachers were always a soft touch. Darla would stand behind her mother looking miserable—easy to do. She was mostly always miserable anyway and then the old lady would go into her story which was usually some crap about her having cancer or shit like that. At the moment, she couldn't be sure when she heard it. Things like that happened to her lots of times—when she couldn't connect the whats with the whens. Something to do with the brain chemistry crap the docs always talked about when she got looked at.

Darla knew there would be a bathroom with soap and towels in there, too. The most important thing, she thought, if the church had been put together like any of the other old buildings in the area, it would have a crawl space somewhere. Unless it had been covered over with Sheetrock or like that, it should be big enough to hide her for as long as she wanted to stay hidden.

That and a supply of food meant she could hole up in there, like, forever. If not? Well, this place right here was pretty good and who'd go looking for her in the bushes around the church? Just as long as she could get some supplies and it didn't rain too hard.

A police car drove in off the street, circled the parking lot, paused for a moment, and pulled out again. She shuddered. She was pretty sure she recognized that particular cop. She shrank back a few feet, deeper into the safety of shadows fighting the urge to stand up and run—run like the wind as far away as possible.

Chapter Thirty-six

Ike's e-mail appeared at the top of Ruth's inbox. It had had been there for days, begging to be read, accusing her of procrastination or worse. She'd ignored it. Doing so wasn't a matter of her putting off tackling a necessary task. She'd intentionally skipped over it because in the past an e-mail from Ike would likely contain a raunchy joke he'd picked from Lee Henry, or a lewd suggestion, or a bit of Percy Bysshe Shelley he'd remembered from Freshman English Lit. As this was one of her busy times and as she had not felt like being regaled, scandalized, or wooed, the message remained unread.

All of which explained why Ruth did not find out about the date she had for Monday at the church until the Thursday preceding it. She nearly fell off her chair.

"Agnes," she yelled, "get in here."

Agnes Ewalt had served Ruth as her personal secretary—administrative assistant, the HR director insisted she now be called—for more years than either would willingly admit.

Agnes flew through the office door ready for combat, to make a call to 9-1-1, or to apply emergency first aid. "What happened?"

"It's Monday."

"No, it's Thursday. Yesterday was Wednesday, you remember because—"

"I know that."

"You do? I thought you said it's...what's the matter?"

"Ike and I will be at Blake Fisher's church on Monday for the ceremony."

"You're getting married? On a Monday? Who gets married on a weekday?"

"You'd be surprised, but in this case we are already married. We're putting on a show like a pair of trained seals to keep the county happy."

"Sorry, I don't understand. You're married. How come I didn't know that? What about your health insurance and—"

"Never mind that now."

Ruth explained the events in Las Vegas, their subsequent need to have some sort of public acknowledgement, and the fact that Ike had arranged a compromise service with the Reverend Fisher.

"And you didn't know he made the arrangements? Why did he wait so long to tell you?"

"He didn't. It's my fault. I have been ignoring his e-mails for, I guess, forever and that bad habit just jumped up and bit me."

"What do you want me to do?"

"I don't know. Stand by and I'll call you."

Agnes left to retrieve the local phone book assuming she would soon be calling caterers and florists with urgent requests for some consideration in the light of a last-minute call for their services. There were vendors who valued, indeed depended on, the university's goodwill and who could be persuaded to perform the near impossible if called upon.

Ruth couldn't really get on Ike's case for not giving her enough time. She'd said ASAP when he'd asked her when she'd want Fisher to do the deed, assuming he'd do it at all. Like a good public servant, he'd trotted down to the church and done his part and notified her. Not counting what was left of today, she had something less than four days, three to be on the safe side, to arrange for food, drink, flowers, a place for a reception/party, invitations, and to clue in her mother. She tried to steady her nerves, failed, and launched into full panic mode. She called Ike.

"I'm in the middle of a man-hunt…make that a girl-hunt, woman-hunt. Can't talk now," he said.

"Don't you dare hang up on me, Schwartz, or there'll be no honeymoon this side of the next Ice Age."

"Not hanging up. So, what's the problem?"

"What's the...I just opened your e-mail about the church thing. It's only four days away. How in the bloody hell do you think I'm going to arrange all the stuff that needs doing?"

"I sent that to you the day I fixed it up with Fisher. Why are you in a stew about it now?"

"I just opened the damned thing."

"You just now read the message? What were you—?"

"Don't ask."

"Okay, I won't. So, what stuff still needs to be done?"

"You're kidding, right? Ike, we need to provide for food, a party, invitations, parents, the lot. You can't slap a thing like this together overnight."

"It's not overnight, Ruth, it's at least three overnights. What is the biggest thing that needs doing and I'll take care of it."

"You will. Hah! What did you tell me about Y and X chromosomes? Okay, the reception or whatever we're calling it. That's food, booze, venue, the whole works."

"How about a string quartet noodling Pachelbel's *Canon in D* as well?"

"Why not?"

"Okay, except for the string quartet and Pachelbel, consider it done."

"Sure you will just like that? Listen, brats, beer, and a polka band in the sheriff's parking lot is not acceptable. This do has to have a little class, if not for the Neanderthals who work for you then for the—"

"The academic pussies who work for you. I got it. It will be nice enough for them, not as upscale as a MOMA reception, but nice, and townie friendly for the rest of the world. No fear."

"I don't believe you."

"You don't have an alternative. What else?'

"Invitations."

"You're kidding. I don't know about the ivory tower and its protocols, but down here in the world of grits and gravy, I need only tell four people about what's on tap and everybody in town will know inside five minutes. Why don't you post something on the faculty bulletin board? Better, have the payroll people slip a note or something in their envelopes."

"We have direct deposit."

"Notify the bank. You'll think of something. Listen, the majority of your colleagues don't approve of me, and will not attend anyway."

"And your townsfolk just love me to pieces. Is that what you're saying?"

"They do. They think of you as something exotic, like a local horse breeder who imports a *thoroughbred* brood mare to improve the stock."

"I'm a horse?"

"Ah, but a very beautiful one, don't forget."

"Thanks a heap. Flowers."

"What?"

"We will need flowers in the church."

"Taken care of."

"What? I don't believe it. You are a man. Men do not do flowers and catering. I'll call my mother."

"Do that and then put her in touch with Dorothy Sutherlin, besides being the mother of two of my frontline deputies, happens to be a primal force in the church. All is, or soon will be, arranged—food, flowers, gala, the works."

"You did that?"

"I did."

"I don't believe it."

"But you must because you have no alternative."

"You called me a horse."

"Metaphorically."

"What's that make you?"

"In this case, the jockey, I guess."

"You're awful."

"Yes, but at the same time, said to be irresistible. *Mazel Tov.*"

"I don't believe it," Ruth said to a silent phone.

"Is everything okay? Do you want me to make some calls?" Agnes stood, phone book in hand awaiting her marching orders.

"He said he's got it."

"Do you believe him?"

"I have to. Agnes, figure a way to invite the faculty and staff without them thinking it's a last-minute thing."

"But it is."

"I know that. You know that. They do not need to know that."

Ike hung up and turned his attention back to the reports that had been coming in all morning. Ask for people to look out for teenagers on the run and you can expect a flood of sightings and editorials mostly from uptight spinsters about the dissolution of the moral fiber among young girls these days. Most of those missives contained several exclamation points. Whoever wrote the BOLO needed to be a tad more specific as to the girl's description and why Ike needed to find her.

Abstinence of any sort did not fit George LeBrun's nature. The girls who alternately tended bar and pole-danced downstairs kept one part of his needs in check, but he missed the crank. When your body adapts to the chemical, even a drying out period in jail will not erase the craving. Addicts, if they conquer their problem, do so by owning it and then suppressing it. It becomes easier to do the longer they work at it. George, like many of the addicted, once made clean, figured he could manage it—take it or leave it. George had started dipping. He inhaled and let the drug assault his bloodstream through his respiratory system which had only lately started to return to normal. He nodded and smiled and mixed cola and vodka in a glass. No ice. He felt great. He stamped on the floor for one of the girls. Betsy didn't work nights Whoever showed up had better be ready to party. He sucked on the pipe and stamped his foot again.

She said her name was Cherise. Her accent said she had probably started out life as Sherrie or Cherry. She did not look as happy to see him as he did her. She had no idea what she had let herself in for when she'd run away from an abusive stepfather and an in-denial alcoholic mother who refused to entertain any thoughts about what her husband might be doing to her daughter after she'd passed out at night. Now Cherise struggled with adapting to this new and very scary lifestyle that she'd drifted into. She would soon find out that as bad as her old situation had been, there were worse things that could happen to a girl, especially if no one cared if she lived or died.

Her body would not be found for nearly a year, and then only because a task force created by the FBI, acting on the events of the previous year which determined that there were sufficient reasons to search the woods in and around Picketsville, had finally begun to sift through the sector where she'd been dumped.

In any case, it would be long after the man who killed her had had his own appointment with destiny. Because of that, the irony of her passing would go unappreciated and her murder, like so many others involving lost children, would go unheralded and unsolved. Hers would be just another life served up on the altar of societal ennui.

Chapter Thirty-seven

Darla waited until the last car drove away from the church and the lights in the office area winked out. A moment later she saw the minister, or whatever he was called, walk to the little house next door. An hour later the same man and this time with a woman left the house all dressed up, climbed into their car, and drove away. She hoped they were on their way to a party or something because she would need some time to find her place and then fix things up. That is if she was right about the way old buildings were put together in this part of the world.

She let another ten minutes elapse, then ventured out from the woods, dashed across the parking lot to the church, and flattened herself against a wall. She froze, waiting, then moved cautiously to the church doors. As she had expected, they were locked. She moved along the wall, searching. The doors might have been locked but that was not the case for the basement windows. She slipped through one near the back end of the church and felt her way to what she took to be a kitchen. If it were any normal kitchen, there should be a first aid kit and it should contain a flashlight.

As it turned out she would need the time the absence of the minister and his wife provided and then some. To her consternation, Stonewall Jackson Memorial Episcopal Church had not been built to the eccentric standards of the rest of antebellum Picketsville. She searched every inch of the building in vain for those crawl spaces, attics with hidden cul-de-sacs and the squirrel nests she'd expected. Someone at sometime must have employed the services of an architect. Nothing even approaching a hiding place bigger than a closet existed on any level. She supposed she could crawl up under the altar. In the old days didn't they give you a pass from the cops if you hung on the altar?

The kitchen was in the church basement and it would be there, if she had the choice, she would have liked to have found a hiding place. None seemed to exist. She reconsidered setting up in the woods and using the church as a supply point. She worked her way back through the kitchen. She noticed, for the first time a second door leading outside. This one opened onto a below-grade areaway fitted with a French drain. The space was filled with leaves and yellowed newspapers. She guessed the church people didn't use that door much. She peered to her immediate right and saw another door cut into the wall which formed a right angle to the main building. This part of the church wasn't as wide as the rest and had its own roof a little lower than the main one. It also held the church offices upstairs. So what was under them?

She stepped out and studied this new entrance. It opened inward and was secured with a Yale snap lock—the kind she could open with a credit card inserted between the jamb and bolt. Unfortunately, the builder had forestalled this maneuver by putting a beading around the entire circumference of the door. She might have given up except she remembered the rack of knives on one of the counters. She retrieved the knife with the broadest blade and stepped outside again. She lined the point with the lockset and, pounding gently with her fist, drove the blade behind the beading and into the space between the jamb and lock. The latch was forced back and the door sprang open. She removed the knife, wiped it, and returned it to its holder. Then, flashlight in hand, she discovered what must have been a boiler room added to the main structure in the century follow- ing the church's original construction. She explored the room, squeezed behind the boiler, but as much as she wished it were otherwise, there would be no hiding place for her in this room either. She returned to the main building.

Darla stood irresolute in the center of the basement gazing at but not seeing the ominous shadows cast by stuffed animals and books stacked in readiness for the weekend's onslaught of children whose parents insisted they be amused by Bible stories rather than taught what they considered to be a politically incorrect faith. Darla had all but decided to abandon her idea of hiding in the church and started toward the door, this time to let herself out. Then she stopped in mid-stride. Had she detected an asymmetry in the boiler room area? She knew the space should correspond in its general dimensions with that of the offices above. She would have to go outside and pace off the distances between the end walls and then do the same inside the boiler room to find out. With care and as quietly as she could, she slipped through the door, climbed the stairs from the entry well and in minutes paced off the long side of the addition. Once done, she returned to the boiler room and repeated her pacing. The boiler room came up short. She could not account for something like six feet. A quick inspection of the wall behind the boiler revealed that the bricks that formed it did not reach the joists above. There must be a space behind this wall. She couldn't imagine why they put up a wall there. Maybe to keep the heat away from something. Unfortunately, the gap at its top was too narrow for her to slither through.

Back in the kitchen she again paced off the greater distance and found herself standing next to what she assumed was a recently installed stove. She aimed her flashlight behind it and discovered another door, this one apparently leading to the space that lay beyond that wall. A room existed behind that stove and because the appliance had been installed in front of its entrance, the chances were good that the room no longer served any useful purpose. If the stove could be moved, she had her hideaway. In fact, the oven moved quite easily and with another application of the kitchen knife to the second door lock, she gained access. It was small but luckily it had been emptied.

The next twenty minutes she spent scrounging through closets and cabinets. She managed to find several worn pew pads. The cross stitching seemed in good shape but stuffing leaked from seams. Probably some lady set them aside to be reclaimed someday. She carried them to her lair and arranged them into a serviceable futon. She brought in two large buckets and, just before the batteries in her flashlight failed, she discovered a ceiling light installed in the room complete with a chain pull. She stole a light bulb from the ladies room. Next she stockpiled some canned food from the pantry, being careful to only take one of each kind. She lifted a can opener and stuffed it into her pocket. She cut a large block from a bar of cheddar and took a loaf of bread. She helped herself to three quart-sized bottles of cherry soda. She would have to drink them warm, at least until the next night. Finally, she rummaged through a closet upstairs and took one of the black dress-like robes that buttoned up the front along with its hanger.

She had just finished giving herself a sponge bath in the restroom when she saw the flash of headlights cross the restroom windows. She dashed to the kitchen, replaced the flashlight in the first aid kit, slipped into her hiding place, and pulled the stove back into line. The door she left ajar. She would close it only if and when she needed to, but for the moment, left it open. It provided a small relief from the room's lingering mustiness.

◇◇◇

Mary Fisher craned her neck as Blake wheeled into their parking space not four feet from Darla, except for the dividing exterior wall and six feet of Virginia topsoil.

"Did you see that?" she asked.

"See what?"

"I could have sworn I saw a light in the basement."

"Someone may have left a light on."

"You were the last to leave. Were there any lights on when you locked up? It didn't exactly look like a light left on. More like a flashlight or something. Maybe someone has broken into the church, Blake. You should call the sheriff. Remember the last time someone broke in and stole the Communion silver."

"We recovered it all."

"Not all. There is still one cruet missing and besides they might be vandals or something. In the summer the kids around here get bored and into trouble. The community swimming pool was paintballed last week and we had vandals."

"Not for a long time. Okay, I'll call the sheriff if that will make you happy. I doubt it will make him happy, but I'll do it for you."

Chapter Thirty-eight

Jack Feldman had signed up for a double shift. It was not something he ordinarily did. He liked the overtime pay, naturally, but the long hours cut into his other interests. Interests he kept to himself and as far away as possible from his boss. If Ike were to get even a whiff of the things his deputy did in his spare time, there would be hell to pay. But Jack was careful and while the sheriff may have wondered what he was up to, Jack made sure he never found out. Tonight Jack figured he needed a clear forty-eight hours and took the double to get it. He knew something big was in the wind and that it would require his services. LeBrun, whether he knew it or not, needed someone on the inside and who else could he trust? Harry Doncaster, the pussy, never joined the insiders back in the day. Him and the Sutherlin kid, the hot dispatcher, Falco, only now she was the Sutherlin kid's wife. None of them were tight with George and Parker. If Parker hadn't lost the election they would have been dumped for sure. Bunch of Girl Scouts.

No, George had come back and he needed his boy, Jackie. He grinned at the thought, something big. Oh yeah. To do what he had in mind meant he needed the extra time to set things up and then make them happen. He drove north on Main Street which was a continuation into town of old US 11, his mind on how he would arrange it all and what he brought to the table. He glanced at his watch—ten forty-five. At this rate, he should clear the sheriff's office a little after eleven and that should put him at Alex's Road House, out of uniform, and ready to deal a few minutes before midnight. His radio crackled. Darcie Billingsley called him out on a 10-25 at the Episcopal Church.

"Do you copy, Jack?" Mental bitch. What did she think he was doing?

"Copy that, on it, 10-4."

The call coming in this close to the end of the shift made him angry. Why couldn't the jerk who called it in wait fifteen minutes and then Picket or some other loser would have to take it? A breaking and entering call, with the paperwork that he would have to do when he was done, would slow him way down and probably make him late. He gritted his teeth and turned into the church parking lot. If there really was some dope in the church, he'd better roll over easy because Jack was in no mood to play nice.

The preacher stood on the porch of his house waiting for him when he drove up. Those preachers had a cushy life. They only worked one day a week, except maybe for going to the hospital once in a while, and they got to keep all that cash in the plate, probably. Also, like this guy, they got a free house. Jack decided he didn't like this dude—lazy college kid with nothing much to offer and hiding behind a dog collar. This search would be quick and, unless the idiot who broke in was dumb enough to still be on the premises, would definitely not require a write-up.

◇◇◇

The two men walked to the church and Blake unlocked the door that led to the offices.

"The safe is this way," he said. "If there is anyone in here, that's the first place he'd go."

They climbed the stairs and went through two adjoining offices and on to the sacristy. The safe seemed undisturbed, but the door to one of the cabinets on the opposite wall stood ajar.

"Anything?" Feldman asked.

"Except for this door being open, no. It was closed when I left earlier, I'm certain of that."

"Step back."

Feldman drew his weapon and used the barrel to push the door the rest of the way back. He paused and then stepped forward to inspect the inside. Robes of some sort, black, white, and one or two red ones, all different sizes.

"Nothing. You're sure this was closed?"

"Absolutely. You weren't really going to shoot if there had been someone hiding in there, were you?"

"Nah, too much paperwork. Usually a kid looks down the barrel of this bad boy and he wets his pants. Can't give up fast enough. Well, okay, then we'd better look around the rest of the building. You tell me if you see anything suspicious, you know, like, if something is missing or not."

"Right."

It took twenty minutes for the men to cover the interior of the church. Blake felt, but could not explain why, the deputy seemed so angry at him. He kept looking at his watch and snapping short, marginally rude remarks whenever Blake asked him a question. He made a mental note to mention the deputy's attitude to Ike when he saw him next. Blake's preoccupation with the animosity surrounding the two of them and the deputy's clear impatience to finish and leave meant that neither would have seen anything amiss even if they had stumbled over it in the dark.

At eleven-twenty, the deputy left grumbling about putting in twenty minutes of overtime. Blake extinguished all the lights and locked up. Neither he nor the departed cop had noticed that two of the basement windows were unlocked and that some alterations had been made to the pantry's stores, not to mention the missing pew pads, a light bulb, one black cassock, and four or five hand towels.

Back in the rectory, Blake mounted the stairs to the second floor. Mary, his wife had already climbed into bed but she sat up, wide awake, waiting for a report, for reassurance that all was well, that the child she was pretty sure had taken up residence in her womb would be safe this night.

"Anything?" she asked.

"Nada. If there had been anyone in the church, they were long gone by the time the surly deputy and I arrived."

"Surly?"

"I don't know this one's name, but I did get his badge number. I will talk to Ike about him next time I see him. Yes, he was rude and short. He obviously didn't want to be out here and his whole demeanor was, like, 'I'm doing you a favor.' I don't think I've ever run across that before, at least not in a cop. The guy at the Department of Motor Vehicles acted like that, but I think rude is in their job description."

"You don't mean that."

"No, I suppose I don't. Still…"

"So nothing was disturbed."

"I didn't say that. I said there was no one in the building. If I had to guess, someone had been in it earlier, maybe even as late as when we drove up, but they were gone."

"Then why—"

"Little things seemed out of place like a closet door I'm sure I closed before I left, was ajar. The first aid kit, you know, has that complicated latch that springs open at a touch when you need to get into it but is nearly impossible to close later, had been fiddled with as well."

"Tonight?" Mary pulled the blankets tighter around her breasts.

"Couldn't say. Maybe not tonight. Anyway, there seemed to be, I don't know, a disturbance in the ether."

"A disturbance in the what?"

"Sorry. Things just seemed…you know how it is when you haven't cleaned your glasses lately, or maybe pick up someone else's prescription that is almost but not quite the same as yours? You can see things but the objects are slightly out of focus, or too big and…well, you see what I mean."

"Something was not quite right but you can't say what or why."

"Exactly."

"Why don't I feel better?"

"There is absolutely nothing to worry about. If, and I emphasize the if, someone was in the church this evening, they're long gone. If an intruder came looking for something other than just stealing stuff from the church, you know, like he wanted to harm you or me, he would had broken in here, not over there."

"Blake, there is something I think I should tell you."

"In a minute. Finally, and I mean this kindly, Mary, but you can't always assume that people are bad."

"I didn't say anything about—"

"You assumed that if there was a break-in, the person was up to no good. But the fact is that most church break-ins are made by desperate people."

"Desperate?"

"They need a warm place to sleep, some food, or a toilet. Picketsville doesn't offer much in the way of social welfare programs. The homeless usually spend the night in jail or in the park. Flora Blevins might give them a cup of coffee and a stale donut, but that's pretty much it."

"Then you should do something about it. This church isn't hurting for money, not really. I know you'd like to build a building for the Sunday school, but a food bank and maybe an eight-hour dormitory for the homeless would be better, especially in the winter. A Sunday school could use the building once a week, a shelter, seven nights, fifty-two weeks of the year."

"The vestry would never buy it. What were you going to tell me?"

"It'll keep. Goodnight."

◇◇◇

Even though it was June and her hideaway only a thin wall and three feet away from the church boiler room and hot water heater, Darla sat shaking uncontrollably in the corner. She'd pulled a tattered blanket around her shoulders. It did not stop her teeth from chattering. She knew those voices. The preacher, he was okay, she guessed, though you can never tell. There was that guy…she pushed the memory from her mind. The other one, the cop. She remembered that one, alright. You didn't forget voices. He had been one of them. And now he had been, like, ten feet away. She grabbed one of her buckets, pulled it close, and threw up.

Chapter Thirty-nine

Ike stared at the stack of reports on his desk. Darcie Billingsley's dispatch log listed seventeen items. He scanned the column again. Darcie's handwriting bordered on the illegible, but there could be no doubt about the number. There were seventeen entries. Most were minor problems that only required a drive-by to settle: noisy parties, barking dogs, suspicious behavior involving neighbors, strangers, or children, and nearly all the complaints from either annoyed neighbors or mildly inebriated adults with TVs on the fritz, who had nothing better to do but stare out the window. Except for one serious notation, a breaking-and-entering, it had been an easy night. The B and E had been assigned to Feldman. There should have been his write-up in the stack on the desk, but Feldman had not filed his report. Darcie's log identified the initial call coming from Blake Fisher. The church had been broken into. Why hadn't Feldman done his paperwork? Not the first time he'd skipped closing out or turned in paperwork late, but…but what? What with the search for the girl stalled while the threat to her life mounted and another body to be accounted for in the morgue, Ike really didn't want to waste time disciplining one of his deputies. He picked up the phone and called the church. Ten minutes later, and only after being assured by Rita who had by now replaced Darcie, that no one else was immediately available to make the stop, Ike pulled up to the church and climbed the stairs to the offices.

"Rev, you had a break-in last night?"

"I don't know if we did or didn't. Mary thought she saw a flash of light in the basement and I thought 'better to be safe than sorry,' so I called. I have to say the deputy who responded could use some training in dealing with the public."

"How so?'

"I would say he came very close to being rude. It seemed obvious that he did not want to be here, that he found the job of checking out the church onerous, and he wanted to be somewhere else. He kept looking at his watch as if he had better-paying options waiting for him at some other crime scene. I know you don't, but you don't, do you?"

"I don't what?"

"Important crime scenes don't involve the deputy receiving hazard pay or extra duty bonuses, do they?"

"Of course not. Is that what he said?"

"No, it's how he acted. Anyway, that was then. What can I do for you?"

"I apologize for Deputy Feldman. He was not one I recruited. He came with the rest of the furniture and is only slightly more useful. As long as I'm here, do you want to walk me through the church? It's been a while since I last visited this place and then I was more concerned with a body in the sanctuary than the rest of the building."

"Sure. The crew is here doing the Friday cleanup and since you and Ruth will be here Monday, Dorothy has called in what she calls her *A* team."

"I'm flattered. The *A* team you say? Who would that be?"

"I don't remember. Actually, I think it is more a description of an attitude than an actual roster. Let's go downstairs and see."

As Blake promised, when they arrived at the basement, Dorothy Sutherlin and a crew of four women were wiping down counters and mopping floors.

"Well, look who's here. Are you slumming, Sheriff, or scouting? By the way, I heard from your future mother-in-law. She's in a dither."

"I'm not surprised, Dorothy. Eden Saint Clare is anything but party-planner organized. Dither is her specialty at times like that."

"Well, we got her all settled. So then, what brings you into foreign territory?"

"Just doing a follow-up visit to the scene of the crime—past and future. How are you holding up with a house full of out-of-town guests and Essie and Billy moved back in?"

"It's a circus and it's sure enough got its share of clowns, but it's all fun so far. I do wish Karl would cheer up a little. He expects some test or other is going to send him into unemployment or something. I told him a bright young man like he is don't have to worry about a job, but he didn't want to hear it."

"It's a problem. FBI is the one thing he's wanted all his life and he's afraid it might be snatched away from him."

"Well, shoot, then he could come and work for you, right?"

"It's hardly the same thing. Anyway, the Rev called in a possible break-in last night. You haven't noticed anything missing or out of place?"

"Ike, there must be forty-teen keys to this church in circulation by now. Folks are in and out of here all the time, day and night. Things disappear and then reappear all the time. Sometimes folks'll 'borrow' a loaf of bread or a can of beans and then put it back a week or month later. Don't ask me why, save a trip to the store, I reckon. And then a mom will get a whiff of the cassock their boy is wearing to acolyte in on a Sunday and they'll take it home to wash and press it. It may not show up until the kid is scheduled to serve again which could be a month or two...you see?"

"I do. So, you are telling me that except for a full-scale robbery of, say, the safe, you can't tell if the church has been broken into or not."

"Nope."

"Things could be missing and gone for good, or not, and you wouldn't know."

"Yep."

"Funny way to run a business."

"It ain't a business, it's a church. Taking stuff if you need it and maybe putting it back with extra is how we do it here."

"You net out more than you put in?"

"Mostly, yep."

"So, I can report that nothing is missing?"

"No, you can report that whatever is missing is probably coming back or being put to good use."

"I see. Blake, there's not much sense in ever calling in a break-in, is there?"

"Well. Dorothy has omitted we have had our safe cracked a few times. Those instances, I would say, justify a call."

"Right. And today? What's missing? I don't care if it's eventually coming back. I want to know anyway."

"There's a chunk of cheese and maybe a loaf of bread gone," Faith Chimes, an *A* team member, said.

"Faith, you're not doing hair today?'

"No, Friday is my day to help out here. Oh, and Sheriff, we keep candle stubs in a box? Well, I can't be sure, but I think a bunch of them are missing, too."

"Candle stubs?"

"Well, we burn a bunch of candles here, you know, it being a church and all, and when they burn down too low, we put in new ones."

"And you save the stubs? Why?"

"I don't know. Why do we, Reverend Fisher?"

"The answer to that comes under the general heading of, 'We Always Have.' I think the Sunday school uses them for projects or something. Maybe that's where they went."

"Okay, so candle stubs and cheese. Not hearing grand theft larceny here. Mind if I look around?"

"Jump right in, only step carefully in the kitchen. The floor has just been mopped. I must say, whoever installed that new oven sure did mess up the floor. We just can't seem to get the scrape marks off the tile.' Dorothy said. "It's like somebody keeps sliding it around."

"Probably needs leveling," Ike said. "Would you like me to have a look?"

"Sure, if you've a mind to."

Ike peered at the stove unit. It seemed in order and level. He peered around it to see if there might be something on the wall that interfered with the stove's proper seating.

"What's behind this thing?"

"Old storeroom. Been locked up for years. Why?"

"Just curious. Locked, you say?"

"Yep. We cleaned it out when we bought the stove. Never really used the room because of how it backs up to the boiler room and was too hot to use as a pantry or practically anything else and, besides, there was no other place to put the new oven unit, so, there you go."

"Okay, thanks. I will let you get back to your cleaning and planning."

Chapter Forty

Karl knocked and then let himself in to Ike's office. He did not look happy. He sat down and focused his gaze on a crack in the vinyl tiles at his feet.

Ike rolled back and slouched a little more in his chair. "Let me guess. The DNA test came in and it is not good."

"Yeah. The body you dug up is our boy Anthony Barbarini. Which means someone in the Bureau will have some serious explaining to do. That someone is not going to be happy since he or she made it very clear to me through an intermediary that I shouldn't find that connection. Now what do I do?"

"You have only two options, Karl. You can tell the folks in the Hoover building the thing they do not want to hear, or you can lie. The only flexibility you have is when you tell them whichever it is you decide."

"Advice?"

"Well, that is a tough one. I will not tell you to lie. I wouldn't lie and I don't think, in the end, you will either. On the other hand, keeping them in the dark a few more days will not materially alter the eventual outcome. It has been ten years since your goombah was planted in our backyard. It can't matter much if you hold off until next week and stick around for my impending quasi-nuptials and the party to follow."

"What's quasi about your...you did say nuptials?"

"It's a long story and one for another day. The real question here is not what you will say to your section chief, but what will you do after you've said it? Are you prepared to pursue a career in the Bureau when it might mean a series of bad, dead-end assignments and pushing paper?"

"I don't know. I am just really angry that the incompetence of some agents a decade ago ends by screwing up my life."

"Ah, a word from someone older and, if not wiser, more experienced in the art of governmental screw-ups. Bureaucrats for the most part are driven by ambition and fueled by political rhetoric. Consequently they never learn history's lessons. We all thought Vietnam taught us something about poking our nose in where it didn't belong and where are we now? Engaged in wars we cannot win, to establish systems that can't be sustained, for people who hate us. It is the nature of the society we have molded in this bright new century to plow headlong into adventures that even a tiny measure of caution would have forestalled and from which we can't seem to extricate ourselves."

"Thank you, Bertrand Russell. I appreciate the worldview. I really do, but what about this poor slob sitting here right now? What do I do in the face of this inevitable landslide of bureaucratic backlash?"

"Stick around for my party. The two of us will get slightly soused and then decide."

"I guess that is the best I can do. I haven't told Sam yet. I guess that can wait until after the party, too. So, you're off the hook on this one."

"Not entirely."

"No? How not?"

"Well the body in the woods begs a question beyond the obvious one: who is he? Or, more properly, who was he?"

"And what question is that?"

"How did the body of Anthony Barbarini, also known to his compatriots as Barbie, find its way down from New York City to Picketsville, Virginia, and thence into our park? Furthermore, since it did, does that imply we have people down here who are connected to people up there in less than legal ways?"

"Oh."

"Indeed. Perhaps you should consider staying on awhile. Your bosses might come to see an investigation into that possibility, assuming it has a positive outcome, as sufficiently redeeming to erase the negatives caused by the unfortunate DNA test and the effects it has on some of the Bureau's more senior members."

"And those 'senior members,' will they be happy by the results of the investigation and let it go?"

"Well, there are two thoughts on that and which one will prevail depends on the options we exercise now."

"Options? We? What options? Ike I—"

"Patience. Okay, number one, let us suppose the sheriff of Picketsville, in the spirit of cooperation, of course, asks for help from the FBI. 'You see,' he, that is I, will say, 'I have a body tentatively identified by the dental wonks in your system as Tony Barbarini.' And suppose further that same sheriff requests files from the original arresting officers. At that point they are officially 'outed,' not by you, but by me. Now, if anything falls back on you, it will have to be very public and embarrassing to them, you see?"

"They wouldn't dare do anything?"

"To you? How can they? I'd be the guy who ratted them out. Assuming a subsequent investigation into the stiff in the woods is launched? They'll be told to get over it."

"You think?"

"Pretty sure. It's what I'd do if I were their boss…and yours."

"Okay, that could work. What's option number two?"

"I'll let you work on that one. See you tomorrow?"

"Probably, sure."

◇◇◇

Ike caught TAK before he left for the day.

"Okay, it's time for your next lesson in policing. This is basic detective work."

"Sir?"

"I have a job for you, son. Make that two." Ike produced the evidence bag containing the dollar bill with the phone number scrawled on it. "This bill was found in the dead man's pocket. You know who I am talking about?"

"Dellinger?"

"No, the stiff who was buried in the woods a decade ago. It has a phone number written on it but no area code. I want you to search the history of this number in metro New York—all the area codes, Connecticut, Long Island, New Jersey. Go back twelve years."

"Yes, sir, twelve years. Can I ask why?"

"Certainly. Police work is mostly about digging and asking questions. Forensics can get you just so far, then the grunt work begins. The bill was in a murdered man's pocket. We want to know who killed him. The number might just lead us to his killer or not. Either way, it is a loose end. We do not like loose ends."

"Right, Sheriff, no loose ends." He turned to leave.

"Wait, I'm not finished." Ike opened the medical examiner's file and pulled out a photograph. He handed that to the intern as well. "This is a picture of the label in the dead guy's suit jacket. It was hand-tailored and the label tells us who made it. The number inside the pocket identifies who ordered it made."

The young man studied the photograph. "A. M. Rosenblatt, and Sons?"

"Of New York, yes. Tomorrow you call them and find out who they made the suit for."

"Sheriff, after all these years, would they know?"

"Oh, they will. If I know about anything, I know about Jewish tailors. You call them."

The boy frowned and left. Ike made a quick call to his father.

"Pop, do you know any New York Rosenblatts? They'd be in Great-uncle Marvin's line of work."

"They're tailors? Let me think. Marvin will, if I don't. I'll call you."

Six o'clock rolled around and he headed out. Ruth wanted to meet and discuss Monday. What she needed from him at this point he could not imagine, but he agreed to meet her in her office. She said she would have food sent in. She also said he was to turn off his phone. That part was not going to happen.

◇◇◇

George LeBrun enjoyed one positive benefit from his addictive lifestyle—stretching the definition of *benefit* a bit, to be sure. Excesses of booze combined with methamphetamine caused him to experience a form of topical amnesia. His "morning after" is somewhat more daunting than the average boozer's. This morning he struggled to recall anything about the previous night's activities. It was not that George was burdened much with pangs of conscience; he'd never experienced a sense of guilt, at least not since he pushed his sister down the basement stairs and broke her arm. His Dad had beaten the snot out of him then. It would be years before he evened that one out. For him, remembering had more to do with establishing his bearings and accounting for his time, should that be necessary, than regrets or recriminations.

Alex, the owner and proprietor of the road house bearing his name, stood at the far end of the bar and grumbled something about missing the girl and why had she left without notice. He shot an accusatory glance at George but said nothing more. Alex knew that George, if he chose to, could make his life difficult or even end it. His current worry, however did not concern possible consequences of an irate LeBrun. It stemmed from George's slide back into using. Like so many addicts who enter detox and emerge "clean," he'd started to dip. Addicts always think that they can manage just a "taste." They can't. Alcoholics, druggies, smokers, you name your personal pollutant, if you're an addict, even taking in a small amount will send you spiraling back into dependency. George had been dipping and the girl had disappeared. Alex frowned, kept his eyes averted, and continued to wipe his counter wondering when George would explode and what godawfulness would emerge when he did.

LeBrun and Alex had a symbiotic relationship. Not a healthy one, like those found in nature, but like flesh-eating bacteria in an old man's leg. George had no interest in or sensitivity to Alex's fears. For him their connection made good business sense and if Alex did not see it that way, there were others waiting in the wings that would. In the meantime, he waited for his scrambled brain to coalesce into some version of normal. Because doing so did not require that he remember much of the previous night, he allowed that time to slip from view, so to speak.

But he did remember two things he considered important. Frankie Chimes had stopped by to cadge some drinks and ask for a small loan. Frankie served as one of George's mules when he needed one. Otherwise he worked at a variety of jobs—none permanent, and managed to embarrass his family by showing up in court to plead to a miscellany of misdemeanors and minor felonies. Frankie had said something he had heard at his brother's house the night before. George thought it was significant, and he struggled to remember it now. This memory connected with Jack Feldman telling him about a call at the church he'd made before he went off duty. That was before he helped clean up the mess in the bathroom, but that didn't have anything to do with the other thing either. He cudgeled his forehead and tried to focus. Failing, he drained his beer and signaled Alex for another. It would come to him in time.

Leota had resumed her position across the road and twenty yards to the south of Alex's Road House at nine that morning. Her watch showed four hours had passed and she needed to eat and use the restroom. How did they do it? Cops sat at stakeouts for hours with binoculars pressed to their eyes and were always ready to start their engines and dash off after bad guys at a moment's notice. They never ran out of gas, never went to the bathroom, and always seemed to have food and supplies.

Leota watched too much television.

She squirmed in the seat and began to reconsider the reasons why she still sat parked opposite the Road House staring at its entrance. Darla's backpack hadn't been in the barn, so that meant she had flown away somewhere and she would be safe for awhile. Maybe she'd come back after LeBrun had been put away, this time for good. She picked up her camera from the seat beside her and shot another series of pictures. She caught the entrance and parked vehicles, making sure that the license plate on the car she thought was LeBrun's stood out in sharp focus. She would have a record of what she did, even if she wasn't sure anymore why she did it. Her camera had come in handy after all. Not for Darla as it had been intended, but for the record she started to compile of her time in Picketsville. No, she wasn't on the girl's trail now. Something else, something more primal drew her to this spot. She had a moment of clarity and realized what she really needed was a reckoning with LeBrun. She desperately needed to make things right, somehow. The past two decades had to count for something, for God's sake. She focused the camera again and ran off four more shots of the Road House—front door, second-floor windows, parking area, and a long shot of all three.

Chapter Forty-one

During her second night hiding in the church, Darla stripped off her clothes and washed them in the kitchen sink. It felt funny standing naked in the near dark. It wasn't that she'd never been like that in a public place before. She blotted out that memory. But this was a church, for God's sake. She sponged, dried off with sheets torn from a roll of paper towels, and put on the cassock she'd taken from the closet upstairs. It was much cooler for sleeping. She wished she could wash her hair but didn't dare soak it in the sink and run the risk of missing a sound or a light. Besides, she hadn't the heart to touch it since Grace Somebody styled and cut it at that beauty salon.

"Now doesn't that look better?" Grace had asked her at the time and spun the chair around so that she could see herself in the mirror. The salon seemed filled with mirrors. Darla never looked at herself if she could avoid it. "Honey, you're beautiful."

Was she? Ethyl the witch said she was ugly and that nobody'd ever want her for anything except for what was "down there."

"No, I'm not," she'd said.

"Not? Honey, well, you just look at yourself in the mirror. See? Let me put a dab of blush and a touch of lipstick—"

"No!"

No, not beautiful. She'd heaved herself out of the chair, stuffed the five- and ten-dollar bills in the woman's hand, and dashed out the door. Thank goodness the damned cop was gone. But… was she, maybe, okay-looking? Leota said that, too. People tell you shit like that all the time and then they screw you any way they can. She shook her head, finished toweling off, and went in search of hangers.

She found some in a closet and hung her wet things on them and placed them on the pipes that crisscrossed the ceiling of her lair. They should be dry by morning. She returned to the kitchen. As long as no one came into the church, she lingered in the kitchen enjoying the space and cooler air. Just enough ambient light filtered through the windows to allow her to move around without lighting a candle. Only if she needed to search for something specific, would she light a candle stub. As long as it didn't flicker, she felt sure it would be barely noticeable outside.

She rummaged through the larder and found enough to make a decent, albeit high in carbohydrates, dinner. She pulled up a chair and sat, her mind wandering a bit. It was a luxury to do so now. She tried to remember what it had been like before. She couldn't remember much about what life had been like before turning six, way too much since. There were a few years when things were, like, good and all. The picnics at the spring in the woods. The woods…that's where. She shuddered. That's where her mother lay now. How'd the bitch ever get there? Who should she thank for sending her to hell?

As she spooned creamed corn from its can, she thought that of all the places she'd lived over the seventeen years of her life, this might be the best. The thought made her laugh. The sound startled her. Darla never laughed. But the thought was too funny. She was living in a self-imposed prison cell, hiding all day and only coming out at night like a vampire or something, and eating food stolen from church people, and this was the best? Too funny.

She knew that Leota tried, but had no way of knowing how painful her tries at fixing her up had been. First showing her the pictures. "See, weren't these good times, weren't you happy there?" And then the other stuff. When you've had to go through what she'd been through, people saying stuff like "forget and move on" or "embrace the bright future" or "become an empowered woman" were like feeding cotton candy to a starving man—pretty, sweet, and would rot your teeth. Darla knew about rotten teeth. What kind of future could she have with this body wrecked by the armies of bastards who made her spread her legs and have sex with them—and worse? And, you can forget the part about finding a nice man, having a family. There were no nice men, only perverts and slimy bastards, and family was not something she had ever known or could have herself. Satisfying her mother's habit had taken care of that.

A flash of headlights outside sent her scurrying back into her bolt hole. As always, she left the door ajar. She would close it, but only if people headed toward the kitchen. Leaving it open let her hear a little of what they said. This time, no one came downstairs. That was a good thing because she'd left her half-eaten can of corn on the counter. She heard the organ groan to life and then singing. She liked singing. It would be nice, she thought, to sing in a choir like that. Those people had no idea how lucky they were. The music lasted an hour and a half and then doors slammed and all was quiet again. She slipped out and retrieved the can, finished it, and dropped it in the garbage. She closed the door and laid down on her improvised futon. Tomorrow, she thought before dropping off to sleep, tomorrow I will find something to read. There must be a magazine or a book around here somewhere.

She rolled on her back and stared at the pipes that held her drying clothes. They made an eerie pattern against the raw sub-flooring of the rooms above. She thought of all the times she'd spent staring at ceilings, disengaging her mind from what was happening to her body. That big pipe would probably support her weight. Maybe instead of a book, she'd look for some rope.

No, not beautiful. How could she be after all that?

"Of all the places you've lived, Ike, which would you say was the nicest?"

Ike and Ruth had taken refuge in the upstairs study of the president's house on the university campus. As the proverbial cat had been let out of the bag, his presence on the premises did not stir the controversy it once had. Some of the faculty still resented it but for a different reason now.

"Oh, I don't know. What qualifies as nice at one age becomes something else later on. I grew up here, mostly, except when my father held some office or another in the commonwealth. Then we lived in Richmond. But definitely here in Picketsville for those years. I liked Hartford and Boston as a student and there are a few places in Europe I could return to. I don't know. All things being considered and except for a blip a few years ago when it seemed everything went south, life has been good to me. Certainly good lately, murder and mayhem notwithstanding, so…here, I think"

"Was that a compliment? Never mind, I won't press my luck by asking. I posed the question because I can't get your missing girl out of my mind. What do you suppose the answer would be if I were to put the same question to her?"

"God knows. I can't imagine."

"Neither can I. Okay, here's another one for you. Consider carefully before you answer. If they find the girl and if she is still intact—"

"Intact?"

"Alive and more or less mentally stable, if she is ambulatory and sentient, I guess…I don't know, just work with me here. If she were, would you consider taking her in?"

"Wow, that came from way out in left field. You mean would we, the newly outed married couple whose behavior has already raised eyebrows across the county, would we further our reputation for outlandishness by adopting this parcel of very badly damaged goods?"

"I wouldn't have described it quite that way, but, yes, that is what I mean."

"Ah, well, there is no easy answer to that. However, for starters, I don't see us, at our present ages…*my* age, then…siring a clutch of children. As much as our parents lust after grandchildren, I suspect it is not in the cards for us, is it?"

Ruth shrugged. "There is no accounting for taste, my dear old Granny used to say. That old saw has nothing whatsoever to do with this situation exactly, but if she were here, that is what she would say. She would mean it as 'who knows what fate has in store for us?' Stranger things have happened and it is a peculiar world filled with unexpected twists and turns, but, no, you're right, little bundles of joy, the inevitable consequence of carefree lovemaking followed eventually by hours of labor pains, do not loom large on my horizon. Does that disappoint you?"

"No. But, on the other hand, if the stork were to accidently hit our chimney or the cabbage patch, should happen to produce one anyway, that would be grand, too."

"One of the things that makes you so lovable, if that word can be applied to a hick sheriff, is that you are easy, Schwartz. So, can you answer my question?"

"Sitting here in this amazingly comfortable den provided by the trustees and endowment funds of Callend University, it is not easy to imagine anything I would want to add to my already complicated life."

"That's a no?"

"Wait. That said, there are times when people need to step up. That girl, should she turn up and, in fact, be eligible for the move you suggest, will have nothing to look forward to except at best a series of foster homes or group homes. Any one of which would be only a marginally safer situation than the one she grew up in. My guess, she'd be on the run again within six months. If we took her in, there would be a slightly better chance she could assemble a life approaching normal."

"Then it's a yes?"

"As long as you understand that as a meth baby she might have some permanent brain damage. Perhaps not, but in any case she will need years of therapy. Also it is likely that she may not trust us, me certainly, for a long, long time if ever. In the end even our best efforts may end with her running away, having a psychotic break, or attempting and possibly succeeding at committing suicide. If you are okay with that, then it is a yes."

"Who do we talk to?"

"You are ahead of yourself. First, we find her, then I get on the phone, my father calls in some favors, and we'll see. But first, we have to find the girl."

"And you have your people looking."

"I do and, unfortunately, I am afraid so do others."

Chapter Forty-two

The office had returned to normal, at least a semblance of normal. Essie was back at her desk. Her brother-in-law Danny sat in a chair in the corner, his eyes trained on the door and a .50 caliber, definitely-not-government-issue Desert Eagle with a ten-inch barrel, in his lap. Ike knew Danny had a permit so he said nothing about the weapon he considered more appropriate for an artillery unit than a Navy SEAL. But his was not to reason why. Danny had also let his facial hair grow out—not quite a beard, more like a souvenir of a three-day binge. Ike didn't know if the whiskers related to his being on a vacation and not on duty, or had become the trademark of the SEALs, or intended as a fashion statement. If the last, he'd failed. To be considered high fashion, a celebrity two-day-old stubble required its owner to be wearing at least a thousand-dollar suit or one that could pass for a cool thou. Less than that and you were just another bum. He smiled a greeting at the second-oldest Sutherlin, beard, cannon, and all, and moved on. If Danny's presence made Essie feel safe, so much the better. Having him babysit her meant, first, Ike didn't have to assign one of his own people to the duty, and second, he had Essie back at her dispatch desk.

He allowed the K-Cup machine to do its angry crocodile sounds and spit out a fresh cup of coffee and headed toward his office. Too many bodies, too few killers in custody, and the missing girl, Darla Smut or Dellinger, still on the loose. Since his conversation about the girl's possible future with Ruth, the last situation preyed on his mind a bit more than the others. He couldn't say why he believed it, but he felt certain she had not gone very far, that she had holed up somewhere nearby. But where?

Essie shouted across the outer office, "Okay, Ike, come clean. What does 'The Blessing of a Civil Marriage' mean?"

"It means that you and all the gang, friends, family, in-laws, outlaws, are invited to the church for a ceremony and then some eats and then finally to stop bugging me about the *when*."

"It's a wedding?"

"Close enough."

"What's that mean, 'close enough'? Is it or ain't it?"

"Yes."

"Billy's Ma said they had enough food to feed the Chinese Army."

"They weren't invited."

"So Monday is the big day."

"Big, yes. Danny, nice piece. Essie, face front and answer the phone."

"It ain't rung…shoot, there you go again. Picketsville Sheriff's Office. Go ahead."

Ike went into his office. The tidy elves had not come during the night and the same piles of papers and reports that covered every inch of his desk had not moved. Still no write-up from Feldman about the call to the church. He punched the call button on his intercom.

"Essie, where's Jack Feldman?"

"He did a double and is off today."

"Find him and tell him I want to talk to him now."

Ike returned to the stacks on the desk. Once a month, he would sort through the mess, rearrange it, dispose of most of it, and start the process of rebuilding the height and breadth of the stacks again. He felt pretty sure that there were no clues in the current piles to the murders of Smut, Dellinger, or Barbarini. The last would be the FBI's problem anyway. When he'd thought about it a while, the suggestion he'd made to Karl about seeking a connection to the dead man and New York had merit. The dead guy did not take a bus to Picketsville and bury himself. Someone went to a great deal of trouble to plant the New York hood in this particular backyard. Why?

"I've got Jack on the line. You want me to put him through?" Essie had mastered the intercom about the same time as Ike, and the office benefitted from it. Until the previous spring, yelling at one another across the thirty feet between their desks had been the rule. Things were quieter now.

"I'll talk to him." Ike waited until the proper buttons were pushed in the correct sequence.

"Sheriff?"

"Feldman, you were sent on a call to the Episcopal church a couple of nights ago. This is Saturday, where is your paperwork?"

"There wasn't nothing there, Ike, just another phony call. That preacher is a little flighty, you know. Hell, all them Holy Joes are."

"Blake Fisher is a lot of things, Feldman, but flighty isn't one of them. The fact there wasn't anything happening does not mean you don't write it up. Paperwork is a pain but we do it anyway. I want the report from your watch on my desk tomorrow morning."

Ike hung up rather than wait for a reply. Feldman had the distinction of being his worst deputy and sat high and alone on the top of his list to be fired if downsizing were to be mandated. The mayor kept threatening to cut Ike's budget citing fiscal hard times as his reason. Ike suspected his motive had more to do with the fact that Ike had caught him on the thin edge of ethical impropriety a few times and he was back at work searching for a much more accessible and pliable sheriff to run against Ike.

Ike turned his attention away from the mountains of paper on his desk and considered his next move. What if the girl had lingered in the area as he suspected? Surely LeBrun or his people would be looking for her by now. He sat upright. Crap, it could be, if the history was right. One of the men working for LeBrun could very well be Feldman. He should put him on some other duties, something away from the office, away from information. Send him out of town for a seminar on customer relations. Lord knows, if Blake Fisher had it right, Feldman could use the training. Or should he put a tail on Jack and see where he led them? Hell of a way to run a department, he thought, when you have to shield victims from the people who're supposed to protect them.

George LeBrun had a room at the Road House, he'd been told. Did Feldman frequent it? That Leota woman had staked out the place. That couldn't be good. Librarians were good at surveillance in the stacks, shushing loud whisperers, and apprehending booknabbers, but staked out at a biker bar and watching a known killer? Lord love us.

Ike stretched and put his feet up. Think. Okay, if LeBrun stayed true to form, by now he should be well on his way down the rat hole of meth addiction. If that's true, I could pick him up and put him back in jail for breach of his release agreement. Then half, maybe more than half, of my problems go away. If I knew that, if I could prove that…

"Danny," he shouted, "I need a minute of your time. Essie, Charley Picket will ride shotgun for a while."

Charley and Danny traded places.

"Yes, Sheriff?" Danny was raised polite and the Navy kept him that way.

"You look like hell."

"Sir?"

"No, no, it's a good thing. Listen, I know you can't hang around Picketsville forever being Essie's shadow. You could be called back to duty any minute, or you will run out of leave time, or something else. We need to free you up."

"I don't mind watching over Billy's wife, Sheriff."

"I'm sure you don't, but I do. So, how long has it been since you spent any time in town?"

"Except for short visits, ten years, maybe more."

"You ever move with the crowd that hangs out at Alex's Road House?"

"The guys I knew growing up who moved in that direction are all dead or in jail."

"Okay, then, here's what I think will solve Essie's problem, free you up for something more enjoyable than guard duty—"

"But I'm okay with guard duty."

"Of course you are. Good to hear it, but I have a bigger problem to solve and Charley and Billy can protect Essie just fine. So here's what I'd like you to do. I need a man inside that bar. This is a small town. There is no one on my staff who isn't known, but you've been out of circulation long enough so they won't know you and, as I said, with that beard you look like one of the barflies that hang out there."

"They'll spot me for a stranger, though."

"I have that covered. I have access to a Peterbuilt tractor. You will bob-tail it to the Road House and make yourself at home. Say you're waiting for a call from your dispatcher to hook up a flatbed. Once you settle in, let on that you might be in the market for some drugs, you know, crack, meth, weed, whatever. That will get the right kind of attention. Then keep an eye on George LeBrun. I am almost certain he's using again. If he is, call me and we'll bust him. He goes back into the slammer and ends your bodyguard duty."

"You think I can do that?"

"I think that you have done a lot more dangerous things than this as a SEAL. If you're up for it, I'll deputize you and we're in business."

Chapter Forty-three

The big truck rumbled up to Alex's Road House, black diesel exhaust spewing from its dual stacks, and country music blaring from the cab. Leota took a picture of it. The music stopped suddenly and a bearded man, by the look of him one of LeBrun's thug friends, dismounted and entered the bar. One more reason to stay out of the place. She realized that decades spent in the safe harbor of library science had insulated her from a society that had changed rapidly over the years. But, she reasoned, how would she ever get at LeBrun if she didn't find a way in? She needed a plan but could think of nothing more to do than to keep on doing what she'd been doing for the last three days—sitting, waiting, and taking useless pictures. She had nearly lost track of the days and hours. It might have been four days, come to think of it. It would, if you counted the first few hours. Perhaps it wasn't just the days. She might be losing her mind as well. If anyone she knew had been keeping tabs on her they would say she was. Ten minutes passed and the truck driver came out and walked around his rig. Those big rigs look ridiculous without a trailer attached, she thought, kind of like a man with his pants down. Not that she had a lot of experience in that department.

The man seemed to be checking the truck—they called it a tractor, she remembered—and reached inside the cab to retrieve something or another. Then he made a call on his cell phone. He nodded and went back into the bar. Leota settled back, took a sip of water, a small one. She had learned her lesson about over-hydrating while sitting in a stakeout.

The bartender nodded noncommittally at Danny's request to be fixed up with someone who could sell him some "painkillers." He leaned forward on the bar and nursed his drink. The Desert Eagle had been too much weapon to tuck into a waistband and he had returned to the truck and swapped it out for a snub-nosed police special. It did not have the stopping power of the cannon, but at close range, a .38 caliber bullet correctly placed would do the same job. He hoped it wouldn't come to that. On the other hand, no one in the joint knew who the hell he was. Why not just plug LeBrun, wipe the truck, dump the piece in the lake, and tell Ike he changed his mind about playing cop? A quick shave and he would be in the clear. If he understood what Ike told him, killing LeBrun meant Essie would be safe and several local problems would be solved at the same time. Ike would guess what he'd done but would not or could not pursue it, not if he wiped the gun and truck clean.

He put the thought aside, but left it open as an option.

A few minutes later, the man in question himself came down from upstairs somewhere. The bartender, who apparently owned the place, asked him about a girl, Cherise or something that sounded like that. LeBrun scowled and said he hadn't seen her and didn't know anything more about her and Alex should stop bugging him about her. The bartender looked as if he wanted to press the point and then he must have read something in LeBrun's face and walked away. A second man joined LeBrun and they ordered a beer each. The new guy looked familiar. Too familiar. Local, for sure, but Danny couldn't quite place him. Someone he'd seen around lately. It would be important to identify the guy. He tried but came up empty. To make sure his cover wasn't blown, he pivoted his barstool away from the two men and stared at the wall with its posters of naked women and accompanying graffiti commentary.

The position made it difficult to hear what the two men were talking about. He closed his eyes and went into SEAL mode. Listening for sounds, alerts, and potential danger were all part of his training and it had saved his ass more than once. He kept his hand on the butt of the pistol under his shirttail.

It would be hours before he had anything useful to report to Ike. In fact it would not be until late the following night that he heard one sentence, but it would be all he needed.

◇◇◇

The afternoon wound down. The three-to-eleven shift came, checked in, and went. Ike fretted. Saturday nights always got busy. Weekends, if normal, could interfere with his search for Darla and his plans for LeBrun. He'd had the call from Danny earlier. He'd settled in the bar and not been recognized. So far, so good, but no news about LeBrun's drug use or anything else useful. All Ike could do was wait. He did not like waiting, not anymore. In his other life, as he sometimes referred to it, he'd once spent three days in an irrigation trench up to his knees in water, a cold, beating rain soaking his clothes, to get a single photograph of an armored vehicle carrying a man in uniform. He did not know who the man was or why Langley wanted his picture. But he shot it, left the ditch, and spent a week on antibiotics fighting double pneumonia. But back then patient waiting defined the job. Now he had a teenaged girl on the loose, and who knew how many men hot on her trail who would kill her without batting an eyelash. One of those men, George LeBrun, through a glitch in the legal system and expensive legal counsel, now sat free as a bird in Alex's Road House instead of serving out a life-plus term for murder. Ike loved the legal system. He had graduated from law school. He knew why LeBrun sipped cold beer on the outside at the moment. He didn't like it, but he understood it. On the other hand, he intended to see to it that the scuzzball's vacation from the penitentiary ended soon and permanently. He thought of Danny sitting within shooting distance of the town's worst nightmare with a loaded gun in his waistband. Would he be tempted to solve one pressing problem and free up Essie on his own? Had Ike subconsciously set up that scenario? Was this another one of those Freudian things? Should Ike worry about that? He decided he wouldn't. There were Ike rules and there were other people's rules. Shit happens.

He pulled up to the parking area next to the Administration Building the same time as a delivery van pulled out. Café Michael, known by readers of *Southern Living Magazine* as one of Lexington's luxury restaurants, had been painted in discreet lettering on the van door. Thank God the food had not come from Frank's Catering. Good food and maybe a bottle of decent wine, and the evening might not be a complete bust after all.

"I hope the box contains the brown trout or seafood Provençal," he said to Ruth when he'd made it through a security check at the main door.

"One of each. We'll share. I also found a decent white in my cooler and there is coffee later. I can't vouch for that, however. Agnes made a fresh pot, but it's been awhile."

"Serve it up and then tell me why we are here in the office planning our almost nuptials and not over at your house."

"Several reasons. In the first place, the house is too easy."

"Pardon?"

"I know you, Schwartz. You would eat the food and before I could say 'guest list,' you'd have us in the bedroom composing sheet music."

"You're easy, Harris, but not that easy. Come on, what's the real reason?"

"Okay, you're right, I'm not that easy. But today, with what's going on at your end—you know, the girl and all—and my current stress level, I think I might be the one calling the tune, if you follow, and when it comes to that area, you really are easy. I need to protect me from me."

"We could lock the door—"

"Forget it. Now, talk to me, Sheriff. My mother says she's been in contact with Mrs. Sutherlin and the arrangements for the…I guess we call it the reception…are all laid on. She said she thought the woman was a little odd."

"Dorothy Sutherlin is about as normal as they come in this town. Your mother is the odd one."

"Hey—"

"Come on, Ruth, she calls herself Eden Saint Claire. Her name is Paula Harris and she is steeped in the process of not-writing a book about academe in the mode of Grace Metalious. Who's the odd one in this picture?"

"Point of view, Schwartz, point of view. The truth is that Picketsville is a hotbed of oddness and you and I walking down the aisle on Monday afternoon may qualify as the icing on the cake of weirdness, to mix a metaphor, if that is what I just did."

"Something to do with parallelism, I think. So which of these two dishes shall we start with?"

"I'm thinking about taking your suggestion and locking the door after all. Which do you prefer, the desk or the floor?"

"The trout, Madam President. First things first. Seafood is garbage if eaten cold and congealed. Then, I think, after the Provençal, some wine, and communal nuzzling, I would prefer the carpet to risking being stabbed by paper clips and ballpoint pens. Or we could just go home."

"Good thinking. So, as Frank, our local ptomaine purveyor, would say, 'bone appatit.'"

Chapter Forty-four

A door slamming woke Ike. He was alone. Ruth had bounced out of bed at five-thirty, showered, had her breakfast, and left for the office by six-fifteen. What important things did she have to do that called her out so early on a Sunday morning? Ike sighed. Too much time had passed and a public commitment had been made. There could be no turning back now. They would share a life together. It had *final* written all over it. But, how long could an extreme "morning person" and a confirmed "night person" expect to stay married? Opposites attract, they say, but two people operating on diametrically opposed diurnal cycles did not bode well for the future of either. Ike pondered this…for him at seven in the morning, a deep philosophical question… then grunted and dozed off again. He would be late getting to the office, but it had been a long and somewhat athletic night and he wasn't as young as he used to be. It was Sunday after all, a day he normally took off.

He did manage to get to the Cross Roads Diner by nine for his pre-ordered breakfast and obligatory sour look from Flora.

"What are you doing in town on a Sunday? You usually hide out on us, lately."

"Busy looking for you goddaughter, if you must know."

Today Flora seemed more out of sorts than usual. The girl and Flora's unacknowledged but very real sense of guilt expressing itself, he thought. Good. She should feel guilty. Most of the problems created by Darla Smut's disappearance stemmed from Flora's suspicious and stubborn nature.

"Before you ask, no news, but I am feeling a little more confident about finding the girl, Flora."

"Why is that?"

"Well, in the first place, consider the possibilities. One, she is on the road and far, far away and presumably safe for now. Second, she is still in the area and if so we will find her and bring her in. I believe the latter."

"Why is that? Did someone see her around town?"

"Why? I can't say, for sure, but there is something about this business that doesn't quite work for me. Because of that, I am taking a different approach and that leads me to believe we have a chance at a good outcome." Ike didn't know if he said that because he believed it or simply to make Flora happy.

"What in the devil did you just say?"

"I said, be of good cheer, I think it is going to be all right. By the way, if the girl does surface—"

"If? You just said—"

"Okay, when the girl surfaces, Flora, when she does, where should she go next? Living with your cousin Leota didn't work out so well. Are you and Arlene planning on taking her in? She's in her teens and she has more baggage than Federal Express. Are you two up to handling that?"

"We will, if that's what's needed. We ain't young no more, that's for sure, but to keep that girl safe, we will do what we can."

"I see. Well, perhaps there will be other options."

"Maybe. Say, how come you didn't ask me to provide eats for your big do tomorrow?"

"Scrambled eggs, grits and gravy, and pancakes just won't cut it. It's a wedding reception, not a prayer breakfast."

"I could do other things."

"Talk to Dorothy Sutherlin. She's in charge."

"Who put that woman in charge?"

"I did. I have to go. Remember, if the girl surfaces, you get her to us somehow."

The sheriff's office occupied space in the Town Hall a half-block north. Ike made it in less than five minutes including a nod and a wave to the few merchants who were open for business along the way. Lee Henry stopped him briefly to say that she thought someone had spent Wednesday night sleeping behind her dumpster.

"You're not open on Sundays now, are you?"

"Just doing some bookkeeping before I head out to church."

Ike tucked away her notion that someone had slept in the alley. It could be important. He just didn't know how at the moment. Karl waited for him in his office.

"The news is not good, I take it."

"Not bad, actually. Not flaming good either, but it could be worse."

'You've lost me."

"Sam and the other Sutherlins are off to church and I decided to use the time to do some thinking. So, while the Bureau futzes around deciding how to deal with the embarrassment of Anthony Barbarini's body turning up here instead of in the Atlantic, I started to look into a New York–Picketsville connection, as ridiculous as that sounds. Hey, it was your idea, don't forget. I didn't get much, but I may have something. It's pretty thin, but with thin, you never know where it will lead."

"What did you find?"

"Did you know that the local BAB's father once ran a butcher business in Buena Vista?"

"Karl, I have no idea what you are talking about. What's a BAB?"

"Bad assed bastard, and in this instance, your own George LeBrun. His father, Henry LeBrun, had a specialty butcher business. He imported and exported meats and so on. Some of his customers were, briefly, restaurants in the New York area, Italian mostly, but not exclusively. Then something went south and the father disappeared. Retirement was the word on the street but nobody knows for sure. Georgie ran the business for a short while before joining your predecessor as a deputy and before his love affair with high octane cough medicine took over his life."

"This is fascinating, Karl, but I am not seeing a connection."

"The meat, Ike, meat processed and otherwise, transported in refrigerated trucks up and down the east coast. So, here's a hypothetical question for you. Suppose you had a body you wished to get rid of and your snitch inside the NYPD tells you that the FBI is watching the docks and local landfills because too many minor league mobsters and associated hoods—"

"BABs"

"Yes, too many of them are washing ashore on Fire Island and turning up in garbage bags, what might you do?"

"Had George taken over the business by then?'

"Theoretically, yes."

"Ah, ha. So we consider the very real possibility that the trucks had an alternative return cargo at least once. That begs the next question."

"Which is?"

"Are there any more dead gangsters' planted around here? The thing about this quiet, peaceful…one might even say idyllic… place is that the woods around here are vast and the traffic through them sparse."

"There may be dozens."

"Or none. And in either case, what are the chances we will find them? We can expect only so much from Andy Lieux's dog."

"I am due to talk to the director's guy about the possibility of heading up a special team tasked with finding that out."

"Are you interested?'

"I don't know. It would keep me in the bureau. After a few months, things could blow over. I don't know, maybe. Sam heard you have an opening in this office. Is that true?"

"It is. Her old spot is vacant and…" Ike glanced at his desk and saw no follow-up paperwork from Feldman. "There is a very real chance there will be another deputy's slot open as well. Can I tempt you?"

"Two slots?"

"Possibly, but before you decide, there is something you should know. I had the intern track down that phone number—the one you gave up on, by the way. Then I had him trace the ID of the tailor who made the dead guy's suit."

"You can do that?"

"You know I can, so could the Bureau, if they wanted to."

"And?"

"He made a list of people who had the number at one time or another. It was not as long as you might think. One of them turned out to be the witness who fingered Barbarini and Murphy. He's dead, of course, but the connection is there. The tailor who made the suit retired but his book is still open and the purchaser was Anthony Barbarini."

"Okay, so you confirmed what we already knew."

"Operative word *you*, that is, I confirmed. You didn't, I did. You see?"

"I'm missing something aren't I?"

"And you call yourself an investigator. Okay, once I had those bits and the ME's dental record report, I dashed off a note to the FBI. I said that it was my understanding that Special Agent Karl Hedrick, was in the area and if they wish us to cooperate with him, I needed to be read into his mission. Then I said that we, that is…"

"You."

"No, the sheriff's office in Picketsville, Virginia, had positively identified a corpse found in our woods as one Anthony Barbarini and that we thought they ought to know because he was reported to be one of their cases some years back."

"You did that?"

"I did. As of now, you are off the hook. Some hick sheriff down in the boonies just pulled the desk chairs out from under some FBI asses."

"My career is not up in smoke."

"Nope. How do you feel about your career prospects?"

"I should say 'pretty good' but here's the funny thing, Ike. I have dreamed about being an FBI agent forever. I've said it a hundred times and I meant it every time I said it. This last run-in has made me wonder. I mean, my career might have ended because someone else's was deemed more important, or because I wouldn't 'take one for the team,' or God only knows what, you see? Right now, I don't know how I feel about it anymore."

"Take your time and think it through."

"I will say this, if it were up to Sam, we'd move back here."

"Happy thought. Now, help me with another problem. My instinct says the girl we are looking for is still local. Any chance we have of solving her mother's murder hinges, I think, on finding her. If we have her in custody, she will tell us something we need to know to get this one off the books. Failing that, the fact we have her could open the proverbial can of worms which would lead us to the killer and, coincidently, a bunch of other men who need to explain to a judge why pedophilia is a necessary part of their lifestyle."

"How can I possibly help?"

"Two brains are always better than one. Assume you are the girl and on the run but the roads are full of cops with BOLOs. What do you do?"

"How well do I know the area?"

"Fair. The people hardly at all and many of the ones you do know are a threat to you at one level or another."

"Does she trust anyone? I assume the threat you speak of means she can't trust too many locals."

"Including the police, us, as it turns out."

"It's a dead end, unless you can identify someone who doesn't fit that mold. Was she a church person? Of course that doesn't guarantee much in the trust department anymore either, does it?'"

"No, but maybe. She talked to Fisher."

Sometime later that night, Ike Schwartz, sheriff of Picketsville, and George LeBrun, the local BAB in question, came to the same conclusion. Separated by some five miles and a chasm of moral rectitude or lack thereof, they blurted to anyone in their immediate vicinity, "I know where she is."

Then Ike received a phone call that confirmed it.

Chapter Forty-five

George LeBrun searched the length of the bar. Only two drinkers stood at the rail: the trucker who hadn't yet heard about his next load and said he wanted to score some crank, and Jocko Fishbein, the old fireman whose wife left him ten years back and who, after a decade of trying, had yet to find the bottom of his bottle of sour mash.

When Feldman walked in, LeBrun motioned to him to follow him outside. Feldman did not look happy. The trucker patted his pockets, looked around, and left after them. He told the barman he needed his smokes. The barman said nothing, but he was pretty sure he had never seen a cigarette in the guy's mouth in the days he'd been hanging around.

Jack Feldman seemed jumpy when he and LeBrun reached the parking lot.

"George, I'm not sure this is a good idea. Schwartz has patrols sliding by here ever since you set yourself up in the place. Besides, it isn't smart for me to be seen with you."

"Shut up and listen to me. Just so you know what's at stake here, Jackie-boy, I figured out where the Smut girl is. You and me are going to that church where you took the B-and-E call and grab her before that Jew sheriff figures it out on his own. You understand what I'm saying here? If he finds her first and she blabs, you're dead meat, Jackie. You'd better just dump any ideas about not being seen with me. I need your help and you need my protection."

LeBrun spun and took in the trucker lurking by his rig. "What the hell are you looking at?" The trucker shrugged, pulled something from the truck's glove box and left.

"You think he heard?"

"That stoner? Heard what? He don't know nothing. We go for the girl."

"Okay, but, what are you going to do when you get her?" Feldman could guess, but couldn't resist asking anyway.

"Well, she should be pretty fresh now, seeing as how she's been out of circulation for a while. We'll have some fun and when we're done, she goes away."

"Goes away?"

"You know, she joins her old lady wherever her kind goes when they die. Skank heaven, probably." George snickered at is joke. "Good one, huh? Skank heaven."

"Yeah, good one. You mean kill her?"

"Jesus, Feldman, Are you that stupid?"

"I'm not too sure about—"

"When did you get to be a pussy? If she lives and talks to the cops, you'll wish you were dead. Do you know what the guys in the slammer do to baby rapers?"

Feldman considered his options. He lit a cigarette to buy some time while he thought them through. "How'd you find out where the girl was at?"

"You told me. You and Frankie Chimes."

"Me?"

"Yeah. You were called to that church, right? And you didn't find nothing. You didn't because the little bitch knows how to hide. Don't you remember how she'd squeeze into crawl spaces to get away from doing her duty back before she disappeared? Her Ma used to drag her out by the hair and beat her ass until she rolled over. Helluva sight."

"Yeah, I guess so. So, you think she's in that church? What did Frankie say?"

"He didn't say nothing. His sister-in-law, what's-her-name, did. She does stuff in that church, cleaning and like that, and she heard the sheriff and some old bat talking about things being missing, food and all, and I did the math, see? The kid is holed up in the church somewhere. All we got to do is go there and you walk me through where you went that night and try to remember anything that looked off, you know, out of place?"

"I don't know, George. I mean, what're the chances somebody would miss a kid hiding out there?"

"Sometimes Feldman, I think you're an idiot. Now saddle up, we're going."

"Okay, okay, so, how about I follow you in the cruiser? That way if the preacher or somebody butts in, I'll say something like it's okay and you're with me or, you know, cover you."

"I guess you're not always an idiot."

The two men started their vehicles and pulled out onto the road, headed to Stonewall Jackson Memorial Episcopal Church.

Leota didn't know whether LeBrun knew he was being followed or not. She'd been watching the Road House for days. A normal person would wonder why she'd kept it up for so long. Well, she had and now at nearly midnight something seemed to be happening. If the opportunity to confront the object of her obsession presented itself, what else could she do? She knew that Mark had been killed and LeBrun had something to do with it. She knew that the girl had fled from a hell created for her by her mother and LeBrun had something to do with that, too. She knew the girl's mother had been killed but because LeBrun had still been in jail at the time, he had nothing to do with that, or had he? Cause and effect is not always easy to sort out. One could argue that the events that took Ethyl Smut to the woods that afternoon had their genesis in LeBrun's polluting effect on those close to him. People like Mark Dellinger, for example, who might have been a good man if he hadn't met George LeBrun, if he hadn't met Ethyl, if he hadn't...but he had and it did happen.

She had started her engine with the intention of giving up for the night when LeBrun appeared and drove off. What she couldn't understand was why a sheriff's car followed LeBrun as well. She'd seen the two men talking but that didn't make any sense. Why would a deputy sheriff be mixed up with LeBrun?

They headed toward town, Leota laying back thirty yards or so with her headlights off. She soon discovered that driving in the dark without them can be tricky. She'd seen it done on television shows and it looked easy. But even staying reasonably close and benefiting from the headlights of the car ahead of her didn't keep her off the shoulder and once she nearly put the truck in a ditch. She did, in fact, clip a culvert and a mailbox and for an anxious moment, she thought she'd been spotted. But LeBrun and his police escort didn't pause. She righted the truck and kept on his tail.

LeBrun turned into the parking lot of an old church. What brought him to this place? She pulled over onto the road's edge and waited as the two men stepped out of their vehicles, circled the building, and disappeared inside. Ten minutes passed. Twenty. Leota had kept the motor running. In horror she saw her fuel gauge slide to empty. If she didn't get to a gas station and soon, she'd have to walk back to her motel and she'd not be able to follow LeBrun when he left. Something stirred at one corner of the church.

LeBrun appeared in his headlights dragging the girl out of the building by an arm. How had LeBrun found her? Everyone thought she'd left town, yet here she was being dragged across the parking lot wearing some sort of black dressing gown. The top buttons had been lost or undone somehow. Funny how you notice things like that. Darla did not scream or even resist. Leota didn't understand that. No screaming, no resistance? She knew that if she were dragged along like that, she'd be kicking and yelling her head off. What was wrong with this picture? Maybe the presence of the deputy had something to do with it. Still, cop or no cop, she'd should be kicking and fighting and calling for help. But Darla stumbled along as if resigned to her fate.

Then it came to her in a flash. Leota understood, finally understood why Darla had never taken to the pictures, had never responded to her assurances of a better life in her future.

All those years of abuse. Of course, Darla believed her old life was the norm for her, an expectation, that the few years out of her mother's sick and twisted orbit had been a promise that could never be kept. She had been drawn back into the only life she knew and had resigned herself to it. She believed that resistance would be futile. That no one would care or intervene. Why should they? No one ever had before.

This revelation hit Leota like a dousing in arctic water. She took all of it in, thought of what she'd tried to do to spare the child, all she'd attempted and how she'd utterly failed. All those hours spent trying to paint a bright future for the girl, hoping, praying for her and it had fallen on ears made deaf by a life of pain and humiliation. The sight of George LeBrun yanking her along by the arm was too much for her. In that blinding moment, Leota snapped and in the next, made up her mind to fix things once and for all.

Without weighing the consequences, she dropped the truck in gear, stamped down hard on the accelerator, and headed straight toward the two figures. The truck's tires kicked gravel and the engine racketed to a roar. Darla looked up and saw the vehicle break into the light and bear down on her. LeBrun, riding a methamphetamine-fortified notion of immortality, ignored it. Darla's mouth formed into a perfect O and at the last second, yanked free from her captor leaving him grasping the empty cassock sleeve. LeBrun turned and would have grabbed for her again except the Ford 150 slammed into him at a speed sufficient to send him sailing into the trunk of an old, and some say historic, oak tree. Leota did not brake. She kept her foot pressed down on the accelerator and the truck followed George into the tree as well. Leota's last thought was, even if it were remotely possible for him to survive, in the end, there was no way George LeBrun would recover from his injuries to stand trial. The result was not pretty but for Leota, it was redemption.

Jack Feldman stood frozen as he watched the truck and George fuse with the tree. He still had not moved moments later when Ike and three more cars skidded on the gravel and came to a halt and discharged deputy sheriffs. Flashing blue and red lights, the steam from the truck's crushed radiator turned the parking lot into a surreal moonscape. Ike had Billy cuff Feldman and read him his rights.

"Wait, what's this for?" Feldman said.

"Aiding and abetting, for starters."

"You got this all wrong, Sutherlin. Look, I saw LeBrun leave the Road House, Okay? And I heard him talking to some guys—"

"What guys?"

"What? Like, I don't know. Just some barflies. There was this truck driver there. Maybe it was him. So, I hear him talking about finding the girl and we're looking for her too, right? So, even though I'm off duty, I say to myself, 'Jack you should follow him.' So, I come out here and I am ready to make the collar when that crazy woman drives in here about a hundred miles an hour and—"

"Shut up, Jack. The only reason you were here was to help him grab the girl. You know that and we know that. You are toast and about time, too. If you were acting like a cop instead of LeBrun's errand boy, you'd have called it in. But since someone else did, here we are throwing the net over the last of the goons who used to screw this town over."

"No, that's not right, I would'a called but—"

"Jack, we had someone in the Road House for a day and a half. We knew what you were doing. How do you think we got here so fast? That truck driver you saw? He's my brother Danny. He called it in, not you, you dirtbag. No, you're done. And think about this while your sorry ass rots in the slammer. The girl will recognize you from back in the day when you and your buddies, including Georgie over there, helped to destroy her. She's going to talk, Jack, and you and everyone else who was a part of that operation is going down. As I said, you, are toast, buddy, now get in the car."

Chapter Forty-six

A small crowd formed, muttering and gossiping outside the yellow crime scene tape. At first blush, the news that George LeBrun had been killed by a runaway truck made no sense, but as they all agreed that the news was all to the good. Most decided they didn't care how he'd met his end, only glad that he had. Ike turned Darla over to Blake and Mary Fisher temporarily, although it probably didn't meet Child Protective Services' protocols and he called Flora to tell her that her goddaughter had been found and was safe.

Billy put Feldman in the backseat of Charley Picket's cruiser and banged on the roof. Charley would take him in, book him, and let him cool off in jail. Whether or not Feldman would receive an appropriately long sentence or only a few years for aiding and abetting, one thing was abundantly clear: the likelihood that an ex-cop and child molester would survive more than a few months in jail was problematic. There is a code among inmates that requires that the judicial system's fuzzy decisions involving leniency in those areas be adjusted to a more stringent standard, particularly for ex-law enforcement officers who happened to stray. Feldman, as Billy predicted, was toast.

One of the EMTs sent to the crash handed Ike an envelope. "We found this on the front seat of the woman's truck."

"You should not have touched it, son. This is a crime scene."

"Sorry, Sheriff, but the chief was afraid the vehicle was about to blow. I don't think there are any other fingerprints on it but mine and they are on file."

"Did the woman say anything before she died?"

"No, sir."

Ike donned the obligatory latex gloves, which he hated and which now seemed superfluous, and pulled out a three-page letter. Leota Blevins had left a message. He scanned the neat librarian handwriting and then read it through.

To whoever finds this, please forward it to the proper authorities.

Where to begin? My life, it seems, has spun out of control. I didn't mean it to. I always thought of myself as a steady, rational person, at least lately, but events from the past caught up with me. Anyway, I write this hoping that no one will ever have to read it. But since I can't be sure how this mad journey will end and since Darla will need answers, should I fail, I feel I should at least write a synopsis of what I did and why I did it.

Like so many tragedies, it began innocently enough. I met with the caseworker overseeing Darla. I tried to explain to her how difficult it was to communicate with the child. That she seemed so withdrawn. The caseworker suggested I try what she called "photo therapy." I was to elicit from Darla if there were any times in her past when she felt happy, or content—positive even. Once I knew that, I was to go to the places where those events took place and photograph them. I should then assemble an album and show them to the girl. Over time, the caseworker said, this would help her remember, not just the events, but how she felt. The theory, she said, was that emotions like joy and happiness, if suppressed over a long time, are often difficult to release and that Darla needed to practice them. I don't know if I believed the woman or not, but I thought it was worth a try.

I see that I am rambling here. So sorry.

I drove to the various areas where Darla had lived and begin taking pictures. Outside Picketsville, for example, there is an old barn where she used to play hide and seek and a picnic area where she and her mother went often. That would be when she was very young but she did remember the place especially. I had just finished photographing it and planning my trip to Luray and the caverns when Ethyl Smut staggered through the woods. She didn't see me at first and it appeared she'd been hurt.

I need to back up. Before she appeared I heard a great deal of shouting and car doors slamming. I did not recognize the male voice at the time but now I know it must have been Mark Dellinger.

Ethyl knelt at the spring and washed what looked like blood from her side or somewhere, I couldn't be sure. Then she saw me. I confess that what happened next is a blur. We had words. Words about what she'd done to her daughter—the sheer awfulness of it. And Mark's name came up, too. If you understand the expression 'seeing red,' you will understand what happened next. I lost my temper; she came at me in what I assume must have been a drug-enhanced rage. I tried to fend her off but she would have none of it. Finally, I picked up a stick I found at my feet and hit her on the head. Somehow I must have hit her in the one place that would be fatal. I read about those blows—a whack on the temple, leaving hardly any mark, but inevitably fatal.

I would like to think what I did was self-defense, but given the circumstances of our rivalry over Mark, I doubt a jury would agree. That thought was in my mind when I decided that the world would be a better place without her anyway, that no one would mourn or miss her, that doing anything other than removing her from this earth made no real sense. There was a shallow depression nearby and I scraped out enough dirt to fashion a grave and I buried her.

I thought I was done. I brought Darla back to the place a week or so later to see her mother's grave. I don't know if that

*was a good thing to do psychologically, but I thought closure
was more important for her than the possible trauma the visit
might create. She seemed relieved and asked if she could stay in
town and visit her godmother for a while. She said she knew
the way to her godmother's place and to just drop her off at
the corner where the Cross Roads Diner was located. I did not
get along with Flora so I let her go and drove back to Virginia
Beach. Later, I discovered that George LeBrun had been
released from prison and Darla might be in danger as he was
one of the (many) men who had sexually abused her as a child.*

*After that, things careened off the tracks, you could say.
I heard from Mark D. and he was telling me that he'd had
a set-to with Ethyl and it had been he who had taken her
to the woods that day and that earlier he'd accosted LeBrun
about what he and his cronies had done to his daughter. I
am guessing about that part, but it fits. I don't know how
many people know Darla was Mark's daughter. I am certain,
though I cannot prove it, that LeBrun killed him and burned
his trailer down to cover the murder. I believe I must have
been on the other end of the phone when that happened. That
was when I think I went completely crazy.*

*Then, Darla disappeared and I was frantic. I have since
been following LeBrun, who I believe destroyed the lives of
Ethyl, her daughter, and Mark Dellinger—God forgive me,
the only man I ever loved. What I will do when the time comes
I do not know, but I have my father's shotgun with me and
I will, if I am given the chance, settle the score.*

*If someone happens to be reading this, you will know,
then, that I tried.*

Leota Blevins.

*P.S. I hope, if the worst occurs, that some stable family will
find it in their hearts to take Darla into their care and give
her what she never had, a real home and hope.*

L.B.

Ike folded the letter and replaced it in its envelope. "We're done here," he announced. "Everybody pack up and head for home."

◇◇◇

"What happens now?" Ruth asked as Ike emerged from the shower.

"Now? Well, let's see. It's Sunday night." He looked at the clock on the mantle. "Oops, make that Monday morning. We have just enough time to sleep a few hours, don our outfits, gather ourselves together, march smartly through our *faux* wedding ceremony, eat too much, drink too much, and set in motion the steps necessary to create a home for the girl. The last, by the way, is the really important thing to get going. That done, we carry on as usual."

"No honeymoon?"

"Taken care of."

"Someone asked what we were going to do."

"I hope you told them that if the honeymoon was anything as successful as the rehearsal, it should be great."

"You never stop, do you? Okay, no second thoughts about the girl and what that will do to our hitherto unsullied life together?"

"Define unsullied."

"You know what I mean. There is a world of difference when it was just the two of us and we could do as we pleased. It's a wholly different situation with a young woman in our care, one who will require, as you pointed out, all kinds of attention and time."

"When I was out at the trailer park the first time, when we found Darla's father dead, I heard the name Dellinger and I couldn't place it. You remember me saying something about that in Frank's last week. The intern had told me earlier that Darla had a father named Dellinger, and I completely lost it."

"What has that got to do with…what do you mean, you 'lost it'?"

"I mean I have lost a step. There was a time when I could tell you something about everyone I ever met. I never forgot anything, at least nothing critical. Now, I hear Dellinger and a couple of hours later, I don't know who he is."

"And that is important because?"

"Declining skill set, I think the psychological wonks would describe it. I am not getting any younger, Ruth. I could not survive ten minutes in my old profession and increasingly, I need help now, in this new one, you see?"

"I don't see. What has you getting older have to do with taking in Darla? I'm sorry as hell you are no longer James Bond but what the hell, you're not that old and who cares about your damned 'skill set' anyway?"

"I do, but more importantly, it reminded me that we all have to grow up sooner or later. Darla does and, sad to say, so do we. It's time to move to a new place, mentally, I mean. So, as for Darla, nope, I have no qualms. It'll be a risk for all concerned, but one worth taking. It's just a damned shame someone wasn't there for her years ago. Flora Blevins may fight us on this you know."

"No she won't, trust me, she will end up here, Ike."

"You're certain."

"A woman knows. So, what about the honeymoon?"

"Ask me tomorrow. Right now, I am beat."

Chapter Forty-seven

It didn't rain. Ruth's mother said it would. When confronted on her negativity, she declared the best way to insure something didn't happen was to bet that it would, tempt fate, sort of. Wash the car—get rain. She said it worked when Ruth was a teenager and it should now. No one believed her, especially the part about Ruth, but it did not rain. Ike's deputies put together a betting pool on the exact time Ike would actually marry the professor. Most people believed he would be late and the only issue was how late. Time slots in fifteen-minute intervals were charted out. Charley Picket won. He maintained a wedding would not happen at all. He won on a technicality. For those who actually paid attention to the words of the service, it soon became apparent that Ike and Ruth were already married and the service simply conferred a church blessing on it. Nobody really cared.

Food and drink were laid out on tables next to the church on the only grass available and guests, crashers, and two tourists from Pennsylvania who, since it was a weekday, thought they were witnessing an historical re-enactment of some sort, joined the celebration.

Townies performed a complex gavotte with the academics. Mutual suspicion and disdain seasoned with the grain alcohol Billy dumped in his mother's famous lemon-strawberry punch heightened the strain, but there were no fights. When enough of the spiked punch had finally kicked in, the mood shifted and one of the town's livelier citizens actually danced with the chairwoman of Callend's Philosophy Department. This was all the more remarkable as there was no music provided at the time and neither dancer seemed to notice.

"Okay, Schwartz, where is he?"

"Where is who?"

"You know. Where is your buddy and mega-trouble maker, Charlie Garland, spook, spy, and ruiner of weekends?"

"Charlie? Did you invite Charlie?"

"Don't go all innocent with me, Bunky. He's here, isn't he?"

"Probably, but in spite of what you may believe, I did not invite him. He called and said he'd see me Monday, that is today, well before I could get around to it."

"Then you were going to invite him?" Ike shrugged. "How'd he know we were doing this?"

"He's CIA. He knows everything. If you don't believe it, ask him. He even knew about the Budding Rose Wedding Chapel."

"I hate him. So, where is he?"

Ike pivoted around and did a quick mental inventory of the crowd. He paused for a moment to watch the tourists from Pennsylvania. They were taking pictures and interviewing some of the guests, notebooks at the ready. The townsfolk were used to this "innocents from the north behavior" and, because of the spiked punch and the general gaiety of the moment, were busy helping them fill their notebooks with some completely fictitious Civil War minutia. Ike and Ruth's wedding would be described a week later on one of the visitor's blogs, as the annual celebratory re-enactment of Picketsville's savior, General Percival Frontain's marriage to Lucinda Lee Picket, great-granddaughter of the town's founder and hero of the Revolutionary War, Horatio Bellweather Picket. Several of his readers would bookmark the story and the reference would later appear in the footnotes of two term papers and the subplot for a bad historical novel.

"Charlie Garland is over there next to the cake entertaining your mother. Do you think we need to mount an intervention?"

"No. My mother can take her chances like everyone else. Who's that with him?"

"Um…that is, if I am not mistaken, Harry Grafton."

"And he is?"

"An associate of Charlie's and more you do not want to know.'

"The woman with him looks familiar."

"She should. She graduated from Callend. Her name used to be Jennifer Ames. I presume it is now Grafton. I'm missing Armand Dillon. He would have loved this."

Ruth sighed. "He would have and you're not the only one. Since his death, the University Development Office has to do actual work now to raise money."

"No more picking up the phone and calling 'Uncle Armand' for seed money, matching funds, outright gifts?"

"Alas, no. Okay, I think we're done here, let's blow this joint."

"We have to cut the cake first."

"Okay, then let's cut the cake and then blow this joint."

"Cut the cake. Right."

"Should we should say something to Darla before we go?"

"We could, but we won't just now. She needs time to decompress. She has had a horrific week which topped off a horrific life. There may still be some, or a great deal of residual enmity directed toward police in general and me in particular. I don't want to spook her into running away again. The Rev is working with her. He's good at that stuff. Give him time with her. When we get back we will see where she is and if and when adopting her or whatever it is we do would be appropriate. It could be some time, Ruth, before that child is wrapped tight enough to deal with you and me."

"And you and I with her, I suspect. You're right. I am used to receiving immediate results, I'm afraid. In this instance, I will have to wait."

Ike was told that Darla insisted she be called Darlene Dellinger, not Darla Smut. They were her birth certificate names after all. She stood to one side between Mary and Blake Fisher in a very new party frock. Since she'd managed to escape her mother and the life she'd been forced to live, she'd worn nothing but slacks and jeans. She seemed uncomfortable in a dress. She held the front down with one hand and kept her feet together. *Vulnerable* would describe her best. The party ebbed and flowed around her. She didn't appear able to take it all in. So many happy people. Blake had spent the previous night explaining to her that the sheriff's office as she knew it had vanished absolutely and that the new sheriff had only her best interests at heart and had been trying to protect her from the LeBruns of the world. She'd given him a weak smile and he'd guessed it would take time before she believed any of what he said, but then she started asking questions about what had happened and what people were doing. Youth, given a chance, has remarkable powers of healing.

"By the way, O groom of mine,' Ruth said, bringing Ike back to the moment, "you said you would tell me where we were going when we finally do cut and run, pun intended."

"Yes, I did. Thank you for reminding me. For the 'unbridled' portion of this inspired Morris Dance, I have arranged for you to take a week off—"

"A week? I can't take a week off. We just got back from too many weeks off already, Ike."

"Nevertheless, with the skillful connivance of Agnes, your loyal and at the moment teary-eyed administrative assistant, I have managed to have you off the books for one whole week beginning today. This afternoon, we head out to Roanoke."

"Roanoke! You want me to spend quality romantic time celebrating this matrimonial crash and burn with a week in Roanoke? Really?"

"Not the city, Miz President, the airport. From there we shall hop our way across the country and spend a rollicking week in Sedona, Arizona."

"What's in Sedona, Arizona? Hell, aside from being in Arizona, where is Sedona?"

"Middle of the state, out of the worst of the heat and very pretty. We will have a week in a luxury resort, complete with a spa, mud baths, and cucumber slices on the eyes if that is your wish, crystal shops with New Age woo-woo, art galleries, good food, pink jeeps, red rocks, and energy vortexes."

"Energy vortexes, you mean like a New Age filling station?"

"Um, yes that would pretty much cover it."

"Right. So, what could possibly go wrong with that?"

Acknowledgment

If you are like a lot of readers, you skip the Acknowledgments in the front of books and go directly to Chapter One. I even know people who will skip Prologues as well. I don't recommend that. Many writers put important stuff in them. You should take the time to at least skim them. Anyway, I decided to put this bit at the end of the book in hopes that you could be lured into turning one last page before snapping the cover shut, figuratively in the case of an e-reader. The folks who make the story magic happen are important and need to be acknowledged. You are the beneficiary of their efforts as much as mine.

There was a time, not so very long ago, when all I needed to do when it came time to thank those responsible for this wonderful literary ride would be to list, at most, a half dozen names. Poisoned Pen Press was a small outfit then. Now it boasts well over a hundred writers banging out classy mysteries and a staff that grows ever larger, as it must. So, rather than omit someone whose contribution played a vital role in this book's production, I will thank the whole slate by Acclamation, as they say in Robert's Rules…or somewhere.

I cannot, however just leave it at that. I have to single out at least three folks and hope the rest will forgive me. Barbara Peters brought me into this writing business because she liked a very raw and rough book titled *Schwartz*. Her patience and steely editing ended with the first of the "Ike books," renamed *Artscape*. Now, ten years later the number of Picketsville books stands at nine. Also I need to thank Robert Rosenwald, who got flimflammed into publishing *Judas* and that led to the Gamaliel mysteries, which I love writing. Then a shout-out to Jessica Tribble who has been the glue, I suspect, to this enterprise and who now reaps her just desserts along with a chronic need for antacids.

Finally, to my long suffering wife, Susan, who has endured endless ramblings about the other women in my life; Ruth and Sam and Essie—all fictitious, but real to me—and Ike and Gamaliel and Loukas and Sanderson and...

Thank you, all.

Frederick Ramsay
2014

To receive a free catalog of Poisoned Pen Press titles, please contact us in one of the following ways:

Phone: 1-800-421-3976
Facsimile: 1-480-949-1707
Email: info@poisonedpenpress.com
Website: www.poisonedpenpress.com

Poisoned Pen Press
6962 E. First Ave. Ste 103
Scottsdale, AZ 85251